Previously published by Aidan Ellis

The Unmade Bed

PAINTING IN BLOOD

PAINTING IN BLOOD

Françoise Sagan

Translated from the French
by Anthea Bell

AIDAN ELLIS

First published in the United Kingdom
by Aidan Ellis Publishing Limited
Cobb House, Nuffield, Henley-on-Thames, Oxon. RG9 5RT

This work was originally published in French by
Éditions Gallimard, Paris, under the title *Un sang d'aquarelle*
Copyright © 1987 by Éditions Gallimard

ENGLISH TRANSLATION COPYRIGHT © 1988 BY
AIDAN ELLIS

First edition: September 1988

British Library Cataloguing in Publication Data

Sagan, Françoise, *1935–*
    Painting in blood.
    Rn: Françoise Quoirez   I. Title   II.Un
    sang d'aquarelle.   *English*
    843'.914[F]

    ISBN 0-85628-172-7

Typeset in Times Roman by
AKM Associates (UK) Ltd.,
Ajmal House, Hayes Road, Southall, London
Printed by Redwood Burn Ltd., Trowbridge, Wilts.

To Françoise Verny
with my admiration, gratitude
and affection

PAINTING IN BLOOD

Part One

I

"Right, this is the last sequence; we'll start shooting right away!"

On the way back to his camera, Constantin von Meck, the most popular director in Hollywood and Europe for twenty years, and in all Germany for the last three, crossed the set again. As he did so the spotlights caught his coppery hair, russet moustache, the wide eyes slanting towards his temples, emphasizing his high cheekbones, and the large nose and full lips which gave his face a Cossack look above a typically American loose-limbed body standing over six foot four — but it was the look of a civilized and smiling Cossack.

At forty-two, Constantin von Meck was as famous for his eccentricities as his films, and it had required a great deal of talent and success on his part for puritanical Nazi Germany to close its eyes and ears to his private excesses and his lukewarm politics. When he had made his name in Hollywood, where he married the super-star Wanda Blessen and lived in California for twenty-five years, his return to Germany in 1937, apparently because he had contracted to make a film of *Medea* for Universum Film Aktiengesellschaft, or UFA, had created an unprecedented scandal in America and the whole free world. What a surprise it was, and how sad, to discover that the independent, witty Constantin von Meck was a fanatic — even in a way a traitor! Germany, however, had made that discovery with pride and delight. But though he had been directing entertaining comedies ever since, they were less and less ambitious, and as apolitical as possible. It was said that Constantin von Meck had refused to make *The Jewess* or any other film of a committed nature, and refused so flatly as to arouse the ire of the dignitaries of the Third Reich; such a refusal would have finished him if his films had not been the only ones to make the all-powerful Dr Goebbels laugh. The protection of Hitler's Culture and Propaganda Minister had been officially bestowed upon him, much to his own advantage. For besides his weakness for Jewish scum, his total ignorance of politics and his lack of enthusiasm for the National Socialist Party, Constantin von Meck was suspected of an excessive appetite for drink, drugs, women and even men, although mention of that last tendency made a good many persons in a good many capitals laugh heartily. All the same, if Goebbels were less amused than usual by one of his films, that would suffice to show Constantin von Meck that only twenty kilometres separated Munich from Dachau.

Meanwhile, vigorous, loose-limbed and smiling as he stood there in his old Western boots, larding his orders and advice with English terms that were as automatic — it was to be hoped — as they were tactless, Constantin seemed not to have a care in the world.

"Right, let's go!" he said. "Now then, Maud dear, let me just remind you that this is the very last sequence of this very wonderful love story, and your lines here are among the most thrilling in the entire script. I want you to be truly memorable. Come on, hurry up!" he added, in English. "Cameras roll . . ."

The pretty starlet Maud Mérival, a slender blonde ingénue who had been launched into the UFA firmament by dint of publicity work, raised to the camera eyes which she hoped looked ardent and tormented, but which were more suggestive, thought Constantin, of a rabbit fascinated by a snake. A technician was holding the clapperboard between her and the camera, much as he might have offered a menu to a cobra. He shouted, "*The*

Violins of Destiny, sequence 18, take 1!'' before disappearing.

"Oh no, I cannot take these roses! Coming from you, Count, even these poor flowers distress me. Their scent is fading. I can't accept them! How could I?" inquired Maud, in an offhand tone which made the ineptitude of her lines more striking than ever. Constantin was beginning to find a certain morbid fascination in the silly sentimentality pervading the plots and scripts of the films he was obliged to make until he would agree to direct something more serious, a film that toed the Party line better. Delivered in such a tone, however, Maud's "How could I?" would move even the most sentimental of German Gretchens to laughter.

"Look," he said, "come over here with me, Maud dear, and we'll just put our minds to the revulsion that girl is feeling."

"Oh yes, let's!" exclaimed Maud, and he automatically took her hand, which in view of her crinoline and their respective sizes made the young actress look like a doll. Constantin tried but was unable to free his hand. He had momentarily forgotten that young Maud, convinced by her mother and her agent that it was a great thing for an actress to go to bed with a director, particularly a director as distinguished as Constantin von Meck, thought her heart was broken by his polite rejection. And as he knew there was not much difference between loving and believing oneself to be in love, suffering and believing that one suffered, he was always kind to her. In passing, for safety's sake, he grabbed the arm of his set designer, who happened to be within reach, and took him along as chaperon. They moved away from the brightly lit set and over to the far end of the studio. "There's something not quite right about it — that sentence, I mean," he said. Maud vivaciously interrupted him again.

"Yes, it *is* rather lame, isn't it?" she said earnestly, vaguely hoping to shift the blame on to the scriptwriter. "I feel something's not quite right — I feel it here," she added, stopping and indicating a point situated midway between her breasts: the site, apparently, of her mental difficulty. Constantin cast it a polite but rapid glance.

"Look," he continued, "it's the intonation you give that 'How could I?' that bothers me. You emphasize the 'How' too much. As if you were summoning a native bearer — 'Howkoodai! Come here!' Or maybe it's that you sound too surprised — as if this was some new exotic fruit you'd discovered. 'Well, fancy that, a howkoodai!' That's the way I feel you're saying the line, if you see what I mean."

Maud did not see at all. She was wondering anxiously how on earth a native bearer and an exotic fruit had intruded into what was supposed to have been a frothy Viennese comedy all along. She nodded.

"Oh, yes, I think I see . . . It's so much clearer when you explain things — isn't it?" she asked, turning to the designer on Constantin's other side. He nodded too, eyes lowered. He saw Constantin put his head back as if to check the lighting. Constantin's hand had just let go of his wrist in order to fluff his moustache out and back against the natural growth of the hair, a device which he always if mistakenly hoped would act as a kind of screen to conceal his mirth. The designer, familiar with these signs that Constantin von Meck was about to burst out laughing, and aware of the infectious nature of his laughter, listened apprehensively.

"Oh yes!" added Maud Mérival, grasping Constantin's arm with both hands as he reached the studio door, turned, and in so doing half lifted her off the ground; she briefly looked like a fishing smack caught up in the wake of a liner.

"Yes, I see, you don't want me to put emphasis on the 'How'," she went on. "But then where *do* you want me to put it?" Constantin and the designer stopped, and then walked on at once without looking at each other or replying. Finally, Constantin grunted, "Don't put the emphasis anywhere — I mean, just take it more gently . . . after all, you're supposed to feel sorry for those flowers, they're no worse than any other flowers. Oh, by the way, Henri, I want that bunch replaced, it's faded. Look, Maud, those unfortunate flowers aren't to blame, it's the Count who makes them a dubious proposition." Maud noticed that he was speaking with some difficulty, and felt inspired by enthusiasm, all the more so because she did not care for the attitude of the designer, who was coldly turning his back on them, and had turned his head away too, just as if he had nothing to learn from the brilliant Constantin von Meck.

"Yes, and these things do happen!" she exclaimed. "In real life, I mean! There was a man once — oh, a really big shot, he thought he could buy me — or anyway, please me — by giving me jewels! Me!" she said, smiling with amusement rather than indignation at such a psychological error. "Well, no sooner had he shown me that necklace than I got the feeling, just looking at his hands and his face — even though it was in a jewel case and everything — I just got the feeling those stones were fakes! Amazing, wasn't it? All at once, just like that, those stones seemed a dubious proposition, exactly like you said." She paused for effect, a long pause, and then added, triumphantly, "And the best of the joke, the best of it all, is that they really *were* fakes! Would you believe it? They really were!"

But this speech, despite its vivacity, did not have the effect she hoped for. Not only did the designer walk away, his back still turned to them, but at present Constantin von Meck himself seemed positively fascinated by the lighting. Head tipped back, voice cool, he asked her to go back to the set.

"Time to shoot this sequence," he said. "Now that we've agreed how to do it," he added, hoarsely, waving a hand towards the camera as if to show Maud where her duty lay. Disappointed, she was about to move off, but now Constantin's glance was fixed on a point at some distance from her, in the studio doorway, and something about his attitude made Maud turn and look the same way. Standing there, arrogant and still, silent out of respect for another man's work but very obviously sure that both their presence and their discretion had been noted, she saw two German officers and their two aides flanking the producer and the French production assistant, come to see the last sequence of the film being shot. Their caps gleamed and their boots shone in the dark, and behind them, in the doorway, French press photographers furtively appeared, disappeared, and reappeared again.

"Gentlemen!" said Constantin — and Maud wondered yet again why the director's voice always sounded so different — toneless, almost dry — when such official visitations occurred. He became another man, remote, stiff in manner, and yet these were his fellow countrymen, after all.

"Well, please go on!" said Constantin, speaking in English as he always did on such occasions. It made Maud smile: really, she thought, he's such a child! She opened her mouth, feeling perfectly confident now, for in front of Germans Constantin always seemed wildly enthusiastic about his cast and his film crew; his Russian rages went away, turning to lavish praise.

"We're nearly through, gentlemen. This is the last take. Mademoiselle Mérival, please go on," he said, in French this time. "And then we'll all have some champagne — we deserve it. We all deserve it," he translated at once into perfect German for his visitors' benefit, though without turning round, just as if the officers, after more than two years in France, were still unable to understand a few simple phrases in the language of that country. There were conspiratorial glances and a ripple of laughter all around Constantin; suddenly, he felt paternal. It was true that all his technicians and the actors had always liked him, and it was true that he liked that. The fact was, though he might not admit it to himself, that Constantin loved to fascinate other people: to cheer, amuse, alarm, protect and cherish them. The fact was, as he would sometimes admit, with ironic indulgence for himself, the fact was that he liked to please. Saying so spared him admitting that he needed to be loved. That was a vague feeling — or no, more of a distinct certainty — which his mind would not even formulate, did not translate into such terms, or not where he himself was concerned.

"Cameras roll!" he cried.

"No, no! Coming from you, Count, even these poor roses have a perfume that distresses me. Oh, no, I cannot accept these flowers! How could I?" Maud protested, and very forcefully this time, contrary to her director's suggestions and despite herself, for up to now she had been rehearsing with an old bunch of flowers which the designer, as requested by Constantin, had just had time to change, but only just, and at the very moment when she raised the bunch towards the Count, no doubt to let him savour both her personal distaste and the innocence of the roses, a piece of wire slipped under her right thumbnail, digging itself in savagely as she lowered her arms at the words, "I cannot accept these flowers!" Her new rendering of "How could I?" was thus far from gentle, but expressive of surprise and anger, indeed, indignation — as if the Count, forgetting his ambiguous role, had put a hand up her crinoline.

This last-minute change of intonation was too much for Constantin von Meck; he collapsed behind the enormous grand piano which formed part of his set, and which most fortunately stood open, so that he could stifle his laughter behind it together with the electrician. A few feet away, the set designer had plunged head first into his packing cases, where he remained, upside down, like an empty bottle in a dustbin. Taking no notice of this little interlude, the officers and their cohorts applauded politely, indulgent eyes bent on Maud.

"Constantin!" she cried, immobilized under the spotlights. "Constantin! I mean Dr von Meck," she corrected herself, with a little look of confusion which suggested to these military hearts Maud Mérival's probable liking for her director and indeed for men in general. "Now what, Constantin? Do you want me to do it again? I thought I was a bit . . . a bit too emphatic, wasn't I? I hurt myself."

Maud had thought of waving her finger in the air, showing the bead of blood on it and putting on a performance of childlike fragility, but in the end she decided against it. After all, these uniformed men were back from the war, they had come from Russia or Africa or some other place where there was fierce fighting, and they might be more irritated than touched by tears over a pinprick. Finally Constantin emerged from behind the piano, red in the face, one hand to his side, his breath coming short, his eyes suffused. Surely he wasn't going to say he was ill? Not Constantin von Meck! That would have all Europe laughing, beginning with Maud.

"Well," he gasped, "well, if you like . . . oh, my God! . . . yes, of course . . . maybe . . . well, another time you might be more careful," he added, with the last word in English. "Careful — oh, what's the French for it?" he apologized to the officers. "Ah, yes — *plus attentive*, Maud," he repeated, and reverted to French. "Though never mind that — you were wonderful, darling, sublime! But we'll do it again just for fun, eh? And for these gentlemen."

He was stammering, breathing hard, he must be feverish, and Maud decided she had better get this finished as soon as possible: the moment the word "Take!" had been uttered she launched into her speech.

"Oh no, I cannot accept these flowers. Coming from you, Count, even these poor roses have a perfume that distresses me. Oh no, I can't accept them. How could I? How could I?" she squawked a second time in agitation, like a chicken, for Constantin, no doubt wild with enthusiasm, had rushed on to the set and folded her in his arms; bent right over her shoulder, he was saying, "Well done, darling! Well done, well done!" in a choked voice. His big body was shaken by dry, silent sobs — so moving, in a man! And Maud gently cradled this tall, famous director, whom the world thought debauched, not to say cynical, as if he were a little boy. "Inside that great frame, behind that tyrannical mask, I felt the heart of a child beating — and the heart of a genius too!" she was to confide to *Cinémondial* next week, delivering a speech dictated word for word by her agent, but which for once expressed her own feelings.

"There, there," she said, alarmed despite herself. "What was it you didn't like, Constantin? What's the matter? Do you want us to do it again?"

Between sobs, she heard him say, "No, no . . . no, no! That was the last sequence!" After a moment's reflection, she thought she understood the director's distress: it was the end of his film, the end of *their* film. Perhaps he loved her after all? Perhaps he knew their respective careers would part them? Perhaps there was something about this film and its history which reminded him of his wife? Meanwhile, face ravaged, Constantin was unashamedly wiping his long moustache, which was wet with tears, on his heroine's curled hair and white cambric fichu.

"There, there, Constantin!" she said. "We'll see each other again. I share your feelings, you know! You must control yourself — there are those men over there, Constantin, those soldiers!"

He disengaged himself, with difficulty, but Maud Mérival whispered something into his ear which seemed to strike him forcibly and brought his face down on her shoulder again, much to the interest of the UFA publicity man, Darius Popesku.

For Constantin, whose private life was so licentious and whose public reticence so marked, had never allowed himself to be photographed in a position of intimacy with anyone whatever. At most, he had once been seen holding his wife Wanda's hand in a dimly lit restaurant. And now all of a sudden, right there in front of Popesku, he was hugging young Maud Mérival and burying his face in her hair. It was the scoop of Darius Popesku's life, professionally and personally. It sent him hysterical!

And yet Maud had not said anything very fascinating to Constantin; she had merely whispered, "You're just a little boy, M. von Meck, just an overgrown little boy!" But Constantin, who stood over six foot four and who used to go to great lengths to avoid his mistresses in hotels, in the street and socially, had succumbed to this ridiculous remark, or rather, his nerve had cracked — and so had his wits. He had, after all, been making these stupid films for some time, films that sprang from the lamentable brains of UFA's scriptwriters, from German minds that were conventional and sentimental to the nth degree. And now he really felt he could take no more of it. He would be demanding again, he would tell UFA he wanted to direct Stendhal's *La Chartreuse de Parme*, and maybe Wanda — Wanda Blessen — would agree to play La Sanseverina? No doubt that was just a dream that couldn't be realized, but so beautiful a dream he just had to believe in it.

Though Constantin might complain of the sentimentality and conventionality of his scriptwriters and of Teutonic conformity, Darius Popesku had every reason to be glad of those very things. Born in Lebanon to a Lebanese mother and an unknown father, Popesku had had many a brush with danger in identity checks because of his hooked nose and his hair. By a recurrent stroke of good luck, if he was insufficiently Aryan in the eyes of the Gestapo, he was still sufficiently Levantine for one simple-minded form of racism to replace another and deadlier form. It was to emphasize to the Nazis the difference between ethnic groups of the Middle East and Jews, a distinction which had become essential to him, that Popesku had taken it upon himself over the last year to provide them with irrefutable proofs — which meant living proofs.

It was in this scientific spirit that he had recently denounced to the Gestapo two fine Jewish prototypes, namely the designer Weil, otherwise known as Petit, and the electrician Schwob, otherwise known as Duchez, both hired by the ill-informed

Constantin von Meck, although for once he was no less well informed than Popesku, since it was precisely because of their race that he had taken the two men on. However, the authorities dealing with racial questions in France had had to wait some little while before making use of Popesku's supplementary proofs — for the Minister of Culture and Propaganda, Josef Goebbels himself, had given orders three years ago that no one was to bother Constantin von Meck while he was shooting a film. For three weeks, Popesku had feared that his living proofs might get away from him (both of them being more Aryan in appearance than himself), but he based his case on their names, for "Weil" and "Schwob" had a different ring from "Popesku", which its owner thought the height of ambiguity, and thus of innocence.

And now, at last, the film was finished, and while the German officers' aides marched on to the set staggering under cartons full of champagne bottles, while Constantin improvised a brief farewell speech, Schwob, otherwise Duchez, and Weil, otherwise Petit, were congratulating themselves in blissful ignorance, and for the last time, on their luck in being alive.

"Hey there, everyone! Come and have some bubbly for a change!" Constantin was leaning against the tripod of the camera, which he held around the neck as if it were a woman, brandishing in his other hand a champagne bottle whose cork he pushed out with his fingers, sending it flying through the air with a loud pop. While the cork shot through the fake window of the set, and struck the huge castle keep on the other side — a dummy castle which would fold flat in a moment like something out of a funfair — while the officers, at the sound, instinctively reached for their revolvers, froth shot out of the champagne bottle and all over Constantin's coat, hands and sleeves; without flinching, he simply raised the bottle and poured its entire contents over his head. He had froth and bubbles in his hair and his eyes, he was laughing, he looked more like a boy of eighteen than a man of forty.

"Friends!" he forcefully addressed his film crew, arms raised, his demeanour wild as that of another orator of the time, something that cast a slight chill on proceedings before he returned to a normal tone — "friends, I want to thank you for your hard work and your patience. But for you," he continued, "I could never have made this amazing specimen of ineptitude, this piece of boundless insanity known as *The Violins of Destiny*. Thank you! Well done!" he said, clapping, and hoping that the words "ineptitude" and "insanity" were not in the vocabulary of the interpreter standing behind him. Apparently not, since the officers applauded while everyone else cheered, and the photographers, back again and unaware of what they had just missed, took picture after picture of the director and his pretty leading lady — who were a good five metres apart by now.

Gradually, everyone managed to get on to the set and inside the square marked out by the spotlights, the one part of the studio where there was any warmth and you were not shivering. And as the entire company was standing shoulder to shoulder, and champagne was flowing, for a moment fatigue, nervousness, hostility and fear — those feelings most prevalent in the city for the last two years — evaporated in honour of this epilogue to a ridiculous film. In that moment there was even a sense of friendship, of cheerfulness, of common humanity between these people who were so different, so full of hatred, so contemptuous of one another: it was a moment which reminded everyone of peace and even silenced the chattering gate-crashers, those uninvited guests who descended like parasites on any party, and whose numbers had doubled with wartime restrictions. That moment of peace triggered off something in Constantin's memory — as a landscape, a piece of music or a perfume might have done — bringing before his mind's eye the back of a woman walking towards water, against the background of a deserted swimming pool, a faded palm tree and a large Buick coupé. Who was she, and why that image? Perhaps it represented peacetime and his American past to him? It was a very fragile image, or anyway an anonymous one.

Constantin was, of course, used to his memory being nothing but a half-empty, insecure left-luggage office; he had become used to finding his most passionate loves represented by insipid images, faces turned away, or vague phrases. He was used to it, but not yet resigned, for, he told himself, if one no longer remembered one's whole life, all one had been and done, all he himself had done, if there was no one to tell him about it, then how could he ever do his great calculation, render an account of the acts of his life, add them up to the figure which was to be the justification and meaning of that life? When and how could he make that summary he always meant to make and was always postponing, take the plunge, do the sum whose answer would tell him if, ultimately, his existence had been necessary or a matter of no interest? Before he died, would he at last be able to see the haphazard, lurching trail of that comet shooting on under its own impetus which had been his life? The idea of not being able to do so maddened him.

He had sworn to himself at the ages of ten, twelve, sixteen and twenty, he had sworn, ridiculously, that he would know before he died if his life had been worth living, and although everything indicated that this was a stupid question, as unimportant as it was unanswerable, all the past in him clung to it: a past like a boy scout, a not particularly bright child but one of whom he was fond, and who was bound to be disappointed, for the memory of his acts, their consequences and their echoes was fading, becoming more blurred all the time, and if he insisted, if he told his memory to make the effort, try another angle, find another trace of that past, a badly adjusted projector clicked in a vacuum, as it seemed, and with difficulty produced shapes once dear to him but now, seen in back-lighting, very distant. "I was crazy about her, though, crazy about that figure," he told himself with a kind of compassionate contempt for the foolish lover he once had been. "There must be other memories of her in my lumber-room of a memory, close-ups, other symbols: she was my first love, I would have died for her . . ." But no; there was nothing.

So he came back to more recent loves, but saw only a blurred, monotonous road, or the face — a very precise and distinct image, this — of the garage mechanic who had come to the rescue when his car broke down, a face seen for a couple of minutes, but selected by his ridiculous memory instead of the face of the woman he had loved for two years at that time, now supplanted by the garage mechanic. And that was his memory of recent events! No, it was a crazy memory, out of control, except where Wanda was concerned, of course, his wife the super-star, before whom his own will had once bowed and his memory still did, always conjuring up at the mere mention of her name a perfect close-up of her face shot from a low angle, sensual and vivid, in which he could make out the gleam of her teeth, her skin, the distracted look in her eyes when at last she admitted that their love might perhaps be different from other, earlier affairs.

Ten minutes and two bottles of champagne later, having listened to the producers predicting the fortunes of his film in the future tense, to one German officer telling the story of the battle of Tobruk in the past tense, and above all to the total silence of the other officer on the subject of Stalingrad, Constantin von Meck set off to raise a glass with every member of his cast and crew. There were twenty of them, and he was slightly drunk by the time he reached the last, when he realized that Maud was no longer present; he made up his mind to find her, feeling slightly surprised at himself. What was happening to him? Just now, taking refuge in that child's arms out of sheer necessity — the necessity occasioned by his fit of hilarity — he had lingered in them, he recalled, with pleasure. Ever since they first began shooting, ever since she had offered herself to him, Maud had inspired him principally with a sense of compassion, a feeling which, in him, was very far from desire. She had offered herself initially as a wonderful, unexpected present, a surprise, but in the face of Constantin's own surprise and indifference she first assumed the role of a woman maddened by desire, a Phaedra, and then came down to the level of an equal: the alluring, amused, modern woman. Constantin, hitherto absorbed by his work on the film, had reacted just in time, stopping her at the point when she was about to resign herself to becoming nothing but a possibility, a one-night stand, an object. Since he hated a woman to be humiliated in front of him, or by his own doing, he had got his word in first, giving her a long account of his unhappy, unrequited, and consequently exclusive love for his ex-wife Wanda Blessen. He had not had to put too much acting into it either, for he did miss Wanda, he missed her badly. There wasn't another woman who could hold a candle to her. There was Romano, of course, but where had Romano gone? Romano was never around; you never knew where you were with Romano.

Unlike Michael, who had always been there: so intelligent, so calm, so gentle, Michael in his rocking chair on the terrace, whistling a jazz tune. Constantin had always felt he was well on the way to dying, and at the beginning of their relationship he had taken him off to ten doctors to assure himself of the stupid improbability of his own theory. Unfortunately, his intuition had been correct, although to prove it Life, like a third party, an obscene, brilliant, unexpected player took a hand in the drama one afternoon, throwing Michael over the guard rail and down to the bottom of a ravine in the black metal machine that was taking him to the studio. That death, that accident in broad daylight, had been all the more terrible for Constantin because at the same time as it destroyed Michael's body, it destroyed his image, his personality, and above all their idyll, which had always been painted in soft pastel hues, in gentle tones, like those grey rocking chairs at twilight, with rain over the sea. That blazing, blood-stained end, with its glaring colours, had nothing to do with the temperate, tender Vuillard scene of their mutual love.

Well, he wasn't concerned with Michael or Romano now, but Maud. Constantin finally found her in her dressing-room, sobbing. It was not the first time he had found her in tears, but it was the first time they had alarmed him, for her tears — and this was another first — swelled her eyes, puffed up her face, made her ugly. So Constantin knew that her grief was genuine.

"What is it?" he asked, kneeling down so as to be on her level. "Maud, what is it?" he repeated, earnestly, for he saw in her eyes a spark of rebellion, something of which he had thought her wholly incapable.

"It's Duchez," she said, sobbing harder than ever and putting her head on his shoulder, for once without the slightest suggestiveness. "It's Duchez and Petit. They've taken them away, those swine," she whispered.

Constantin was briefly bewildered, before remembering she was talking about Schwob and Weil.

"But why?" he asked, foolishly. "What for?"

"Because they're Jewish!" Maud shouted furiously into his face. "Didn't you know?"

There was a note of contempt in her voice which elicited from the actor in Constantin a sardonic smile worthy of the silent cinema, a smile which he instantly regretted.

"Well, yes, I did know, Maud," he said. "I should know if anybody does — I got them their false papers. But how can they have been taken away without anyone telling me?"

"They hardly had time to drink their champagne," sobbed Maud. "We'll never see them again! I had a friend like them — a

Jew — they took him away . . ." And she began to hiccup. "You never get to see them again, never! None of them's been seen again, not for two years. You'll see . . ."

"Well, yes," said Constantin. "I am indeed going to see about this."

And he strode out into the corridor. He went back from the dressing rooms towards the studio, his old boots ringing on the concrete floor. But long after he had turned the first corner of the corridor he could still hear Maud's little sobs and gasps of grief in the distance — sounds which, God knew why, reminded him of swallows calling just before nightfall out in the country, when they swoop low over the fields and houses, as if afraid of the gathering dusk.

He had left the studio in a cheerful and exhilarated mood, and found it much more sombre now. The sound of his own footsteps, gradually warning the others of his approach, the fury of his strides, had progressively imposed silence on them, and that silence was complete when he stood in the studio doorway: immensely tall, lit by a spotlight glancing off a mirror and off his hair, his eyes full of anger, with that irascible, juvenile look he still retained at the age of forty, exactly the same as it had been twenty years before. It was mere chance that the brunt of his wrath was borne by Popesku who, intoxicated by the compliments he had just received from both UFA and the Gestapo, trembled at this encounter. Constantin grabbed him by the tie.

"Where are they? How did they get taken away without my knowledge?"

"Who are you talking about?"

"I'm talking about Duchez and Petit," Constantin shouted furiously into his face. "Where've they gone? Why didn't anyone tell me?"

"But," said Popesku, struggling, "but M. von Meck, what you don't know is, you've been deceived. Those two men had false papers. The fact is, they were . . ."

In his fury, Constantin almost tore his collar off.

"They were Jews, yes, I know! And so I should, seeing I gave them those false papers so that they could work for me and not be bothered, understand?"

Popesku jumped. "You got them their false papers? But M. von Meck, you shouldn't say things like that! You'll get yourself arrested! You'll . . ."

"Idiot!" shouted Constantin, flinging Popesku violently against the wall, where he collapsed and sat back on his heels, motionless; he had almost mentioned his own part in the matter, he had almost claimed credit for the arrest, and he realized, with retrospective terror, that Constantin might well have killed him for it. He had seen as much in his eyes: that half-Russian was no man, he was a mad wild animal, a moujik! With mingled relief and alarm, Popesku saw him march up to the German officers and the producers, who themselves were stiff with embarrassment, while the rest of the company moved away from the group and gathered in a far corner of the set, whispering.

"I've had two men taken away!" Constantin barked at the party of four. The tallest of them, one of the German officers, scarcely came up to his shoulder. "I've had two men taken away! My best designer and my best electrician, on the grounds that they were Jews! I want them back! I'm not making another film without them, not for UFA or anyone else, you hear me?"

"But . . ." said the French producer, "but listen, it's the rule — you know that, M. von Meck — it's the rule not to hire any Semitic personnel for . . ."

"I don't abide by your rules," said Constantin, contemptuously, "and I didn't know the French ever had any rules of that sort either!"

"Well, let's say it's a German rule," suggested the UFA

producer, who always had a small, satisfied smile hovering about the corners of his mouth, usually hidden by a cigar which made him look like a caricature of his profession. Constantin turned on him.

"M. Pleffer," he said, "I believe you're a scientist. You must have heard of Darwin's theory of evolution, according to which Man, I mean the human race, is descended from the monkeys; I believe that theory's generally accepted. Well now, M. Pleffer, I don't suppose you ever heard anyone speak of Jewish monkeys, did you? So could you kindly exert your influence to get me back those two descendants of monkeys, my electrician and my designer, and hand them over to me here on this set before I chuck UFA up for good? Go on, go on, hurry up about it, will you?"

And with a wave of the hand, a director's wholly theatrical gesture, Constantin von Meck sent the two producers and their hangers-on off towards the telephones. The only man to remain beside him, unmoving, as if he had heard nothing, was the captain back from Stalingrad; he looked sad and tired, not to say abstracted.

"What about you?" inquired Constantin. "Don't you have any influence on the Gestapo or the SS?"

"No, monsieur," said the officer, in a flat, neutral voice which imperceptibly calmed Constantin. "No, monsieur, I've been serving in the Wehrmacht."

Constantin looked him up and down, but there was something resigned about the captain, something careworn in his bearing and his features, which stopped him bawling the man out in the same way as the others.

"M. von Meck," said the officer, in an unexpectedly gentle tone, "M. von meck, you strike me as very excitable . . . or very ignorant."

Constantin breathed slowly to calm himself.

"Look, can you tell me just what it is the German people have against Jews?" he asked, in a voice which even to his own ears sounded childish. "What's going on, for pity's sake?"

The officer's voice, replying, was still neutral, almost pedantic.

"The main thing that's been going on, M. von Meck, is that when we wanted to get out of the 1919 Treaty of Versailles which brought Germany to her knees, we needed the support of money and the press, and both, as you know, were in the hands of the Jews."

"In the hands of German Jews among others, I believe," said Constantin. "Some of whom died at Verdun, am I right?"

"You may well be right," said the captain. "But they were German Jews whose brothers worked in London, Milan, New York. As I'm sure you know, banking families go everywhere, and that prevents them from feeling whole-hearted, complete, absolute patriotism such as we needed. The press was in similar hands, M. von Meck. Perhaps history's to blame, and those dreadful pogroms in the old days, but you know very well that we couldn't leave power in Germany to people whose loyalties are international."

Constantin was watching him closely; he tried to light his cigarette, but it was no good: his hand was trembling nervously. "But was that any reason to arrest grocers, hairdressers and dyers too?" he asked.

"We couldn't pass a law solely for rich Jews," said the captain, in the same expressionless voice. "We couldn't do that. It would have been against all our egalitarian principles."

He did not even smile in saying this; he was reciting a text. Constantin made one last effort.

"But," he said, "but how did those principles of yours, 'our' egalitarian principles, how did they come to lead to such atrocities?"

There was silence at last. The captain was tapping his right boot with his left heel. He had an ugly scar low down on his neck, quite new and very red, as Constantin noticed when he bent his head.

"We missed out on a generation, you see, M. von Meck," said the captain. "In between the defeated men of the 1914–18 war and their children of 1939, in between resentment and rage. We missed out on peace, on a generation that wanted peace. Germany went straight from the memory of one war to the desire for another without any period in between. There was misery and resentment, and next thing we knew we had a generation trained and ready for war — which has given us the finest army in the world, the strongest and the most effective. Or so we think, anyway," he murmured, as if to himself. And bringing his complicated foot manoeuvres to an end, turning abruptly and leaving Constantin at a loss, he left the studio.

The producer came back a couple of minutes later looking pleased, even cheerful, and assured Constantin that everything would be put right tomorrow, he had been in touch with the right people and Constantin's vital assistants would be returned to him at the end of the week. Constantin protested, insisted on having them back next day, and the producer promised everything he asked for: he even said he would send them round to Constantin's hotel tomorrow. But the promise was made in so friendly a manner, so airily, that Constantin, unhappy with the ease of it all, decided to go higher. He would apply to General Bremen, as Goebbels had advised him to do in case of any trouble, and General Bremen, he knew, would be dining with Boubou Bragance, an old friend of Constantin's, as he did every Monday evening.

Elisabeth Bragance, Boubou to her friends, had had the most brilliant salon in Paris fifteen years before the war, and it was still the most brilliant now. All the top French collaborators and the Wehrmacht élite met there. Looking at his watch, Constantin saw that he had time to have a bath at his hotel, change and arrive in good time at her apartment on the Quai d'Anjou. Before he left, however, he went round to the dressing rooms and took Maud Mérival's arm.

"Come along," he said. "Make yourself pretty, and then we're off to Mme Bragance's elegant salon, to intercede for our friends with a very powerful general. So you come with me, Maud dear!"

And Maud, who had read about the big apartment on the Quai d'Anjou, had seen pictures of it and heard tell of it in fifty journals (not *Cinémondial*, but journals more along the lines of *Comoedia*), was delighted. It was just as chic, her mother and her agent had told her, indeed it was even more chic than going to Maxim's for the evening. Her grief disappeared in an instant. And yet it was because of that same grief that Constantin was taking her. He intended to drink that evening, and knowing himself, he was afraid intoxication might make him forget what he had to do, the wine might make him forget the blood: he was taking Maud with him as one might take one's conscience, as Pinocchio took Jiminy Cricket. Very likely it was the first time the poor girl had played such a part. And in the darkness of the car which he was driving himself, she turned to him, her eyes bright with curiosity.

"Look, Constantin, there's something everyone's been wondering at the studio: you were tremendously successful in Hollywood! So why did you leave the Hollywood studios, and the stars and all that, to come and make films in Germany? You're partly American, aren't you?"

"Well, it's a long story, Maud, my dear. I arrived in Germany in '37 feeling disgusted with everything, including myself. I'd been very badly treated by the American press; as I told you, my wife had thrown me out; I had no friends left, I had no money, I'd fallen from the heights as low as I could go, and just because I wanted to make a film that was a little ambitious! America is a country of money, my dear Maud. And those who forget it are punished . . ."

The sad dignity of his own voice carried conviction even to him for a moment, and it had a shattering effect on Maud, whose eyes brimmed with tears yet again.

"Oh, poor Constantin!" she said. "Tell me about it. Can you tell me a little about it? Maybe it would do you good."

Constantin von Meck shrugged his shoulders.

"Why not?" he said. "It all happened when I came back from Mexico. When I got back to Los Angeles."

1937 Return to Los Angeles

Standing up in the dusty, frantic train as it crossed the desert, which was like an inferno of sand dotted here and there with poor little stations with white rough-cast walls, baking hot, forgotten, and in any case left behind too fast for even their names to be seen — standing in that train as it crossed the desert between Mexico and California, Constantin von Meck was thinking. This journey was taking far too long; the confidence and lightness of heart that had entered the compartment with him in Mexico, like a couple of charming young travelling companions, had turned as they rode the tracks to uneasiness and remorse, two angry, cruel old women with whom he was inevitably going to be saddled. He knew it; indeed, he had known it since last weekend, when he spent two days and two nights in Cuernavaca waiting for Wanda in the hotel where they had both spent such wonderful nights when he first began shooting. But that was two years ago; it was now three months since he had had any news of Wanda, and the telegram he had sent her, the telegram asking her to cross the desert with him — and return to Hollywood like lovers in the Buick convertible — that telegram now suddenly struck him as the height of odious pretension. Had he really believed that on receiving his telegram Wanda would board a plane, have the car sent down and wait for him, heart fluttering, in that hotel — after he had spent a year roving elsewhere? Had he thought, had he really believed, she would clasp him to her breast and thank him for his boorish conduct? Had he forgotten that Wanda Blessen was not only his wife, his great love, his mistress of the last ten years and a forbearing woman, but also the greatest Shakespearian actress in London and the most famous film star in the world? Had he forgotten that beyond the roles of executioner and victim — depending on the circumstances — which she acted out with him in their amorous relationship, she was also a cultivated, sensitive and proud human being? The fact was, his telegram had been a monumental piece of conceit and impudence.

Without even having to stretch, Constantin took his bag from the luggage net above him, got out a bottle of tequila and took a long drink — noticing, in passing, how light his baggage weighed: he was bringing back two old pairs of boots, a pair of duck trousers, a few Aztec objects, some books and photographs, and that was all. He had left with six full suitcases, with suits, books and luxury gadgets chosen by Wanda to amuse him when he was not working on the film during those six months on location in Mexico from which he was now returning a year late, looking like a bandit or a tramp — on the whole, more like a tramp. Constantin bent down to the level of he mirror in the compartment and examined himself: he was thin as an old cat, his body hair scorched by the sun, his skin tanned and scored with white wrinkles at the corners of his eyelids, his eyes reddened by wind, sun and alcohol. What a fine present to bring back to Wanda! In addition, he didn't have a thousand pesetas or fifty dollars on him, and he had no more than a thousand dollars in Hollywood; his film had been a failure — hard enough to bear morally speaking, and catastrophic from the practical viewpoint. Maria de Aleya, his conquest, his rich conquest, had been ruinously expensive, like all rich women; you always had to give people used to luxury presents as good as their own. In the long run, nothing could be worse for a man's wallet than going around with an heiress, Mexican or otherwise! Oh God! Constantin dropped on to the seat, where he had to curl up or at least bend his knees if he stretched out, even with it to himself, and he closed his eyes; he genuinely felt he had reached the extreme limit of grief.

He searched around for adjectives to describe his character, came up with raffish, disdainful, self-opinionated, scornful, swaggering — and stopped there, tired of it all. What lay in store for him now, other than the life of a tramp? He obviously needed to make a new film in a hurry, since the Americans had entirely failed to understand his last one. They were so used to his comedies, the idiot audiences were so accustomed to laughing at the stupidity of their own customs that they couldn't take any interest in the soul of another nation, a nation interesting in a different way. And yet Constantin's present misfortunes had high-minded origins. He had been seized by a passion, a true passion for the civilisation of the Aztecs, its rituals, its pride, its excesses, its folly: in fact, for everything that represented a change from Hollywood, awash as the place always was with milk, whisky and petrol, three fluids in which he had been wallowing since the age of thirteen. He was in his mid-thirties now, he wanted other liquids, and he had discovered tequila and blood. No, that was going too far; he had never thought much of the rite of human sacrifice, but he certainly knew a lot about tequila . . .

Well, since this was his situation, since one needed money to live in the USA — ten times more money than one needed in Mexico unless one had lumbered oneself with the likes of Maria de Aleya — once he was back he would make one of his comedies, one of those sophisticated, humorous farces at which he was apparently so brilliant, bringing the famous von Meck charm to bear on both mass audiences and the most esoteric of criticism. Although he had had enough of the von Meck charm.

Yes, he had definitely had enough of it. The desert, the pampas, the solitude and ruins of Mexico had cleansed his soul, if not his body.

That being said, however, he would do better to resort to his charm rather than his soul where both Wanda and the film producers were concerned: it was safer. Not that he minded about the producers. He wanted just one thing: he wanted to see Wanda. He feared just one thing: he was afraid she wouldn't want him. And suddenly the thought of the woman, her body, her mouth, her hands, her voice, her way of moving, her way of sleeping and of dancing with him . . . and her laughter, the thought that all that might not be his any more, that he might have lost her (an element as essential to him as water and air) and it was his own fault — that thought made him rise, bend over in actual physical pain, and cling to the luggage nets to left and right of him with both hands, trembling as if in hysteria. He was mad, that was it, mad about her! How could he have lived without her for almost two years? He was sick, very, very sick. What was the point of it all — liberty, the Aztec civilisation, interminable horse-back rides, physical fatigue, solitude, alcohol, baked beans? What had he been thinking of? Why did he always have to be acting a part of himself, flinging himself into such fatal escapades, such supposedly romantic flights of fancy? Why must he always act out his life like a farce, allotting himself an amusing or a sinister part as he pleased, but one which always ended up leading him, if briefly, away from what was really important and necessary to him: his love, Wanda, his work as a director? Although at this precise moment, as he carefully knocked his head against the window pane with a view to disfiguring himself, although at this moment he would willingly have sacrificed his career to his wife; he would have sacrificed everything to Wanda, "if only she would share with him whatever tiny remant she let him keep!" He would tell her so . . .

Share with him a tiny remnant of what? How could he go

putting things so vaguely? What exactly did he think he meant by a "tiny remnant"? A hovel in the desert? A menial calling in life? Why did he get such ideas — "share with him whatever tiny remnant she let him keep"? What on earth did he mean by that? When he tried to express himself, he did it like a bad writer; when he tried to make a film, he did it like a bad director; and when he tried to love he did it like an oaf. He was nothing, nothing, NOTHING! And for the first time since the beginning of this (unusual) conversation with himself, much struck by finding a simple and plausible word, Constantin stopped knocking his head on the window, straightened up, and sat down quietly like any ordinary traveller. Nothing. NOTHING. Perhaps it was just as well that way: NOTHING. A man of no account. A nonentity. A nonentity who had made a Mexican film which he had wanted to be very good, which he had thought was very good — and which had been a failure; which he had wanted to be enthralling, and which had bored everyone (although the critics had praised it "on the aesthetic plane"). The hell with the aesthetic plane: he wanted people to laugh or cry or marvel at his films. The hell with people anyway, the hell with everyone but Wanda. He had been an idiot; he had thought he could do without her, and it looked as if he was going to pay a high price for thinking so. That was the whole truth.

Constantin rose, reached for the bottle again and swallowed a third of it in four burning gulps. It was horrible stuff to drink in this heat, but the unpleasant taste calmed him. He did not even feel nauseated, his body was in good condition; he opened his hand, closed it again, noticed the strength of his fingers; he had become very muscular this last year. Yes, well, he had developed his muscles in Mexico. He might have lost his wife, his work and his zest for life, but he had acquired muscles. Better than nothing. Oh, really, he felt disgusted with himself, and wondered vaguely just why his intelligence, so keen when turned on other people, so ready to grasp, comment upon and analyse everything that passed before it, became so confused, garrulous and foolish when he asked it to focus on himself.

The fact was, his intelligence was not at his own command, as he had long known. It was something, a faculty, entrusted to him for his lifetime but which had nothing to do with the being of flesh and blood that was himself. That being was only the mouthpiece or standard-bearer of the swift and unrelenting intelligence which was no actual use to him or anyone else, operating like one of those extra-terrestrial characters occasionally let loose on the screen by the directors of science fiction films: monsters or robots with no resemblance to anything human, and usually bent on total destruction. Constantin knew quite well that this weapon he had in his head, aided by his two eyes which saw things so quickly (and which did, incidentally, allow him to make quite good films, if only so that he could lead a pleasant life and get material nourishment), Constantin knew quite well that this weapon was not there solely to destroy him; it was given him for some more important purpose, of which he would never be more than the humble, blind servant. But what purpose, and on whose behalf?

Good God, he was going out of his mind today! Round the bend. Maybe far enough round the bend to crack up, give in. "Wanda!" he groaned, voice high as in some Teutonic romance, but something physically squeezed his heart and made him sit down. It's love, he told himself, with a mixture of crazy hope and great scepticism. It's love, "a young man's trembling emotion, an old man's cynicism, a grinning rictus, a child's glance . . ." Dear Lord, it was about time this train arrived, time it stopped and he got out. He shouldn't be left alone with himself so long; he wasn't used to it, it was intolerable. And Constantin wondered how a human being of any discrimination at all could bear his company as he had now been bearing it for over four hours.

At this point the cruel, intelligent bird perched on his shoulder woke painfully, like an owl woken in broad daylight. All it could do was offer him a little sensible advice, no more, no less. "You had better calm down, Constantin," it said. "You had better calm down. You've been drinking too much and you've spent too long in the sun. How long since you last had anything to eat or any sleep? Going without those would unbalance anyone. What's more, if you want to find Wanda and get back together with her you don't want to frighten her, which you will if you're sick and hysterical and look as ghastly as you do now. Don't think of anything else: just think of what you want and how to get it. Forget about yourself. You were never very interesting, but you're amiable enough, pleasant enough, so just shut up! That's about enough thinking for one day. About enough for one year, in fact . . .

"And what's more," added the exasperated prompter, with the swift, dry manner typical of it (when it was not shut up in a train with Constantin's confused and tiresome thoughts, when it was facing people, ideas, books and events), "and what's more, do us a favour, forget about me, will you? What's this latest notion of yours? Just what is this faculty you're going on about, this impressive, deep-thinking, lofty faculty perched on your shoulder? I think you are being extremely presumptuous. It's not just peculiar, it's downright pretentious . . . Idiotic, in fact! What the hell would make you so intelligent? Why would you have been given this weapon, as you put it, when as you yourself realize you don't make any use of it? Right, you'd better forget all that. There's a touch of psychiatry about it, my poor friend. If I really wanted a laugh, I'd send you off to see a psychiatrist, but you'd find it so tedious. Go to sleep now, do . . ."

Drained and soothed, Constantin von Meck fell asleep with his head on his shoulder.

After passing through a Los Angeles three times bigger than before, the train came into a station which was also three times bigger, and where Constantin's agent, the inimitable Norman Griegson, was waiting for him on the platform. Norman was a small, stout man with gold-rimmed glasses framing innocent blue eyes which were a deception on the part of nature. He had known, liked, and made excuses for Constantin for ever; he therefore submitted without flinching too much to the embrace Constantin bestowed on him, an embrace which was a trial to all who received it. The fact was that Constantin hated to be touched by anyone he did not find physically attractive, and as embracing had come into fashion, first between women, then between men and women, and finally between men, he had briefly resigned himself to accepting certain embraces before choosing those whom he would embrace himself.

Norman Griegson was one of these privileged souls; accordingly, he courageously advanced. Constantin bent down, took him by the waist and drew him close, which naturally left Norman with his legs dangling; then, clutching him to his chest, gripping him like a rabid dog, and thrusting out his chin, he brought it towards Norman's right cheek and rested it there. Next, jaw still thrust out as if he were afraid of being bitten in passing, he applied the said chin to the left temple of the unfortunate Norman, whom he suddenly dropped. It took all Norman's familiarity with this manoeuvre, his agility, and three hasty little steps at the end of it all to keep him on his feet. As for Constantin, he was wearing an expression which, as usual, he believed to be one of the utmost affection.

The full horror of this process was that Constantin applied it only to a few hand-picked persons whose number he occasionally increased, to the alarm of one and all. No one had yet ventured to complain or ask where he had picked up these peculiar notions: it was known that they were dictated by affection and thus could not be avoided, that was all, but as for the criteria which determined their form, those remained a mystery to everyone: they did not include age, or the duration of the friendship, or physical attraction, or anything of that nature. There was something which set off in Constantin this alarming need to show his affection in the Hollywood manner. Even Wanda, who discussed everything with him, had never dared to question him on the subject: at least, when an old lady complained mildly of such treatment, which made her heart — a weak heart — flutter, she had confined herself to asking Constantin idly why he kissed that particular woman and not her sister, who was about the same age and did the same job at Warner Brothers.

"Good God, no!" had said Constantin, forcefully. "It's bad enough kissing *her* — you can't expect me to kiss her sister too!"

And Wanda, baffled, had not continued the conversation. Hollywood society was amused when Constantin's arbitrary choice fell on Dimitri Wallers, the tyrannical little dwarf who was studio manager at Twentieth Century Fox, and who had been flung up in the air like a cork, struck hard on the skull twice and then dropped back on the grass by the gigantic Constantin von Meck with a mixture of revulsion and goodwill. But apart from such moments of comedy, everyone trembled at the thought of becoming one of those obliged to suffer Constantin's embraces.

Having recovered his balance, though not without some flailing of his arms, the result of being out of training — the result, that was, of Constantin's absence — Norman Griegson signed to Constantin to follow him. There was a mysterious and secretive look of ill omen about him, thought Constantin, the look of a bearer of bad news, and he followed the agent without protest to a magnificent convertible into which they climbed, Norman fussing nervously as he adjusted the seat so that he could both drive and give Constantin room to stretch his long legs.

"Came on your own, did you?" said Constantin, in the same airy tone he would have employed to ask, "Fine day, isn't it?" And he added, at once, "I'd say Los Angeles has been multiplied by three, or am I dreaming?"

"You're not dreaming, no," said Norman, eyes on the traffic.

"I guess the people have multiplied by two, anyway."

"Are you taking me to the Siren?" inquired Constantin in the same tone, "You're looking well, by the way."

"Think so? No, I'm taking you to the Brewster."

The Brewster was a pleasant, unassuming hotel where Constantin had lived for some years, but it could not compete with the luxury of his Hollywood house, known as "The Siren", which he and Wanda had rented for nearly ten years.

"Why?" he asked. "Wouldn't I be welcome at the Siren? Doesn't Wanda want to see me?"

"The Siren's been let to someone else. Harold Mason," said Norman, with some difficulty. "The rent wasn't paid for three months," he added in a hurry, as Constantin frowned.

"I see," said Constantin. "So where's Wanda living?"

"In Lilian Gish's old hacienda near Monterey," said Norman, sweating, his eyes still fixed on the road.

"Who with?"

At this Norman suddenly turned on him, furious. "With nobody, Constantin! You know very well Wanda wouldn't have left you for anyone else. It was *your* fault Wanda left you, she didn't leave you *for* anyone! As you must be aware."

There was an ominous silence. Then Constantin put his head back, sighing.

"Well, let's go to the Brewster," he said, and a moment later, "Are my funds as low as that, then?"

"Worse," said Norman. "Worse, old fellow!"

"And you've got a film for me to make right away? Some sugary Hollywood fantasy served with whipped cream? That film you were planning — *Iced Tea*, wasn't it . . . ?"

"No," said Norman, between his teeth, "no, Bernard's making *Iced Tea*. You remember Bernard, the Austrian director? Very gifted . . . he came over from Austria, and *he* was on the spot when the actors were ready. Had to run for it from the Nazis," he added in a hurry, as if this were an excuse for commandeering the film and the script which Constantin expected would boost his finances.

"And what about the producers? Tell me all," said Constantin, head resting on the back of the seat, eyes searching the sky as if to find an unknown avenging god who would do something to improve on this dismal return of his.

"Well, I guess that is about all," said Norman, swallowing. "Look, it's this way: Wanda's left you, your film was a failure, though the critics praised it, you don't have any money and right now you don't have the prospect of a job. Well, except one I found you. It's in collaboration with Lilian Hellen. An adaptation of . . ."

"Shut up, will you?" said Constantin. "Just shut up. Let's go to the Brewster and get drunk."

Which they did. The train from Mexico to Los Angeles had been right to sound so frantic.

Hitherto Hollywood had forgiven Constantin von Meck practically anything: his manner, his supposedly Russian charm, his gaiety, talent, couldn't-care-less attitude and total lack of malice had won him the friendship of his peers (in so far as such a thing was possible in Hollywood) and as much fame among the general public as the biggest stars; his private life, his dissipation and his follies had brought him the popularity of a Barrymore. He therefore found it hard to believe in his reception now: of course, there were friendly, smiling faces everywhere, but no more of that enthusiasm, understanding and instant complicity he had always known in Hollywood. It was as if he had gone just one step too far, as if he had done something absolutely forbidden. And yet what *had* he done, apart from staying away on location a year longer than expected? What had he actually done except waver between continuing on his gilded way and burying himself in the existence of a peon, an obscure life on a hacienda lost beneath the

Mexican sun? Perhaps it was that hesitation between two ways of life, that liberty of choice, which his Californian acquaintances unconsciously penalized. In short, Constantin found welcoming faces and closed doors. Wanda was not in Hollywood; she was away on location, and Constantin's telegrams remained unanswered. According to Norman, the last time she mentioned him had been at Christmas. On opening a Mexican magazine which printed a picture of Constantin drinking tequila in a stable with Maria de Aleya, she had said merely that he didn't look unhappy, and not another word, which in itself was extremely disturbing — horribly disturbing. Constantin tried to get on Wanda's trail, to revive memories of her, even as he hoped for her to arrive in person, to send telegrams, for any sign of her. There was nothing.

The first help that came — or rather, the first offer of work after a long fortnight of solitude, during which he had had to borrow money right, left and centre — was a telegram from Germany, from the powerful, indeed the all-powerful UFA studios, offering him a contract to make Euripides' *Medea* in Greece, with a budget to be fixed by himself, and at a salary which it was also left to him to decide. This was on a day when Constantin had been drinking too much, was disgusted with himself and everyone else, and when Germany seemed a country no more hostile to his future than anywhere else in the world. Without a word to anyone, without consulting another soul, Constantin von Meck, the most talented, famous, free and independent film director of the free world, boarded a plane, boarded another and then another, and landed in Hitler's Germany to make a film of a play by Euripides, under the auspices of Goebbels.

The reverberations of that flight and his decision were more than loud, they were deafening, throughout Europe and America. Constantin did not even know it: no sooner had he landed than he was dispatched to Hydra, a Greek island cut off from the rest of the world where he worked like a man possessed, under a leaden sky, with Andreani Pallas, the great Greek tragic actress. Far, very far from cruel America, and above all far from cruel Wanda.

II

Maud had been weeping all the way, and throughout this story. Constantin was feeling friendlier towards her now; he even felt a certain regard for her, as he did for everyone who willingly fell into his toils. Contrary to the claims of her detractors, Maud Mérival's recent resounding success was not due solely to her looks. She did indeed have the blonde hair, pink skin, blue and ingenuous eyes fashionable at the time in France, if not quite so wildly fashionable as in Germany. But she also had an innocence, a candour in her affectations, an innate lack of character — you might call it impertinence, ingenuity or stupidity as you pleased — combined with the glow of childhood, the laughter of childhood, the silly, pert responses of a child. Ever since her possessive, ambitious mother and a stroke of luck had launched her into show business and established her in that world, Maud Mérival, who felt nothing deeply and genuinely except boredom, discomfort and timidity had been able to call her boredom and discomfort the price of fame and thus bear them more easily. Practice had taught her the gestures, intonations and expressions necessary to her character as a star. She knew how to laugh very loud, fling out her hands, toss her hair back, bend down, pout, frown, and so on — make all the movements proper to her charming, deliciously sensual, and even (if you liked to think so) slightly depraved prettiness. She played at being herself all day, or more precisely, she played at being her reflection in other people's eyes, in mirrors, and her only moments of spontaneity were desperate reactions to the vast vacuum which any unforeseen situation created for her. For instance, if she happened to have a bedroom to herself, she could not go to bed or sleep in it unless someone came to tuck her in — or throw himself on her; solitude terrified her. In fact, her rise to fame was slowly killing her, but no one realized that, least of all Maud herself. Even Constantin, another human being who had been working with her for three months, did not realize it.

In sweeping furiously out of the studios, taking Maud Mérival with him, Constantin had made a mistake. After so eventful an end to the shooting of the film, Maud was stimulated, amidst all the drama, by the idea of the society gloss the refinements of the Bragance salon would bestow on her. For Boubou Bragance's salon figured regularly in the fashionable journals. She dried her tears of emotion and indignation with a handkerchief too wet to be any use by now.

"Do you know her well?" she asked Constantin eagerly. "They say her salon's stunning!" Then, thinking this sounded too naive, she added, "Well, the snobs say it's stunning!" — the term "snob" deriving, so far as Maud was concerned, from the domain of language which was both complimentary and obscure. Constantin shook his head without replying, and took her back to her place to change, having commandeered the UFA producer's car.

Maud was dressed and freshly made up in less than three quarters of an hour, which was a record for her. Then she accompanied Constantin to his room in the Lutetia Hotel, where, impelled by the tide of his anger rather than by desire, he made love to her, but without crumpling her dress, which struck poor Maud as the very height of gallantry. Afterwards, when he apologized for his unexpected ardour, she replied, eyes shining,

"Oh, I've waited so long for this moment!"

"You weren't too disappointed?"

"I — disappointed? Did I seem it?" And Maud assumed a languorous smile to which there was no reply.

She had not seemed anything much, thought Constantin; she had heaved great sighs and uttered little cries, she had done everything to perfection, and he kissed her forehead in the car while she nestled into her white fur coat. How much longer, he wondered, would she keep up the habit of conversing in interrogatives, like the heroine of his film, saying "How could I?" rather than "I couldn't"? It might be some time: when Constantin signed her on for *The Violins of Destiny* a year before, she had just finished playing a woman of easy virtue, a part which left her talking to him and his team like a fishwife for a good three weeks. At least her present stylized manner would be less of a strain than *that* ridiculous lingo. Constantin was also secretly, sadistically, relishing in advance the expression Boubou Bragance's face would wear: stage actors might be accepted in fashionable society these days, but film actors were still considered rather vulgar, more showy than artistic.

Boubou Bragance's house in the Ile de la Cité was a sombre building surrounded by water almost as sombre. The porch was illuminated by two tall candleholders in which two luxurious candles burned, even more luxuriously repeated all the way up the stairs, outlining the romantic, ornamental patterning of the superb flight in black shadows cast on the long, shallow steps. In Maud's eyes, as she clung to his arm, Constantin saw a childlike expression, half dazzled, half afraid, which touched him; just as sensuality followed anger in him, so sentimentality followed sensuality. Having left their coats downstairs, they went up to the first floor and found themselves on a landing with a polished floor, leading to two drawing rooms: out of one of them floated the melodious, sentimental sounds of a Charles Trenet song, with dancers shuffling their feet not quite in time to it.

"I say, this place is quite something!" whispered Maud. "Shall we dance, Constantin?"

"Ssh!" he said, for Trenet was singing *En écoutant mon coeur chanter*, and the trumpets took up the tune like an echo:

> Je vous retrouve à mes côtés
> Me serrant très fort pour danser
> Et dans la nuit pour m'embrasser . . .

The gentle notes of a piano slipped in, accompanying the next verse:

> Murmurant des folies tout bas
> Me forçant à rire aux éclats
> Et me faisant fermer les yeux . . .

"Where's the lady of the house?" Constantin shook himself; he felt that this languorous music and these soft words were suitable only for dance floors for ever removed from him, a thought that saddened more than it actually disturbed him.

"Constantin, do you know where I can comb my hair?" Maud said for the second time behind him. Constantin indicated a door and promised to wait out here for her.

He was watching guests going into the drawing room opposite, the one where there was no dancing, and whistling quietly, when a hurricane came swooping down on him from the far end of the ballroom. It was the lady of the house, Boubou Bragance in person, who had been clasped in the arms of a nervous and passive dancing partner and had abandoned him in the middle of the floor to launch herself at Constantin.

"Constantin! Why, it's Constantin!" she announced, before flinging her two arms like a lasso around her friend's waist. Tilting her head back, she inspected him with small, round, bright eyes like a bird of prey's.

"Now, Constantin, first of all, tell me — are you divorced? Are you a free man?"

"No, first of all," said Constantin, amiably, "first of all *you* tell *me* — is General Bremen here?"

"I asked first!" said Boubou Bragance, firmly. "So you have to answer first."

Constantin began to laugh; amidst all the extravagances of society, she could still act like a schoolgirl.

"All right, I will: yes, I'm free, but I'm not on my own tonight."

"Then I'll answer you too," she said. "General Bremen's here, but there are a lot of people with him."

And they both started laughing.

"I don't think we have the same thing in mind," said Boubou Bragance. "Indeed, I'd be surprised if we did. You old rascal!" she said, trying to slap Constantin on the back, but as her arm was too short to reach his shoulderblades she confined herself to a punch in the region of the solar plexus, which earned her a nasty look from Constantin.

Swathed rather than dressed in what was surely a magnificent black satin Paquin 1935 gown, Boubou Bragance forcibly called to mind a little barrel mounted on piles. But a very rich, very powerful little barrel, able to inspire such terror that nobody dreamed for a moment of mocking her. Married first to a member of the Duval steelworks family, who died young and left her everything, she had then married one Louis Bragance, an obscure literary man who had swiftly disappeared from the scene, and in his turn left her a sketchy kind of salon which she had soon made the most sought-after salon in Paris. Her reign had lasted twenty years, and by now no one knew whether her authority, her alleged aristocratic connections, her flair or her intelligence were to be admired most. In fact, Boubou Bragance was very far from being a fool, and had a remarkable instinct for fashion and those who were going to be in it — even under the Occupation.

She had gradually evolved a series of charming phrases and very efficacious dodges: for instance, she used to say, "I simply call myself Bragance, without the aristocratic 'de'." Which, while it was perfectly true, allowed the hearer to assume that she had the right to use the aristocratic "de", and she had not. Or she would say, "I have to confess I'm well past forty," which again was more than true — since she was sixty — but allowed the gullible to put her age at around fifty. In any case, she reigned over Paris, its salons, its intellectuals, its chroniclers and its politicians of all parties.

For all that, in two years not a German uniform had been seen in her house. She insisted on all her guests, military or otherwise, wearing formal civilian clothes. Accordingly, you met German officers there, but German officers in dinner jackets, very well-bred German officers not all of whom, apparently, were fanatical admirers of Hitler. If by any chance their love for the Führer became too obvious, Boubou Bragance put on a fine display of authority and composure. She would tut-tut, remarking, "No politics in my house, if you please!" in a Verdurin-like voice and laughing, as if Hitler were no more than an issue in some local election. Then, taking the trouble-maker by the arm, she would lead him to her boudoir and brazenly make such explicit advances to the Nazi as very soon sobered him down. This was one of her strengths: she made use of everything she had, including her physical defects, which she actually enjoyed inflicting openly and without shame on handsome young men if she found they could be bought. It was now ten years since Boubou Bragance had discovered, and begun practising, this new form of voluptuous-ness; the dark pleasure of parading her swollen, obscene, fat body, her disgusting and naked body, at length and shamelessly before alarmed young men who would suddenly draw the satin sheet of her bed up over their shoulders, lowering ironic or scornful eyes whose lashes were always too long.

"Boubou," said Constantin, briefly, "I've brought my star along, Maud Mérival. She's no Einstein, but she's charming. Be nice to her!"

He stopped, for Maud, elegant and full of enthusiasm, was emerging from the bathroom.

"Look, the bathroom's all glass and marble!" she exclaimed, abandoning interrogatives for once and turning to Constantin before she realized that the little barrel standing next to her lover, the little barrel with the eyes of a bird of prey, was the lady of the house. The realization stopped her in her tracks, her pretty cherry-red mouth open, and while showing deliberate goodwill, Boubou Bragance shot Constantin a sharp glance. Oh, not bad, my dear Constantin, it seemed to say. She's pretty — stupid, of course, but pretty! And she shrugged her shoulders slightly, as if to ask: why that "be nice to her"? What are you afraid of? You think I might attack your little bird here? Well, really! And she appeared genuinely kind and friendly as she took Maud's hands between her own.

"Well, well," said Boubou, in her powerful hostess's voice — her welcoming voice, which conveyed to all around and to her regular guests that Maud was a newcomer, and under her protection — "well, well, at last! We've heard so much about her, and hoped to see her here for so long, while that naughty Constantin was hiding her away . . . what a lovely surprise for us, oh, what a lovely surprise!"

Boubou Bragance always delivered her platitudes in the first person plural, saying "we" and "us" as if the plural enabled her to shift responsibility for a good many of these stupid remarks to some third party concealed among her guests, an indolent and anonymous third party. "We must drink her health," she added, turning to those of her guests present in the first drawing room, who dutifully approached. "My dears," she cried, "just look at our surprise visitor — Maud Mérival!"

And in the ensuing noise, Constanstin saw the left-hand side of

Maud's throat, the nape of her neck and her cheek blush naively, while Boubou, beaming, the very picture of goodwill and generosity, gave him a satisfied look which demanded his approval. A look to which Constantin returned an ironic and glacial glance. He had noticed everything she put into the word "surprise" in making that announcement to her guests, and between his lips, looking her straight in the face, he enunciated "Bitch!" quite clearly, although without making any sound at all. For in plain language, Boubou was actually saying, "Well, my dears, fancy that: a film actress in my salon! Whatever next? Of course she wasn't invited, but of course I know my duty as mistress of the house." All this was conveyed by her intonation, and she would have had to suppose Constantin very provincial, or very stupid, or perhaps very German not to notice. She flushed slightly under the director's gaze, turned her head away hastily, and took Maud's arm with an affectionate gesture which was intended to say, "Think what you like, but there's solidarity between us women!" It was a gesture which made Constantin shrug his shoulders before he strode off towards the buffet, where he thought he had glimpsed the label of a bottle of vodka standing among some carrot and walnut cakes.

Unfortunately, the bottle was empty. Constantin turned back towards the women: still standing beside the black, gleaming, thick-set, hawk-like Boubou Bragance, and vaguely disturbed by this dangerous proximity, Maud, that gentle dove, had a new kind of smile on her face. Her agent had plenty of imagination, and had also taught her the smile of the modestly successful, a warm, cordial smile, a smile sadly lacking in any ulterior motives. Maud opened her mouth wide enough to show her gums slightly. At this modest smile a young man fell victim to her charms and went over to her: a young man dressed in Teddy-boy style with a long jacket over wide trousers, a cord instead of a tie and thick shoes, or as thick as possible given the shortage of leather: a young man, therefore, who was the very pinnacle of elegance and modernity. He bowed brusquely to Maud and swept her into a wild jive, taking no notice of her widened eyes. Relieved of his duties as escort, Constantin turned to his old friend Boubou and at last gave her a really warm smile: her close-set little black eyes were gleaming with curiosity.

"Now don't tell me," she said, with a laugh in her voice that conveyed no amusement at all, "don't tell me you . . . well, I mean . . . that you and she . . . you're not going to tell me that . . ."

"What exactly don't you want me to tell you!" inquired Constantin politely. And Boubou Bragance tilted her head back, thus obliterating three of her five chins, and uttered sounds of a very strange nature, harsh at first and then rippling.

"Doesn't she remind you of someone?" she said. "With such fair hair, and such pink skin and such blue eyes . . . don't you see what I mean?"

"Yes," said Constantin, "she reminds me of Marshal Pétain as a young girl."

An astonishing kind of cooing noise burst from Boubou's throat even more powerfully and shrilly than before. The witty Constantin turned aside: he had certain principles, acquired very young, principles which, once he had gone to bed with a woman, made him if not her devoted squire at least her protector.

"We're at war, you know," he said gravely, smoothing his moustache with his hand, "and alas, one can't talk of love properly in wartime. You know," he added at once, as her face darkened, "you know you have a remarkable laugh, very curious. First you squeal like a pig, and then you make a sound like cracking nuts."

"Oh, you cheeky devil!" she helped, trying to moderate the tone of her laughter. "Impudent as ever, I see! Careless too, someone told me yesterday. Now who was it? Oh, yes, that little idiot Fario. Did you know Fario was here, your enemy the critic? He's still around . . ."

All of a sudden Constantin brushed his moustache up the

wrong way, pinching its ends and turning them back against his upper lip, so that he instantly and involuntarily resembled a furious fox terrier.

"Oho, so Fario's here is he?" he murmured. "My old friend Fario. With Villeneuve in attendance as usual, I suppose. Laurel and Hardy still wreaking havoc in the Parisian press! Still guiding Hitler's footsteps? Now there's a pair who deserve instant decorations! But," he said, becoming serious again, "but first of all, tell me about General Bremen. Where is he? I need to talk to him."

"What for?"

Dear Boubou Bragance was as frankly and persistently inquisitive as ever. She was used to having her questions answered at once, and Constantin did not intend to thwart her today. He had not come here for fun, he had come for the liberty and perhaps the lives of two pleasant, trusting young men whom he had taken under his wing, and whom he could not imagine being maltreated or even insulted by the SS at this very moment. He refused to believe it; his mind, his imagination always dodged away from the possibility of unpleasantness, something that had prevented him from venturing upon many a love affair that might have been more dazzling than those he had actually had.

"I want to see him," he said, "because I have two men in my film crew called Weil and Schwob — well, I got them papers in the names of Petit and Duchez, or something like that. They were picked up this afternoon and I want them back."

Boubou Bragance shrugged her shoulders.

"Oh, my dear Constantin," she sighed, "you don't yet realize there's a war on, do you? You think you can get your two Jews back from the SS just like that, simply because you're Constantin von Meck and they'll want to do you a favour? Don't you realize it's like taking a bone from a pack of fierce dogs? Don't you realize the SS are raving lunatics? No, of course, you don't realize anything at all! Well, never mind that, my dear; right now, the

General listens to Fario. He's the only Frenchman he does listen to. Go and talk to Fario and ask him to introduce you to Bremen. And I'll mention you to him myself. That's the way to do it. Off you go, my dear! I'm sure Fario and Villeneuve are saying the most dreadful things about me and my guests at the far end of the left-hand room. The general's in the back drawing room, in the middle, near the window. He likes views of Paris — 'Ach, Paris, zo picturesque!' All right? Off you go, then!"

And she set off herself at a resolute toddle in the direction of the window she had mentioned, while Constantin crossed the landing in two strides and inspected the left-hand room. Sure enough, there he found the two most sought-after film and literary critics of contemporary Paris, talking in low voices but laughing very loud, casting casual but sharp glances around them: Jean-Pierre Fario and Henri de Villeneuve, both of them leaning against the fireplace. Although "leaning" was not exactly the right term; if he had ventured to lean on it, Henri de Villeneuve would have fallen into the meagre fire itself, his short stature and the considerable height of the fireplace inevitably tipping him in, since his head did not come as high as the mantelpiece.

Henri de Villeneuve was at present a count, would soon be a duke, and had been congratulating himself on the fact for ever. Particularly of recent years, when his curly hair, his Bourbon nose and his manner of speech had obliged him, like Darius Popesku, to lower his trousers a dozen times before fanatical German Gestapo men. Since 1940, however, as opposed to that occasion in May 1936 when a gang of louts had also debagged him (though that was only to throw him in the family lake), his coronets, which before the war were embroidered only on his shirts but were now scattered over all his underwear, had changed German suspicions into respectful consideration: it showed the pervasive and constant prestige enjoyed by the aristocracy on all social strata of the German nation. Nowadays

Villeneuve no longer wore his nobility just as an innate privilege: it was an extra passport, a talisman whereby he could avoid the police and death.

He had thus come to see in the occupying forces a certain sense of values and a moral hierarchy too often lacking, alas, in the French mentality. Discharged from the army for nervous disorders which were certainly genuine, and a coward too, Henri de Villeneuve had been brandishing the late lamented nationalist Charles Péguy in one hand and Joan of Arc in the other since the fall of France, a dismal date, of course, and one which had seen his anglophobia and germanophilia rising in inverse proportion to the distance between the Nazi tanks and the towers of Notre Dame. Stupid, but no fool — or at any rate well aware of the savage anti-Semitic denunciatory pamphlets being published along with his literary writings — Henri de Villeneuve was later to meet with disproportionately savage retribution: de Villeneuve, too frightened by those who might be said to be of his own way of thinking to have any time to fear the opposite camp, would be shot when France was liberated, convicted of incitement to genocide, whereas he was only a snob and but for those ten years, but for the war, might well have died peacefully in his bed convicted of nothing worse than snobbery.

His alter ego, Jean-Pierre Fario, collaborated with the occupying powers for less puerile and, one might say, less obvious reasons. He too was obsessed with nobility and genealogies, but being wholly unable to add any aristocratic "val", "mont" or "fort" to his own surname, Jean-Pierre Fario had found only one way to connect himself to the aristocracy, namely on the wrong side of the blanket, by way of bastardy. The son of an unknown father, said to have been Spanish, he had always emphasized the semi-anonymity of his birth, dropping copious hints that it was at the very least princely. The fact was, he had been born a bastard like any other, but unlike most bastards he proclaimed it from the rooftops. As a good and magnanimous friend, Villeneuve would let Fario talk at length about his origins, since Fario was the only other journalist who could stand his own conversation, pomposity and foolishness.

In any case, the arrival of Constantin von Meck aroused their curiosity and what they called their high spirits. This great, Germanicized, American colossus, in whose company they had eaten carrot cakes with other patrons of the arts, of whom they had had to hear many complimentary things said while they ate their own hearts out, this colossus Constantin seemed the perfect target for their irony, particularly this evening, when he was accompanied by Maud Mérival, who had her photograph in all the papers . . .

"Well, well, just imagine, a film star in this house!" exclaimed Villeneuve, allowing a hint of reproach to creep into his voice only after casting a circumspect eye around him (for Boubou Bragance could materialize beside you in a split second).

"Yes, we've certainly seen everything now . . . poor Boubou!" replied Jean-Pierre Fario, after scrutinizing the room himself. And they both raised a hand in greeting to Constantin and Maud, who were steering a course towards them, much to their surprise; hitherto, Constantin had seemed more anxious to avoid them than to enjoy their company.

"Good evening, M. von Meck!" cried Villeneuve, who always spoke first by virtue of his indisputably noble birth. "Good evening, mademoiselle. May I introduce myself?"

"Maud, meet Henri de Villeneuve, and this is Jean-Pierre Fario the film critic, maybe soon to be a literary critic too," said Constantin, good-humouredly. The two men bowed with ex-aggerated deference over Maud Mérival's hand; she herself was delighted, and made no objection, even casting them a grateful glance. Constantin was beginning to feel irritated.

"Mademoiselle," said Villeneuve, "Mlle Mérival, I have to tell you I absolutely *adored*, your film . . . what was its name, now? *The Column of Old, The Golden Column, The Column of Gold, The*

Well of Gold? Now what *was* it?" he asked, with insistent incivility.

"Oh," began Maud, very happy to be in a position to offer such erudite men any information, "it was called . . ."

"*The Column of Gold*, that was its name," Constantin interrupted.

"I do assure you, I had to see it two or three times," Villeneuve went on, in the same tone of lively surprise. "I just had to see that film two or three times . . . I really did!" he added to Fario, as if making a confession. For his part, Fario looked amused, and incredulous to think that his brilliant friend could have sat through such nonsense three times running.

"Yes, I did, I honestly did," continued Villeneuve. "Though I must confess I'd been working hard the night before, and lulled by the music of your film — *The Golden Well*, wasn't that it? Or the *Pillar of Gold*, or some such thing — well, anyway, I have to admit I missed part of the plot. Is there a happy ending, mademoiselle?"

"Oh no!" exclaimed Maud, apparently unperturbed to find anyone could so easily drop off to sleep during a film of hers, not even taking an interest in the outcome. "Oh no, I die — I mean, *she* dies," she added, with a small smile of confusion and in a friendly manner which, whether assumed or not, triggered Constantin's fury. Reaching out his arm, he grabbed the collar of the unfortunate Villeneuve's jacket with his right hand and lifted him up in the air like a rabbit. In anger, as in his friendly embraces, Constantin's strength was enough to hold the unhappy critic pinned against the wall like a big butterfly, legs kicking slightly above the floor.

"My dear, good Villeneuve," said Constantin, in a loud, harsh voice which made Fario, who was preparing to pull his companion in misfortune down to earth again, flinch away. "My dear Villeneuve, are you telling us you fell asleep at the end of that excellent film?"

"Here," said Villeneuve, wriggling harder than ever, "here, von Meck, let go of me, will you? You're ruining my dinner jacket, you're hurting me! This is ridiculous! That *Pillar of Gold* film wasn't one of yours, was it?"

"No," said Constantin, "but Mlle Mérival starred in it. It does surprise me, as you are so fond of women and women are so fond of you, to think you were unable to see that superb film through to the end. I wouldn't advise you to do any such thing at the première of my *Violins*."

Constantin had a powerful voice: the guests, one by one, turned slightly to look their way, most of them both surprised and delighted to see Villeneuve pinned to the wall.

"Look here, you're hurting me!" Villeneuve repeated, but not so loud this time, for he felt ridiculous. "Put me down, M. von Meck, put me down or you'll be sorry!"

"Right," said Constantin. "I only wanted to get a little closer to you. You seemed so very low down, so very far below me this evening. Excuse me!"

Opening his hand all of a sudden, he dropped the unfortunate critic twelve inches to the floor; only with a desperate wriggle of his loins did Villeneuve avoid sitting down heavily. However, Boubou Bragance was already on the scene, mysteriously alerted by her notorious personal radar; her guests' glances had attracted her attention and warned her something was going on.

"Good heavens, Constantin!" she said. "Don't say you're still picking people up in the air and waving them about in front of your face to talk to them? Really, it's too bad of you! I do hope he hasn't hurt you, Henri dear?" she added, with an imperious little flick of her finger against Villeneuve's dinner jacket, which made him flush with anger. However, Fario took a step forward — a firm step, since the presence of Boubou Bragance was reassuring.

"Our friend Villeneuve," he told her curtly and indignantly, "was ill-mannered enough to ask Mlle Mérival how her last film, *The Column of Gold*, ended!"

"But," said Maud, who did not really understand any of what was going on, "but I'd already told you: I die. I oughtn't to have died, mind you — it was so silly! It wasn't a happy ending," she added, to Villeneuve, who was dusting himself down nervously and did not so much as look at her. "I ought really to have married the brigand and gone away with him, but the scriptwriter insisted on my death! And mind you, that's not surprising, he was a pansy!" she went on, vivaciously. "So like all pansies, he wanted the heroine dead: it seems that's their standard reaction . . . oh dear, I'm ever so sorry!" she suddenly exclaimed for no obvious reason, and putting a hand to her mouth she glanced apologetically, distractedly, imploringly at Villeneuve and Fario, as if she had dropped a terrible brick. The two men looked at her in bewilderment, as did Constantin and Boubou Bragance, and it was a good ten seconds before Constantin let out a great shout of laughter, bent double with mirth and gasped, "No need to apologize, Maud dear. These gentlemen's tastes don't run that way. You haven't been tactless. Still, that's the third delightful thing you've done for me today: I'm much indebted to you! Come on, Boubou!" he commanded. "Your cheeks are all swollen! You come with me."

And he went off, followed by Maud, doubly embarrassed by her blunder and Constantin's intimate reference to their love-making — also followed by Boubou, who was indeed having great difficulty in suppressing her hilarity. He would manage all right with Bremen by himself, and never mind those two toads.

At the far end of the room there was an oasis in the form of three Louis XVI armchairs standing around a table upon which stood a whole bottle of vodka. The sight of it stopped Constantin in his tracks like a gun-dog pointing at a pheasant, and without consulting his companions he dropped into the centre chair. He was already reaching a lordly hand out for the bottle when Boubou stopped him.

"Don't touch that, for goodness' sake, it's sheer poison! Italian vodka made from potatoes and aluminium. Don't drink it! Aimé," she called, and a butler hurried up, with that shifty expression on his face typical of, or inevitably acquired by, all Boubou Bragance's domestic staff.

"Get M. von Meck some proper vodka," she whispered. A moment later, Aimé came back from the other drawing room with three clean glasses and a dusty bottle, from which he poured drinks.

"Ooh, I say, isn't it strong?" exclaimed Maud. "Oughtn't we to give those poor men back there some? Are you sure I didn't drop a brick, Constantin? Oh dear, are you cross with me, Mme de Bragance?"

" 'Boubou'," that lady corrected her, secretly mollified by the use of the "de". "No, my dear, you didn't drop a brick! Or not as far as I know! I don't suppose they'd know it either, even if you did — backbiting's their usual substitute for good manners . . . Do take it easy, Constantin!"

Constantin, holding the huge glass of vodka Aimé had given him, was drinking it in small sips but continuously, and apparently without drawing breath. Eyes closed, face serene, moustache drooping on either side of his mouth, he appeared calmer; suddenly he seemed twenty, and the two women looked at him appreciatively.

"Don't you think he looks like Christ?" whispered Maud.

"Maybe, but a philandering, alcoholic, Russian Christ — ah, yes, charm personified!" said Boubou Bragance, with the melancholy pride which her unsatisfied desires inspired in her when she thought well of their object — and she did think well of Constantin. She turned her head.

"Well, well, here comes your dancing partner, my dear," she told Maud. "Little Brehagne — he's rolling! He may dress in that ridiculous fashion, but he comes from Brazil, and you might as well know he owns three quarters of all the coffee there."

"Brazilian coffee?" exclaimed Maud. "You mean that young man comes from Brazil? How amazing!" And Boubou's bewildered expression made her add, "Isn't Brazil very far away?"

"Yes, but the coffee gets here all the same," said Boubou. "In the form of beans, too, so why not a biped? Come over here, Séverin!" she called, and the young man hurried up, looking anxious. Without a word, he guided Maud on to the dance floor; she put up only a feeble resistance, for the unfamiliar vodka was already making her legs and spine feel shaky.

She did manage to say, looking at Constantin, "This gentleman wants me to dance," but Constantin, face impassive, only opened his green eyes, already dilated by the alcohol, and let out a feeble, "Can't help that — how could I?" which made Maud blush with shame and a dimly felt anger. Shrugging her shoulders, she followed her fashionable Brazilian millionaire.

"Alone at last!" said Boubou Bragance. "Do you realize we never seem to be alone, Constantin? We never have been. Apart from that one night, of course . . ." And she began to laugh, the same grating laugh as before, but this time Constantin was not amused, for a dreadful doubt suddenly assailed him: had he or had he not really once made love to Boubou, in Vienna or somewhere? It was quite possible. He had done plenty of other stupid things.

Boubou Bragance was in the habit of making men believe (at least if they were drinkers), whether or not it was true, that there had been something between them, on an evening which could not actually be pinpointed. She did it for two reasons: first because it aroused a vague kind of fond, distant gratitude in them, and second because on reflecting that they had not actually died of it, they might think of returning to the fray some day. Constantin smiled weakly, and assumed a melancholy air just in case — that is to say, his moustache drooped a little lower on his chin.

"Constantin, you're not going to sleep, are you?" Boubou Bragance spoke severely. "Constantin, let me remind you there are two Jews you want to get back, two individual Jews out of all the millions who've been arrested. I didn't tell Bremen you were here, or praise you to the skies, just for you to get drunk first. Particularly not on vodka I've been keeping stored away for two years. That may be my last bottle!"

"Oh, come now," said Constantin, husky-voiced, "come now, don't tell me various brave officers back from the Russian front and Stalingrad aren't bringing you crates of the stuff!"

"Don't mention Stalingrad to me, please!" said Boubou, sharply. "I've lost two very good friends there, you know — former lovers, in fact, a Russian and a German. Dreadful thought, isn't it? Maybe they killed each other?"

"You'd have preferred them to fight a duel over you, wouldn't you, darling?" said Constantin, yawning and stretching with unfeeling but deliberate detachment: it was the only way, he knew, to take Boubou's mind off this sad subject. If she ever did show the slightest sentimentality, it was advisable, indeed essential, for her companion of the moment to laugh her out of it at once (before she did so herself, alone with her pillows and perhaps her tears) unless he wanted her to be furious with him later for having witnessed such a thing.

"You're a brute," she said cheerfully, straightening up inside her corsets, eyes bright with pleasure and anger. "Come along and I'll introduce you to the good, worthy, bourgeois Bremen. He runs all the police forces here in Paris, or at least he knows about them. If anyone can get you back your two Jews, Bremen's the man."

Her voice told Constantin that if she did not say "Jewboys" it was only on account of a dislike, natural or acquired, of slang, and not of the term itself.

Bremen looked a melancholy old man, his face covered with fine wrinkles, but his comparative youth showed in his glance and his hyperactive hands. At first glance he seemed more like a Johann Strauss character than a henchman of Hitler. He uttered small, dry bursts of laughter, had a way of turning his head like a bird and rubbing the palms of his hands against each other which, curiously, recalled to Constantin's memory the heroine of a Viennese operetta. Bremen signed to him to join him on the large sofa where he sat enthroned, surrounded by a court of attentive young Germans in evening dress, young men who were sufficiently unnerved by the tall figure of Constantin looming over them to move away one by one, looking annoyed. Constantin sat down with Bremen and met his gaze, a gaze of mingled sympathy and curiosity, but mainly curiosity.

"Well, M. von Meck, so here you are within our walls? Not that we see you on the social scene much . . . our friend Boubou regrets that, and very understandably too!" he said, with a small smile of approval which threw Constantin off balance.

"I can't go out socializing while I'm working," he replied. "Making a film is quite exhausting work, you know."

"How lucky you are!" continued Bremen, without listening to him. "Living in a world of pasteboard sets, surrounded by illusion, cut off from life and its horrors . . . *ach*, war is a terrible thing," said he, with an air of conviction so quaint as to seem comic.

"Yes, indeed," said Constantin forcefully. "In fact that's just why I wanted to talk to you, General! I . . ."

However, there was no doubt about it, Bremen was not listening to him.

"Yes, M. von Meck, war is a terrible thing for a man: not just because he has responsibilities, but because if he has any imagination he fears them; war is most terrible of all for a man at night, before and after battle. Solitude, you see, is the soldier's constant companion, yes, solitude!" he asserted, frowning, chest thrust out, and he tapped his knee with the flat of his hand as if to drive home this platitude (which in Constantin's opinion was better situated on his knee than in his head). The poor man was going senile.

Constantin made another effort at entering the conversation, less directly and more generally this time.

"There's solitude everywhere, sir. A director feels it too: I myself feel very far from my life, my friends, the people I know and . . ."

"Yes, yes, how true!" cried Bremen abruptly. "Married too, are you? A terrible thing, eh? A dreadful thing, leaving one's home behind! My wife, my children, my children, my wife — I think of nothing else. Outside working hours, of course," he added, with sombre pride. Constantin wondered uneasily whether Nazism invariably led to mental debility. He sought Boubou Bragance's glance, but she was some way off, feeding like a bee on the dubious nectar of her guests' conversation.

"Personally, I'm divorced," he said flatly.

"Divorced? Oh, what a mistake!" The general appeared scandalized. "Divorce is sacrilege! How can you leave a woman? How can you get divorced from a woman when you've vowed to live with her for ever?"

"Alas!" murmured Constantin, cautiously. "Alas, alas, alas!" he added in a louder voice, by way of counterbalancing things. He had had all he could take of this old wreck made of iron, military crosses and gold braid: no doubt his officer's cane was down in the cloakroom too . . . The General at last gave him a puzzled look.

"Our friend Boubou told me you wanted to see me about something," he said. "May I ask what?"

"Yes," said Constantin, 'it's about two friends of mine, my designer and my electrician. The Gestapo arrested them this afternoon on the grounds that they were Jews, and I want them back."

There was a silence. Bremen was rubbing his nose from top to bottom; he stopped at the edge of his nostril, looking deeply interested.

"And are they?" he asked.

"Are they what?" inquired Constantin. "Jews, you mean?"

"Yes."

"Well, of course," said Constantin, surprised. "Of course they are. Jews, I said, not masochists!"

"All right," said the General. "All right . . . though I don't know that 'all right' is quite the way to put it . . . I'd sooner they hadn't been, so far as your little business is concerned."

"In which case they wouldn't have been arrested," said Constantin, logical for once. "I don't follow you, General."

Bremen began to laugh, a crafty look in his eye, forefinger raised: he couldn't be more than fifty-five, sixty at the very most, it must be something other than time that had aged that face.

"Well, the Gestapo do sometimes make mistakes on purpose, my friend. Deliberate mistakes, I mean. I personally saw a young man called simply Schneider arrested at Drancy as a Jew — which he wasn't. Schneider! Yes, Schneider? Well? Does that seem Jewish to you, eh? Schneider?"

Constantin recoiled: the man's mental weakness, senility and epileptic manner were alarming.

"Schneider," he repeated automatically. "Schneider? I don't know. Nothing seems particularly Jewish to me. What does racialism mean, anyway?"

"Oh, my poor fellow," said the General, amused, "it means that you won't be seeing your two employees for some months — well some weeks, anyway: as long as it takes for Germany, *our* Germany, to finish winning the war."

Constantin restrained himself from saying that the prospects for their Germany did not look to him too bright. He persisted. "Then you think we *shall* soon be seeing them again? What is the Third Reich going to do with them? Where are they now? All those trains leaving and never coming back — it's bound to cause some anxiety, don't you think?"

Bremen sat very upright on the sofa, so that the top of his skull reached the level of Constantin's chin. He raised his forefinger again, but this time he pointed it at his companion's face like a pistol.

"What do you mean?" he asked arrogantly. " 'Never coming back' — what do you mean? You think that's bound to cause anxiety, M. von Meck? Well, let me tell you, it's not just Jewish men we're taking away. We are also taking Jewish women and children! We are taking Jewish babies! What do you suppose we do with them? M. von Meck, do you really believe that Germans, our own fellow countrymen, are capable of inhumanity? Do you take the German army for a set of sadists?"

Luckily for Constantin, Bremen's voice was rising higher and becoming weaker at the same time, while his face reddened with excitement. But he began again almost at once. "Do you think we would let anything happen to them — we, officers of the Third Reich? We who come from Essen, Jena, Elendorf?"

"No, no," said Constantin, crushed, "no, I know you wouldn't. Only the Wehrmacht isn't the whole of the German army, there's the SS too. Personally, I find them rather disturbing."

"The SS in France have been under my command since 1942. So have the Gestapo. I am in charge of the political police," said Bremen, as he might have mentioned that he had a Persian cat. But he had slumped again, and was sitting almost hunched on the sofa, eyes vague, hands dangling between his knees. Once again he looked a powerless old man, and he also — it suddenly flashed through Constantin's mind — he also looked, quite simply, like a man terrorized. But by whom? Or by what? What did he know? Acting on an impulse of pity which surprised himself, and which was due to the vodka, Constantin put his hand on the General's sleeve.

"Are you unwell, sir?" he asked, lowering his voice. "Can

I do anything for you?"

Bremen sat up, tried to inject a martial light into his blue eyes again, but then lowered his eyelids and turned his head away as he muttered, "No, there's nothing you can do for me, M. von Meck. And there's nothing I can do for your friends. Or maybe there is! Ask my ADC," he added waving an aristocratic hand in the air and dismissing Constantin at the same time as he indicated a flabby-faced young man of rather unlikeable appearance, stolidly crunching a synthetic pretzel a little way off.

Bremen repeated this gesture three times, in a manner that was not very courteous, but chiefly seemed weary. Taken aback, Constantin went off to find his bottle of vodka (which he had been watching out of the corner of his eye throughout the conversation, and which he now finished off very quickly all by himself). It enabled him to think the aide pleasant enough after all when he eventually joined him, and even to believe the man straight away when he promised to fix everything: Bremen had all the necessary signatures, he said, and he himself would be pleased to free Constantin's two friends — whose names he took down in a little notebook — and send them round to him at the Lutetia. He could say that for sure, he added.

And thus, despite the unlikelihood of this promise, Constantin persuaded himself that he would have Schwob and Weil back next day. Just as his intelligence sometimes impaired his preference for happiness, his optimism sometimes impaired his lucidity. How could he believe that despite the implacable laws of the Third Reich, implacably put into practice, despite the part so tirelessly played by the Gestapo, his two Jewish friends, arrested in possession of false papers, would ever be returned to him? And yet he did believe it. First because it was what he wanted, and it was unusual for him not to get what he wanted; second because even if he did not wholly believe in the power of his name and of his star status as a film director, he was sure of his luck. Constantin therefore got deliberately drunk that evening, several times spurning the tearful and sentimental lamentations of poor Maud, who was trying to get him away. He ended up drunk and dead to the world on the bed in his hotel room.

In the middle of the night he woke up, clear-headed and desperate. He was all alone. Nobody loved him. If he died, no one would be sorry: not Wanda, his beautiful, crazy, egotistical wife, nor Romano, that suicidal and violent youth, nor poor little Maud with her childish ambitions. His future looked bleak and nasty: he would have to answer for the crimes which he guessed his compatriots were committing as if they were his own. And no one would want to defend or protect him, since no one had ever tried to do so yet — except that grim-faced, harsh-voiced nonentity, that fanatic Goebbels, the perfect symbol of the absurdity of his own life. The stupid films he had to make, so complacent in their sugary artificiality, could no longer distract him or hide the fact that his life was dismal, lonely and pointless; a bleak life which was nothing but a long and ineluctable slithering towards death, a slithering which would soon accelerate until it ended in a brutal, horrible, unmerited fall. Writhing with fear and grief in his bed, Constantin von Meck, who at forty could still suffer the panic-stricken despair of a boy of eighteen, surprised himself by calling out for his mother, and realized he was guilty of having done it in English.

Sitting up in bed with the light on, Constantin tried to retrieve his image of himself as Constantin von Meck the director, the devil-may-care, invulnerable character who, he well knew, would be laughing at these fancies tomorrow, laughing at the shivering old man he had prematurely become that night. The trouble was that at this particular moment, that light-hearted, all-conquering Constantin did not exist: he was nothing but a reflection, a cardboard cutout, a straw dummy set up to keep the fierce, squawking birds at a distance — Hollywood producers of yesterday as well as Gestapo officers of today. A dummy who sometimes managed to scare off a few of those dangerous predators, but who never frightened away the eagle, persistent, always there, who crushed him and was only himself, Constantin, a man of forty without genius, without a country, without ties, a thousand leagues away from his audiences, his mistresses and his friends: a Constantin devoid of grace or mercy, a Constantin without courage, unable to manage without a mask, a Constantin who was not now the man he had been all his life, not the man he had been only three years before.

1939 Berlin

Although the month of April had hardly begun, Berlin was basking in warmth and sunlight that afternoon; summer before its time, but too mild a summer to slow the pace of life in the city. There was an atmosphere of tension and frenzy about the streets which seemed to have nothing to do with the seasons.

At the wheel of a splendid black Duisenberg convertible, a present from Goebbels on his arrival, for which he must soon thank him, Constantin von Meck was driving through the city and smiling despite himself: Berlin in military mood, he thought, had a touch of operetta about it. Fifteen years in film studios, including Cecil B. de Mille's, had given him an eye for certain areas where the Third Reich had overdone the decor and direction: too many soldiers, too many flags, too much saluting! And too many swastikas in the streets, too many monuments, and too much martial activity! Constantin smiled, as if at an error of taste.

Having arrived that morning at Tempelhof airport, still dazed by Greece and its inexhaustible sun, Constantin was feeling tired, happy, and pleased with himself, in spite of those comments in the press which had followed his departure from the United States, and which he had not seen for six months — for as soon as he arrived UFA had sent him straight off to Greece, to the island of Hydra, to write and direct *Medea*: his superb *Medea*, the marvellous film he had edited himself in Athens, remote from civilization, the film now enjoying a triumph throughout Europe before going on to conquer America. Constantin felt cheerful, in spite of the faintly exotic impression he felt in all foreign capitals, though he ought not to have felt it here: he was in his native land, surrounded by fellow countrymen who spoke the language of his childhood, and he did not like to find himself feeling the globetrotter's instinctive, condescending curiosity; in fact, he felt it here more than in Paris, certainly more than in New York. But apart from these questions of patriotism, Berlin was ten times more tolerable than during his last, very brief stay in the city: the poverty-stricken people wandering among the ruins at the time of his departure in 1921 were now a solid, well-dressed body of men and women, walking their streets with energy: with rather too much energy, perhaps, for Constantin's liking. There seemed to be not an idler left strolling along the pavement, or a woman stopping to look in a shop window, transfixed by desire. The entire city appeared to be populated by soldiers, officers, their mothers, their wives and their children.

Of course, Germany was at war, or soon would be; it showed just a little too much, even in his hotel, the old Kampeski palace, where the chambermaids on his floor, instead of chatting brightly with him — like chambermaids in hotels the world over, in his experience — or exclaiming at his wardrobe as it deserved, had hung up his clothes without comment, and with the busy, intent look of women soldiers. No, Germany at war was not a very cheerful place. Well, he hadn't come here to amuse himself . . . And Constantin was driving towards the Ministry of Information when a woman on the pavement at a road junction, seeing the golden-blond giant sitting in his open car, met his green eyes and instinctively returned his smile, thus restoring Constantin von Meck's zest for life and his patriotic fibre.

He was whistling as he entered the Minister of Propaganda's courtyard, where his pass, signed by Goebbels himself, earned him a dozen of those abrupt, noisy salutes, arm raised, heels clicking, now customary everywhere, even in the bar of the Kampeski. He parked his car in the sun, roaring its engine. And the stupid soldiery, those idiots with their heads full of tanks and Bren gun carriers, did not so much as glance at the big headlights, the long lines, the excellent design, the sheer pedigree of his wonderful car. An officer instantly appeared beside the car door and opened it, not omitting to give him that apparently military salute, here accompanied by a fervent "Heil Hitler", a greeting to which Constantin replied only with a small wave of the hand, purposely effeminate and provocative, though it failed to shake his guide's impassivity. The officer did, however, look startled when he saw the car's occupant get out: a broad-shouldered colossus of six foot four whose three-piece suit, though of impeccable classic cut, was made of russet corduroy more red than brown in colour.

"It's called Burnt Sienna," Constantin informed him, with a friendly smile. "Kwickers Taylors of Beverley Hills made it for me. Did you have to wait long?" he then politely inquired in English, before clapping a hand to his forehead and adding apologetically, in the purest German, "Oh lord, I'm so sorry! I really must break myself of that dreadful habit of speaking English, or I'll end up shot. How are you, Herr von Briek? It *is* Lieutenant von Briek, isn't it?"

For this same aide of Goebbels had met Constantin von Meck on his arrival at Tempelhof airport ten months ago, and had very civilly escorted him to the Athens-bound plane. No doubt he was the man whose job it had been to observe him and perhaps work out why this famous, brilliant director, at the height of success and living a life of pleasure in his adopted America, had taken into his head the preposterous idea of coming back to make films for the Nazis, defying the opinion of a Europe he adored, and for principles and an ethic which seemed contrary to all his previous statements and his work as a whole. Despite his good breeding, therefore, von Briek had been startled by the sight of Constantin in bright red, and he paused for a moment before going on in his usual tone.

"Herr von Meck," he said, "the Minister is waiting for you in his office. You are right on time. Will you follow me, please?"

"With pleasure, my dear chap, with pleasure," said Constantin, running on the spot to loosen up before the astonished eyes of the sentries and the soldiers, and he fell in behind his guide. He followed him down miles and miles of marble corridors, with men on duty planted along them every twenty yards or so at regular intervals like fruit trees, but armed fruit trees: they thrust out their chests and clicked their heels as Constantin and his companion passed, and Constantin murmured, to von Briek's back, "What sort of nervous tick sets them all saluting like that? Wouldn't it be an idea to teach them tap-dancing too, or some other kind of step? What will you do with the habit when the war's over?"

Constantin had raised his voice as he put this last question in German, but von Briek increased his pace, without turning. Constantin went on.

"I mean, von Briek, when the war's over and you've sent this lot home, what's to become of them, lumbered with that silly, useless habit, eh? Their boot leather will have worn thin as cigarette paper around the ankles. And there's always a chance peace may come, don't you think?"

He was openly raising his voice now, and just as openly, von Briek was quickening their pace. They passed NCOs and private soldiers, their bodies held rigid by discipline, but their eyes showing amazement at the sight of this outlandish, vivid character striding down their corridors.

"I say, Lieutenant," Constantin remarked at last, "we must have gone a mile or so by now — shall we be there soon?"

Pale but undaunted, von Briek pointed to the end of the corridor. "We *are* there, Herr von Meck. His Excellency's office is just in there."

And all of a sudden they came into an antechamber, also guarded by two soldiers with fixed bayonets, who presented arms to von Briek with the usual pantomime, but did not so much as flinch at the sight of Constantin. Their jutting jaws, dull eyes and smooth foreheads had nothing really human about them, he thought, as the soldiers automatically withdrew before von Briek and himself, as at last he entered the holy of holies — where his guide left him.

Yet again, he was glad he had worked on large-scale Hollywood productions, or this immense empty room, containing a desk, two chairs and a picture of Hitler on an equally large scale which hung on the wall behind the small, very small figure of Goebbels might have impressed him. That small, misshapen figure rose and came to meet him.

"Herr von Meck," said Goebbels, "you have no idea how happy I am to welcome you to Berlin in person! I was very sorry to be at Berchtesgaden when you passed through Berlin before . . ."

As one of them was too tall and the other too short for their mutual comfort, they made haste to the armchairs, as to a haven, and sat down, one each side of the desk, before venturing to look one another in the face. Goebbels' eyes were a pale blue-grey, Constantin's were light green. They were as different as they possibly could be, but they felt a momentary pleasure in their exchange of glances, as can happen between two rather keen intelligences used to grappling with the predictable stupidity of strangers.

Mouth closed, eyebrows raised, manner faintly arrogant, Goebbels scrutinized his companion, employing tactics which must have proved successful before, but which irritated Constantin. Ignorant of the protocol, he was the first to break the oppressive silence, although with a friendly remark.

"That Duisenberg really is a splendid toy — no, a superb toy!" he said, in German. "I don't know how to thank you."

Surprised, but amused, Goebbels looked deprecating. "Don't mention it, Herr von Meck. The Third Reich owes you a great deal, if only from the point of view of the international press. Your leaving Hollywood to come here was like a disavowal of the aggressive policies of the enemies of the Reich, and an endorsement of our nation — an important consideration."

Constantin's face did not show any particular satisfaction. The reasons for his return were too precise and too personal for him to be able to claim that he had earned the disapproval of Europe on such grounds. It must have been obvious, for Goebbels continued, "Contrary to what certain newspapers say, no cheque can repay you for that, any more than a banker could direct *Medea*. You have had a great success with that film, Herr von Meck, a well-deserved success; I felt as if it had been made in red and black rather than black and white. A superb film!"

Constantin smiled his thanks, for the compliment summed up his own intentions well enough.

"Thank you," he said. "My present ambition is to make *Oedipus* in black and gold — if possible."

"I think," said Goebbels, "UFA has other projects for you."

Constantin sat up straight in his chair. "I don't want to hear about that kind of project. UFA wants me to make *The Jewess*, an anti-Semitic film."

"So?" said Goebbels.

"So it's not at all the kind of thing I feel like doing," said Constantin, smiling. "And believe me, no cheque would make any difference to that either: there isn't a man in the world rich enough to make me change my mind."

There was a short silence.

"You ought not to express your . . . opinions so clearly," said Goebbels, quietly. "To me, perhaps, but not in public. Or to the police."

"Nor any instrument of torture atrocious enough," said Constantin, accentuating "atrocious" in such a manner as to remove any suggestion of melodrama from the phrase. "I shall not make *The Jewess*; I'd rather go back to America."

This was Constantin's trump card, and he knew it. Goebbels was not at all anxious for him to leave again, thus offering the Third Reich a slap in the face. Or at least, so Constantin hoped . . .

"It would be a pity," said Goebbels, raising a soothing hand, "it would be a pity if you went back to the USA before your *Medea* is released. It would be better to return with a success to your name — crowned with laurels, as it were. Don't you think so?"

"Well, yes . . ." said Constantin. It was true; he did not want to go back to Hollywood unless he could do so in triumph.

"It would be a pity for the Third Reich too," said Goebbels. "Indeed, a great pity. Your leaving would make the Third Reich seem a country inaccessible to artists, one they could not tolerate, and that, as I will not conceal from you, Herr von Meck, would do us great harm."

Constantin was surprised. This cunning little man was revealing his own weak points, giving him, Constantin, weapons to fight with. In short, the man meant what he said. And his own plans for leaving again were not so serious as all that, thought Constantin, who had never attached much importance to himself or his fame, or the possible repercussions of his commitments where the public was concerned. He hedged.

"Well, let's wait and see. *Medea* will have its American

première in a couple of months. Meanwhile, I might revisit the scenes of my childhood. After all, I could do with a holiday . . ."

Goebbels lit a cigarette, slowly, looking straight at him.

"You don't really want a holiday, Herr von Meck. I know why you came here, you see."

And changing his tone, he spoke in a friendly voice.

"Herr von Meck, wouldn't you have expected me to make my own inquiries, considering that your return to Germany has made headlines in the world press? Don't you suppose I too must have wondered why you would come back to Germany now, when you've made your career elsewhere, when the whole world is wondering why you returned? It was my duty to find that out, Herr von Meck, and I believe I have."

Constantin scrutinized him. "Well, well!" said he, smiling. "So you know my reasons — but are you sure I know them myself?"

Goebbels began to laugh. He had a small, dry laugh, which he concealed behind his hand as if he were coughing.

"If you don't know your own reasons, Herr von Meck, perhaps it will be my privilege to reveal them to you. You didn't leave the USA out of resentment or wounded vanity, as certain newspapers have implied. Your reasons lie much farther back, don't they? Let's see, now . . . you left Germany in 1912 with your mother, who was getting divorced. You were eleven or twelve at the time, weren't you?"

"About that," said Constantin, intrigued.

"And when Germany declared war on France in 1914, you were already in Hollywood. Your mother had married a producer, and when the Great War broke out, she kept you in America; in any case, you were too young then to fight."

"Exactly."

"So the war went on, but you were just beginning on your career, weren't you? You were already an assistant to the directors of the time, one they valued. Your course was already set for success, at fifteen! Such things can happen only in America."

Constantin nodded, without replying.

"You didn't know that Germany was bled white, she had no soldiers left, that boys of fifteen to eighteen from the officers' schools were volunteering in spite of their age . . ."

Constantin von Meck had lowered his head and was looking at his hands, examining his nails attentively.

"No," he said. "No, I didn't know."

"So that when you came back to Germany in 1921, Herr von Meck, and you decided to pay a visit to your old school in Essen, you found that while you had been gone, all your schoolmates were killed at the front. Some of them were older than you, of course, but some had been your own age, and none of them had wanted to survive defeat. You discovered then, Herr von Meck, that you were the sole survivor of your class, except for a young officer with an amputated leg. For you had been to a famous school for military cadets, Herr von Meck."

"Quite true," said Constantin.

And he dug into his pocket for a cigarette, taking a very long time to extract it, his eyes still lowered. Goebbels was watching him with evident enjoyment. When the cigarette was lit at last, he went on, in icy tones.

"And this one-legged officer, your former fellow student, called you a coward in an Essen café in front of everyone; he even challenged you to a duel. As for you, you felt guilty; you had incurred a debt to Germany that day, a real debt, for intelligent or not, no one forgets an insult of that kind, or not at the age you then were, am I right?"

Constantin was inhaling deeply, still looking down. "How did you know all this?" he asked in a tragically choked voice which rather embarrassed him.

"From one of your teachers who was in that café. And then, I know everything on principle, Herr von Meck; it's the principle of the thing, you see."

Constantin looked up again; Goebbels was no longer smiling.

"You are quite right, Minister," he said. "Yes, that wretched memory is still with me, and it leads me to do some strange things . . ."

"But now it has led you to do something upon which I congratulate you," said Goebbels in a strident voice — an orator's voice unexpectedly issuing from this shrivelled little dwarf racked by nervous tics. "Something which does you and all Germany honour!"

Constantin relaxed, and sighed; it was the first time since the incident in 1921 that anyone had reminded him of that humiliation — disagreeable at the time, but something he had in fact forgotten a long time ago. Certainly the class photograph taken in Essen in 1912, where he figured at the age of twelve with his fellow pupils, and on which, when he saw it again, all the heads were marked with a black cross — all but his own and his tormentor's — certainly that photograph had haunted him for a while, but then, like all unpleasant memories, it had faded from his mind; after all, he had merely omitted to do what he still saw as a barbaric and useless duty. Since then, he had had many chances of proving that he was no coward. However, he was perfectly happy for Goebbels to attribute his return to the enormity of a memory of his schooldays suffered in 1921 and not the enormous size of a cheque from UFA offered in 1937! These Nazis were very romantic, ultimately very moral in a heroic kind of way . . . When those directors and scriptwriters who had recently fled from Europe to exile in California painted a terrifying picture of the dimwitted, blood-thirsty brutes who now ruled Germany, they were forgetting Josef Goebbels; the small, glum, puny man who made all Germany tremble but who surely must tremble himself before a woman. Goebbels certainly had a moral intelligence, even if he admired and followed the nonentity whose picture hung above his head, Hitler the dictator with his motheaten moustache and the cowlick adding the last touch to his ridiculous appearance. Moreover, if like so many others, but for reasons of his own, Goebbels deferred to that vociferous tradesman, he must have a plan. Constantin toyed briefly with the idea of making friends with the little Minister; he would teach him how to get on with women, how to dress well, he would get him to throw away those boots which made him look even smaller; he would make him want to whistle as cheerfully as a blackbird all along these aseptic corridors. It couldn't be much fun for a clever, cultivated mind, putting up with this martial show . . . On an impulse, Constantin gave Goebbels a warm smile. Surprised, Goebbels twitched, blinked, and bent nervously over a large file open in front of him.

"Here's the basis of my discoveries," he said, pushing it towards Constantin. "There is your past, your ancestry, your friendships, your achievements: in short, your history! You may keep that file, Herr von Meck; I have no further use for it."

"Nor have I!" said Constantin cheerfully. And without glancing at it, he threw it in the waste paper basket under the desk. Then Goebbels fell to discussing films with his guest — *Rain of Steel*, *The Golden Tears*, *Dead Calm* — various different films Constantin had made, and always with a keen but admiring critical faculty which in other times would have won him the approval of any film director. They spent almost an hour talking about the cinema, and Constantin was the first to pull himself together; being now well launched into a mood of romantic heroism, he asked, if war came, to be swiftly sent to some position of danger in the German Army. It was as friends that they made for the door, the one still towering above the other.

In the doorway, Goebbels held out his hand to Constantin, who did not, however, take it, but turned towards the desk. Goebbels looked disconcerted rather than angry, for Constantin had raised his eyes to the picture of Hitler at the other end of the room: slowly raising his right arm and holding it out in front of him, clicking his heels as best he could in a pair of leather mocassins, he executed a perfect Nazi salute before the curiously disappointed eyes of Goebbels; then, however, he glanced at his own rigidly extended hand and spread its fingers in an exaggerated manner before, suddenly looking very cheerful, he turned to Goebbels.

"Still not raining, Your Excellency," he whispered, as if confiding a secret.

Rooted to the spot, motionless, Goebbels looked at him for a moment and then began to laugh: nervous, shrill, hysterical laughter, laughter which followed Constantin far down the corridors, so that as he went his way he met subalterns in whose eyes he noticed a uniformly incredulous look — a look of alarm, more often than not, at those unfamiliar sounds.

III

The telephone in his hotel had an intolerable, fretful ring; next morning the still drowsy Constantin reached his large hand out to the bedside table and knocked over various different objects before finding the receiver. He put it to his ear, cautiously, since although that ear seemed to be floating somewhere a thousand leagues away from his shoulders, his head felt fragile and heavy.

"Hullo?" he grunted.

A fresh, crystalline voice, the voice of youth itself, Maud's voice, made him grimace; such an echo of spring, such bubbling high spirits could only emphasize the fact that his mouth seemed to be made of wood.

"Oh, my goodness, is that you Constantin! Am I glad to hear you! I've been so worried! Can you hear me?"

"Who is it?" he growled, for form's sake rather than out of any curiosity.

"Maud! It's Maud . . . me, Maud!"

"Maud? What Maud?" he asked in his deep, husky voice, his alcoholic's voice.

"Why, Maud! Maud, of course! Constantin, just how many Mauds do you know?"

Indignation made her raise her voice, and Constantin hastily held the receiver farther from his ear.

"So?" he inquired, teasing her. "You think you're the only Maud on earth? There are dozens of Mauds in some countries —

Kenya, for instance. It's a very popular first name in the overseas colonies, Maud is. It's English, it's bright, it's fresh: Maud. It's rather . . ."

But Maud Mérival, that fragile-looking star of the French cinema, interrupted him with unexpected vigour.

"Here, you're laughing at me, aren't you? Can't you please be serious for once, Constantin? Where were you last night? Do you know I spent a whole hour looking for you all over that mansion, with Mme de Bragance, the mistress of the house herself? Do you know she's very cross with you? Do you know . . ."

"I don't know anything, darling," Constantin groaned wearily.

Leaning back on his pillows, he felt aware of the weight and precise shape of every bone in his skull and his face: that must be due to vodka. He was familiar with its after-effects.

"What were we drinking last night?" he asked abruptly. "Vodka was it?"

"It was indeed!" said Maud forcefully. "It most certainly was! Oh yes, that was vodka you were drinking! Good vodka too, Boubou Bragance told me, or she said it might have killed you. M. von Meck, you are totally crazy!" she said in a light tone that made Constantin grimace again.

Why, however, was poor Maud scolding him so lovingly? All of a sudden he remembered making love to her in this very room yesterday evening: she was merely telephoning her new lover, that was it! Now he'd got himself into a nice mess! And on the very last day of shooting, too! Feeling remorseful, but more wakeful now, he assumed a more affectionate tone.

"My dear Maud, I'm really sorry about last night — Boubou's party, I mean — but the fact is I *had* to get drunk. Speaking up for Schwob and Weil . . . in front of those Germans . . . those officers, that is . . . it left me fuming."

"It's the result that counts, Constantin. You were marvellous! Remember what that general promised you! Thanks to you we'll have Petit and Duchez back in the studio in a week's time. And remember, they'll have escaped those dreadful labour camps. You were just *fantastic*!"

"Yes . . . at least, I hope so," said Constantin, drily and in an almost business-like tone, as if to bolster up that hope. "Yes, of course, the end of the week, that's what they promised. The end of the week . . ."

But there was already doubt in his mind: how could he have felt so confident last night, celebrating a vague promise extracted from two strangers in the space of five minutes as if it were a definite success? Why hadn't he insisted on details? Written details? Why had he been so easily satisfied — unless it was egotism, his feeling for other people's troubles combined with his passion for amusing himself and his ability to disregard every-thing not calculated to help him to that end? He had always been the same; he flung himself into magnanimous crusades, but the least little victory, the smallest apparent success appeared to him definitive and wonderful, and then he would quit the field.

"What are you thinking of, Constantin? What obsession is haunting you?" murmured Maud at the other end of the line. "What's going on? What's on the boil beneath that lion's mane of yours?" she suddenly inquired in lyrical tones.

Surprised, then pleased, Constantin came fully awake now.

"Beneath my lion's mane, as you put it, I'm feeling the electric shocks and short-circuits of an evening spent drinking vodka. And how about you, my dear Maud? What's simmering beneath your own blonde mane? What have you been reading this morning to inspire you with your romantic vocabulary? *The Jungle Book*?"

"Oh, I read that when I was a little girl," said Maud (delighted that Constantin had hit upon one of the items in her not very well-stocked literary store). "Well, I just wanted to send you a little good-morning kiss, Constantin. There, now I've done it! You'll call me later, won't you, darling?"

"Yes, yes," grunted Constantin, who had closed his eyes and clenched his fists at the mere sound of the little good-morning kiss being dispatched down the receiver. That innocent, caressing little noise was now going to soothe his future awakenings. He hung up hastily, as if the telephone were red-hot, realized it, and laughed ruefully. What he urgently needed was a coffee or a vodka to get his head into working order. He stretched his arms and legs, and decided on first an aspirin, then a bath, and finally a vodka.

He made sleepily for the bathroom, meeting his full-length reflection in the bedroom mirror as he passed. He stopped, examined himself from head to foot and then back again with a critical but paternal eye: that big body with all its hair, that moustache, those teeth, those nails, that large, bony body, reliable, sturdy and (by an indispensable piece of luck) attractive to others was his own! A hale and hearty body able to run ten kilometres without getting puffed, drink two bottles of vodka in a session without falling over, enjoy someone else's body all night and sleep only three hours out of the twenty-four for a month. A body that could chase, pursue, resist or endure people, shocks, accidents, even excesses. And heaven knew he had indulged in enough of those; his body, urged on by his mind, had thought up some fine varieties! Scrutinizing himself, Constantin began to laugh: his laughter was for the gaze he was bending on himself as if on his double, a gaze supposedly intelligent and superior to that reflection. What was he but a machine made of flesh whose sensations were conveyed by the lightning speed of his nerves to that little box known as the brain, whence they set off again at the same speed, by way of those same nerves, but transformed into reflexes, before ending in a small, or a noble, or a pitiful human action? There was no need to add an eternal soul to this remarkable ensemble: the length of time lived by the instinctual human body and that little box of awareness seemed to him quite enough, the duration of human existence was the thing, since it sometimes — both physically and mentally — seemed too slow or too fast, too long or too short, but was always possible to imagine.

It was mid-day; what was Romano doing? It was not like Constantin to worry about anyone, but the absence of Romano always set his imagination to work: Romano's secretive manner, his subdued violence, his deceptive calm presented Constantin, and indeed everyone else, with a perpetual question, which neither his embraces, nor his departures, nor his returns could answer. Where the hell had he gone? Disappointed by Romano, exasperated by Maud, Constantin von Meck ran his bath, an operation usually carried out for him by his intimate friends — of either sex — with much caution, for since Constantin measured six foot four and weighed thirteen stone, he regularly overflowed the bathtubs of the Old World, and indeed the New World too.

On this occasion, as so often before when he was alone, he ran too much water and paid no attention to the way it splashed out and flowed over the floor as, closing his eyes and singing an old Mexican tune, he rubbed himself with a pebble described by the hotel as soap. The water, of course, after collecting below him and thus above his neighbour in the room below, suddenly burst through the floor and fell into the bathroom downstairs, which was occupied by none other than Hans Dietrich Schultert, a lieutenant-colonel at twenty-eight and notorious for his bad-tempered ferocity towards his own men as well as his enemies. Schultert, sitting in his own bathtub, watched as a cataract fell from the ceiling all over both his superb grey-green uniform, carefully placed over a chair, and his highly polished boots.

Schultert started shouting and swearing in German, and his orderly Otto Schmidt, who had been silently awaiting orders in the room next door, hurried in. Urged on by his master's hoarse and furious yells, Otto Schmidt ran along the corridors of the

Lutetia, went up one floor and knocked at the door of the suite directly above. He heard someone call, "Come in!" in French, which made him thunder on the door harder than ever, until at last it opened so suddenly that he almost fell through the doorway. The hand of a russet-haired giant in a dressing gown, like Schultert, set him on his feet again, and he heard himself shout at this figure, in German, "What the hell are you doing, you idiot?" before he could even get his breath back. "*Was ist das?*" the stranger inquired, in a voice even angrier than his own, although Otto's uniform could have left him in no doubt of either Otto's nationality or his rank. "Don't you speak French?" continued the giant, "after two years of the Occupation, don't you know a single word of French? Well, what is it?"

"Herr Doktor —" began Otto, in German, his glance straying beyond Constantin in search of a garment, a collar, an epaulette which would tell him the rank of this Hercules — "Herr Doktor, my officer, Leiutenant-Colonel Schultert . . . the water from your bathroom . . . your bath overflowed into his . . . he's down there . . . he's complaining . . ."

"Complaining of what?" inquired Constantin, speaking German himself and shouting angrily. "Complaining that European bathtubs are too small? You can tell him I don't like it either, but all he has to do is mop up the water or complain to the management! And tell him Constantin von Meck is not to be bothered in the mornings! Got that? Then go and tell him!"

And Constantin brusquely shut the door in Otto Schmidt's face. Schmidt went miserably downstairs again, resenting the reprimand: it was not the actual insults which bothered him, but the fact that two men in dressing gowns would venture to offer them to a uniformed German soldier at all. When he got back, Schultert did refrain from doing so again. The lieutenant-colonel confined himself to adding the name of Constantin von Meck to the long list of enemies he had drawn up in a black notebook bought when he was twelve — a notebook he had never abandoned, but to which he kept carefully adding, thanks to his unremittingly malicious character. This black notebook had a red counterpart, listing his lovers — if that gentle word might be applied to conquests each of which was noted down with comments of a more or less obscene and contemptuous nature. He had begun that one at the age of nineteen, and from a comparison of the thickness of the two notebooks one could deduce that malice had developed in Schultert earlier and more strongly than sensuality. If Constantin von Meck could have known of it, the fact that he figured in the black notebook ought to have alarmed him, for it was a dangerous honour.

Lieutenant-Colonel Hans Dietrich Schultert resembled Constantin von Meck's idea of the perfect caricature of an SS man. Schultert had in fact been a convert to National Socialism very young; orphaned at birth, he had been taken in by good people whom he happily denounced, once he had found his true home in the great Nazi family, as opponents of the regime. Free of these second-rate associations, duly enrolled, and a favourite with his group leaders for his good looks and his sporting prowess, Hans Dietrich had narrowly and simultaneously escaped both pederasty and athleticism. One morning he lost the final of the four hundred metres freestyle in a Paris swimming pool, and on the evening of the same day he lost his Hitler Youth virginity in a brothel. It was thus out of chagrin and a spirit of revenge rather than from inclination that he had abandoned sport and close friendships with men. With the help of his blond good looks, his strength and his cold manner, he had subsequently acquired a reputation among women frigid or frightened enough to confirm his virility; this was at the time of the fall of Röhm and the suppression of the SA. Now Goering's protégé, and part of his team, Hans Dietrich had rapidly risen in the SS. The war had reinforced his ambitions — which were many — and his two good qualities of courage and quick-wittedness. Now, late in 1942, after campaigning in France and in Africa, whence he had just come, he was marking time in Paris while he waited to leave for Russia, a battle arena which seemed worthy of his ferocity. He had been one of the youngest lieutenant-colonels in Hitler's army for two years, and was regarded as one of the most gifted of Nazi soldiers. In Schultert's eyes that decadent character the famous Constantin von Meck was the representative of a Europe and an art that were equally corrupt, Nazi Germany being the only fatherland and war the only vocation worthy of a man who *was* a man. And pretty soon now, he thought, the whole world would see how right he was.

Buttoned up in another uniform as impeccable as the garments just drenched by Constantin, he climbed up one floor, marched along the corridor and knocked on Constantin's door. Constantin, who had had time to get dressed himself, opened it. Despite his composure, both native and cultivated, Hans Dietrich Schultert took a step backwards and let his jaw drop at the sight. Constantin von Meck had decided he would dress like an Englishman this morning — a rich Englishman of the thirties — and so he had. He was wearing plus-fours and a beige and black checked jacket, he had on one of a pair black calf-length boots, and around his neck he wore a kind of pale, pastel-coloured silk cravat, which did not go at all well with the rest of his sporting attire. He was a combination of Little Lord Fauntleroy, Byron, and the Scarlet Pimpernel, as seen through Texan eyes. As a finishing touch, when he opened the door Constantin was carrying a dark wooden cane with a gold knob — obviously a genuine gold knob — a detail which made the eyes of Hans Dietrich (who outside the area of his fanaticism was wholly venal) widen first with astonishment and then with envy. However, he rapidly pulled himself together, clicked his heels, flung out his right arm and hand, and cried "Heil Hitler!" in a clear and sonorous voice ("what's called a brazen voice" commented Constantin to himself) before introducing himself: "Lieutenant-Colonel Hans Dietrich Schultert."

"Constantin von Meck," replied that gentleman, still standing in his doorway and obviously extremely disinclined to let him in. "Did we meet somewhere?"

He said this in English, smiling. Hans Dietrich winced.

"I would prefer to use our mother tongue, if that doesn't inconvenience you," he said curtly in German, although being so ambitious a man, he spoke fluent English, French and Italian. He had been tackling Spanish too for some months, but Russian did not interest him, in spite of his forthcoming posting; you don't talk to corpses.

"May I come in, M. von Meck?"

"Yes, of course, but what for?" inquired Constantin, now speaking German — and no doubt intimidated, for he spoke it with a strong peasant accent which at this point amused Schultert.

"As you can see," continued Constantin, "I haven't quite finished dressing. I've lost a boot. You didn't see it anywhere along the corridor, did you?"

Despite himself, Hans Dietrich Schultert looked down at the feet of the giant facing him; sure enough, one of them was bare. Hans Dietrich straightened up and stood stiffly erect.

"I had the pleasure of getting a shower from your bathroom on my head an hour ago," he said, adding acerbically, "I did not particularly appreciate it. I sent my orderly up. On returning, he informed me that you didn't seem to care."

"Well, I did suggest he could complain to the hotel management," said Constantin, beginning to feel faintly amused by this odious and prematurely old young man. He must have been in his late twenties, he came up to Constantin's chin, and he seemed to be in a vile temper. The perfect Nazi, as pictured by the anti-Nazi press.

"I am indeed going to complain to the management," said Schultert coldly. His mind was beginning to tick over, and he was trying both to assess this man, this mocking red-headed giant, and to calm himself down, in both cases with difficulty. This was certainly that grotesque seducer the film director, the one on whom Goebbels was said to be so keen; it wouldn't do to put a foot wrong. The fact that Goering thought highly of himself, Schultert, counted for nothing; no one, he knew, came before Goebbels in Hitler's estimation, for Goebbels was incorruptible in his devotion to the Führer, Goering was not, and Hitler knew it. None the less, it was in a firm voice that he said, looking Constantin in the eyes with an effort, "My orderly did report your advice to me, but not your excuses or your apologies; I had some difficulty in believing him, M. von Meck, when he told me what you had said. A great deal of difficulty."

"Oh dear, that was wrong of you," said Constantin. "If one can't believe one's gentleman's gentleman, then who *is* to be believed?"

He was smiling, but without warmth, and certainly without the least embarrassment. Schultert was losing his temper.

"He is not my gentleman's gentleman," he said. "He's my orderly."

"You know, you'll find yourself quite at a loss after the war, then," said Constantin. "You've no idea how quickly one gets used to having a servant about one from morning to night!"

And turning his back, he walked over to the window with his shoulders ostentatiously shaken by laughter; not for nothing did he work in films. What was more, as Schultert saw only too clearly, no irony or insolence could touch him; Constantin von Meck was too clever and too contemptuous. For what that turning of his back and that silent laughter displayed was contempt, contempt for him, Hans Dietrich Schultert, who had risen from nothing to be here in his own hotel suite at the age of twenty-eight, with a Mercedes Benz awaiting him downstairs and a regiment ready to be cut to pieces for him, for fear of being cut to pieces *by* him.

"I would have preferred an apology," he said with some effort, in so flat and hostile a voice that the surprised Constantin turned back to him. They looked at each other for a good five seconds, both their faces set. Then Constantin raised a cigarette to his lips and lit it slowly, before saying, in the most perfect and courteous German, without any trace of peasant accent now, a refined German which this time, as he knew, Hans Dietrich Schultert could not emulate, "I really am sorry we can't fight a duel, Colonel, since as I'm sure I don't need to remind you, your life belongs to the Führer, and it would be out of the question for you to spill a single drop of your blood for any other cause than that of the Reich. I hope you won't quarrel with that statement, Colonel?"

"And what about your own blood?" said Schultert furiously. "Who do you owe that to, then?"

"Why, I owe it to the Führer too, of course." Constantin had assumed a pious manner. "Besides, I like this suit; I'd hate to soil it," he concluded, smiling at himself in the mirror and at Schultert, who stepped to one side and turned to leave so violently that he collided head on and full force with a young man who was striding through the doorway. Hans Dietrich's still unappeased wrath was instantly vented on the newcomer, who was a civilian into the bargain.

"You swine! You damn idiot, where d'you think you are? Clumsy oaf! Bloody Frog!" he yelled, raising a hand to strike this ridiculous person, this wretched passer-by, when to his great surprise the latter seized his wrist in mid-air with one iron hand and took him by the throat with the other, pinning him to the door in a single movement, while that swine von Meck, moving just as swiftly, immobilized his other arm before he had time to draw his revolver from its holster. They stood there motionless, all three of them, Lieutenant-Colonel Schultert held against the door frame by the two breathless civilians, and all three looking defiantly at each other, as if intoxicated with fury, incomprehension and an exhausting violence. The two civilians were panting as quietly as possible, and he, Schultert, was panting too, instead of yelling for help in German, which would have made him look ridiculous. He felt silly as it was, immobilized by a film director in his stocking feet and a slender, youthful stranger. How could he call for help when he had a gun, and neither of the others was armed?

"Let go of me!" he said in German to Constantin, who had straightened up. "Let go of me!" he repeated, glancing towards the face which he sensed was looking down at his own, amused. "Let go of me or I'll have you shot!"

"Oh, you couldn't do that," said Constantin's voice. "All right, I'll let go of you, but I'm going to borrow something from you first, just until you calm down."

And with a rapid gesture Constantin von Meck, that pretentious film director currently specializing in sentimental Viennese romances, put a hand down under his arm, opened his holster and removed the revolver in a very professional manner; then, letting go, he took a couple of steps backwards. The other man, however, the newcomer, was still holding Hans Dietrich against the door, both hands on his wrists now, one knee against his stomach, in a very efficacious and if the truth were told very painful position, from which Hans Dietrich, used to his own muscular superiority, was exasperated to find he could not break free.

"Let him go, Romano," said Constantin von Meck gently. "Let him go. I've got his revolver, we're in no danger now. Let me introduce Lieutenant-Colonel Hans Dietrich Schultert."

The unknown adversary stepped back, looking surprised and respectful, as if the name of Schultert were one of the greatest renown, and ceremoniously inclining his head, he gave him a mocking salute. Schultert slowly straightened up, adjusted his tight-fitting uniform over his shoulders and brushed it down carefully, face impassive. Then he turned to Constantin, saying in the same toneless and formal voice he had used at the start of their conversation, "Herr von Meck, we shall meet again!" Staring straight ahead of him, he saluted a phantom, sticking out his chest and stretching his arm out once again and shouting "Heil Hitler!" at the top of his voice. Then, after taking several steps down the corridor, he hesitantly and as if he had forgotten some tiresome detail turned back to Constantin, who was still leaning in the doorway.

"Can I have my gun back?"

"Of course," said Constantin von Meck, and still with the nonchalantly loose-limbed gait of the aristocratic Englishman, but as swiftly as he had moved just now, he tossed the revolver towards the officer, who by some miracle caught it in mid-air. Hans Dietrich Schultert realized that if he had missed, if he had had to stoop to pick the gun up himself, he would instantly have emptied its entire contents into those two bastards. They might have ruined his career! He would kill them one day soon, and slowly.

"Heil Hitler!" he shouted again, clicking his heels and looking straight into Constantin's smiling eyes. Putting his revolver back in its holster, he walked away with measured and confident strides. Or so he hoped.

IV

"Be a good fellow — lock the door and push the wardrobe in front of it," said Constantin, stretching as he went back into the bedroom. "That idiot's quite capable of changing his mind, turning round and coming back to empty his gun into us, don't you think, Romano?" But Romano, looking abstracted, had already closed the door. He nodded without even smiling. He had that gentle, thoughtful, pious air which Constantin knew heralded extreme violence in him, or rather a wish to indulge in extreme violence, although also, curiously, it gave him the candour of the childhood he had never known. His face and skin became smoother, the lashes fringing his eyelids seemed longer, his mouth opened as if artlessly, seemed to savour some sweet promise in advance, but the promise was of vengeance, not a kiss. It was at such moments, when Romano looked like a boy taking his first Communion, like a young bridegroom or a serious student, that he was most dangerous — and thus most in danger himself, as Constantin was also well aware. It was at such moments that his disguise became most transparent and Constantin had to step up his stratagems.

For in spite of the genuine papers acquired for him by Constantin, which said he was German (the one European nationality which ran no risk of investigation), Romano was of pure gypsy blood. Being a Jew under Hitler made you first a guilty party and then a parcel which the yellow star, itself now become a label, dispatched to those unknown camps — a process which took a more or less brief period of time, but a period of time all the same. Being a gypsy, however, made you an instant target, since the relatively small number of persons of that race facilitated their individual execution.

Constantin, therefore, had disguised Romano as a young German assistant employed to find locations for his filming, and equipped with enough warrants and stamped documents to get him past any checkpoint; but the soft curls of pale, fair hair cut short above his fine-boned, angelic guttersnipe face, his bony wrists and slender neck emerging from his blue-grey jacket, the black gleam of his eyes under lashes which, like his hair, were bleached by Constantin with peroxide every ten days, all this sometimes, at moments such as the present, made a very strange creature of him. Oddly enough, this came in useful: as seen by a suspicious official Romano was too improbable, too haphazard a mixture, not to be innocent. And as seen by anyone else, his inborn beauty, his mingling of Latin agility and Slav speed, the black fire of his eyes combined with his fair hair, all darkness and light, his cunning tricks and his wild nature made both men and women more concerned with what his desires might be than with his nationality. As for Constantin, even though his profession had left him with little patience for extravagantly bizarre characters, he spent two hours on that head with scissors and bleach every ten days, thought highly of his own work, and was as proud of his blond gypsy as Frankenstein had been of his monster.

"You look so odd sometimes!" he said. Lying on one of the beds, amusement in his eyes, arms folded under his head, he had well and truly creased his splendid English gentleman's suit now. "You really do look odd." And he started to laugh.

"Yes, well, of course I look peculiar," agreed Romano.

Lean and muscular, thin to the point of skinniness, he was twenty-two and still growing. Walking around the room, he gave his reflection in the glass a severe, critical look quite devoid of any charm as he passed it. Constantin liked the fact that though Romano more or less lived by his physical attractions, he had no idea of his beauty, the beauty of a man still almost adolescent, sometimes of an adolescent still almost a child. Romano's skin must always have been as smooth and matt as it was now, with small blue veins visible beneath it, always as pale under the permanent tan which came from the open road and the wind rather than the sun, from the open air he had breathed for twenty years, so that he would never lose it, and perhaps it was the most dangerous clue to his race, although such a tan was now quite common in the vast German army that had been exposed by war to extremes of heat and cold.

Romano had been part of Constantin von Meck's life and luggage for nearly two years now, since the night watchmen in the Victorine company's Nice studios had caught him stealing various expensive items of equipment one night. It had taken three of them to tie him up and pen him in a corner of the studio, like an animal. He had looked like an animal too, when Constantin first saw him, with thick, fine, black hair like fur, a hunted look in his eyes, matt skin quivering over muscles in perpetual movement, and a long blue vein beating with alarming speed at his throat; the grace of his movements, his refusal to listen to Constantin, see or hear him, the whole aura of violence and disorder about him together with the vulnerability he disowned, but which sometimes appeared in his face — all this had aroused in Constantin the feelings of someone who was neither a father nor a lover, but would instinctively protect this animal, this carnivore, a little wolf lost in the war, stealing cameras in film studios in the dark. Instead of taking him to the police, therefore, Constantin took him home and gave him food, drink, and a bed to himself. He even promised to get him some papers next day: all this before the boy had said a word. And so Constantin took him under his wing, in so far as a falcon can be taken under anyone's wing, for Romano, though not yet twenty, knew more about life and its vicissitudes than Constantin himself. He had seen everything, had travelled all over Central Europe in his family's caravan since his birth; he had slept with women, little girls, little boys, mature men, he had stolen, plundered, cheated, perhaps even killed. He was unmanageable, was certainly an orphan, and was obviously desperate, although he hid the fact, for while before the war his life had been a game of hide and seek with poverty, he was now playing the same game with death — and it was a game he was sure to lose at the time when he met Constantin. The latter, all-powerful, proclaimed him German, gave him the name of Romano Woltzer, after a cousin of his own who had died in obscurity in a Hamburg slum, and took him on officially as his personal chauffeur, valet, secretary, factotum and location finder, a job which accounted for his frequent absences and disappearances, since Romano scoured town and country to cover his own expenses. He might accept shelter and sometimes food from Constantin, but he would take nothing else. To that end, he seduced and fleeced willing victims of either sex, whatever their charms or their age, with equal ardour and indifference. Romano had been living by his own charms for quite some time in any case — for five years, ever since his parents, his brothers and sisters and cousins, his whole family and their caravan had been swallowed up in a pogrom that destroyed a Central European village where they happened to be camping. He had gradually made it a profession rather than a game, but one he exercised with such open cynicism as to be quite honest about it. "It's sensations I offer," he had once told Constantin, when he expressed surprise at his detachment, "never feelings. Or if I do I don't mean to, and then I get out, fast."

After their first encounter, after he had spent a week with Constantin without opening his mouth, perhaps reassured by his host's indifference or attracted by his promise of false papers,

Romano calmly and gracefully turned back Constantin's bed one evening to slip into it. Much to Romano's surprise, and indeed to his own, Constantin sent him back to his own room.

"Once you've got your papers and some money," he had told the almost offended boy, "once you have a choice in the matter, then we'll see . . ."

So Romano had had to wait until he had that choice before giving himself to Constantin, abandoning himself with him in sensual and depraved games which first entertained them both a great deal, and subsequently brought them very close to affection: a virile, rough affection transformed into pleasure only when one or other of them wanted it, or felt bored, or needed warmth. By now this erotic companionship had more attractions for Constantin, more than many a supposedly romantic love affair. He was happy with Romano and trusted him, although sometimes, seeing him come in at dawn whistling to himself and with dark circles under his eyes, Constantin felt vaguely guilty, as if he had let a wild wolf loose on a vulnerable society.

This time, the wolf had been gone for over three days, which was unusual but would not be explained. Neither of the two men ever told the other anything about his amorous adventures. It had certainly been known for Romano, knocking on Constantin's door and finding him engaged in dalliance, to murmur an abstracted apology and go away again. It had also been known for Constantin to search their rooms for Romano in vain and swear furiously when he failed to find him. But otherwise, they were as discreet as two chance-met travellers sharing a sleeper in a train for a single night.

"I'll have to change," said Constantin, from the bathroom. "That Hun ruined my beautiful spring outfit. Romano, what the hell made you forget I was finished with the film, and I'd be bored to tears in the evenings? Aren't you racked by remorse?"

He adopted a humorous tone, but let a hint of melancholy into his question, which he knew would make Romano sorry. By now he had a fairly good idea of the way to manage this wild colt of his.

And in fact Romano did reply with some remorse in his voice. "I know, but I was involved in one of those interminable things — someone who took ages to decide — but never mind, it was worth it," he murmured. "You know that fake Dufy you bought from your sensitive and disreputable friend — the little blue one, remember? Well, I've resold it!"

"You haven't!" exclaimed the astonished Constantin, who had just come back into the room dressed like a normal human being in black trousers and a sweater. "You haven't? That appalling copy? I mean, no one would be taken in by it! You must be joking! How much did you get?"

"Twenty thousand," said Romano triumphantly, and Constantin dropped on the bed, arms folded.

"Twenty thousand? But how the hell would anyone pay twenty thousand francs for that thing? How could anyone be fool enough? Was she blind or what, this client of yours?"

"It was a he, actually, said Romano placidly. "Oh yes, he could see it was a fake all right. I practically told him so myself." He started to laugh. "All the same, it took him two days to make his mind up, and then he offered ten thousand. I had to get him to add the rest myself, when he wasn't looking."

"*All the same* is pretty rich," remarked Constantin. "Are you really telling me — I mean, even ten thousand, for that awful daub? It's incredible!"

Romano took offence. "What do you mean, incredible? I never lie," he said, with a certainty that surprised Constantin. He got up, took a long envelope from his coat where it hung on the peg, and tossed it to Constantin laughing, but defiantly. Banknotes carefully held together in two bundles by rubber bands slid out; so did a small photograph hidden between them, which fell upside down on the bedspread under Constantin's nose. Constantin did not move. Romano had frozen; he too looked at it in surprise.

"May I?" asked Constantin, casually. When Romano nodded, he picked the photograph up and turned it over. It showed the calm, serious face of a smiling middle-aged man in a sports shirt.

"Good God," said Constantin. "Good God. I don't believe it. It's Bremen. Bremen himself. Now that, my dear fellow, that is a master-stroke. When I think that . . . hold on, what's the time?"

"Twelve noon," said Romano.

"Right, when I think that scarcely twelve hours ago this upright citizen was telling me about his wife and his children, his children and his wife, whining away about the loneliness of the soldier's life! My God, what a hypocrite! It was well worth twenty thousand francs . . ." And tossing the notes up in the air like flowers he started to laugh, but Romano stood where he was, face sombre.

"What's the matter?" Constantin finally asked. "What's bothering you?"

"I don't like you to think," said Romano, between his teeth, "I don't like you being able to think of somebody with me — somebody you can actually visualize, I mean."

"Why not?"

"Because I wouldn't like thinking of you that way, I suppose," said Romano in a tone of exasperation, before starting to pace up and down the room again. Constantin had bowed his head, feeling moved and rather pleased. It was the first time he had ever heard Romano, wildcat that he was, mention any kind of feeling. He was pleased, but Romano was not. Therefore Constantin must apologize because of the wound he himself might have suffered, although as it happened it would have caused him no suffering at all. Constantin had no visual jealousy; he did not have a jealous imagination, had never been jealous at all in the masochistic sense of the word. The notion that Romano might be jealous on his account, and could say so, both surprised and delighted him . . . as if they had been speaking of the future.

"I'm not thinking of it," he said. "Anyway, the man's not so bad. There's nothing to be ashamed of."

This, he realized, was not the right thing to have said, but he could find no argument to mollify the sentimental, cruel little thief Romano had suddenly become.

And indeed, Romano said morosely, "That's not what I mean," and swept his right arm over the bedspread, sending the beautiful French banknotes flying everywhere. But first, he picked up Bremen' photograph and put it in his pocket — much to the relief of Constantin, who had feared for a moment that he might toss it in the air with the notes, with the same scornful, easy gesture, and although he did not know why, that would have somehow have displeased him; he was glad that his lover too had instinctively sensed the slight, very slight vulgarity of such a gesture.

Constantin lay back on the bed again with his hands under his head. What with Schulter's raging and Bremen's sentimentality, these Nazis certainly had their entertaining side. He suddenly felt perfectly happy. The world lay beneath him, soft and round, warm as a cake; human beings had warm hair, large hands, small feet; there was music, there were oceans everywhere. He began to sing out loud, at the top of his voice, so that Romano, showering in the bathroom, could hear him; he sang a Charles Trenet song popular in the streets and salons of Paris, but changing its words: "When Bremen talks as Bremen can, I think of him, a married man, dreaming of you but not of me, with his fat children on his knee." He repeated this ditty three or four times, at increasing volume, until Romano shot furiously out of the bathroom, shirt unbuttoned, hair untidy, and flung himself on him. They struggled in earnest for a couple of minutes, and ended up falling to the floor, taking with them the bedside table and the bedside lamp, which broke. Romano had suppleness, agility and exasperation on his side, Constantin had weight and strength on his, and would have won in the end if laughter and affection had not got the better of him.

"Stop it!" he cried. "Stop it, for God's sake!"

They lay there side by side on the carpet, each dreaming his own dreams, and now and then singing ridiculous or obscene words to the music of Charles Trenet, doubling up with laughter like sex-obsessed schoolboys.

Romano was sleeping the sleep of the just on the carpet, but the vodka had come back to knock at Constantin's temples, and kept him awake. At last he rose and went to look idly out of his bedroom window at the Boulevard Raspail and the Rue de Sèvres, which were both deserted. In this strange new Paris, a Paris with its streets and avenues full of posters whose wording the Parisians could neither read nor pronounce, Constantin felt more like an irritated civilian than a proud member of the occupying forces. Not for nothing had he moved from film to film over the past two years, preferably in the free zone of Europe — or what had hitherto been the free zone. He could feel neutral in the empty countryside, surrounded by papier mâché sets, especially when his human companions were as varied as the sets. Living with his technicians, his film crew of perpetual vagabonds, with film producers, who were naturally exotic people, and with actors, fundamentally rootless characters whose places and dates of birth had no reality about them, any more than the dates of their marriages and deaths, who had no real existence until they appeared in *Cinémondial* — living with such people Constantin could ignore political problems or tensions, except for those caused by *them*. *They*, in Constantin's mind, were the SS, that small group outside the Wehrmacht, the SS, who, he suspected, were capable of great cruelty. Romano was the only person he knew who was wholly uncompromising on the subject of the SS, who said this cruel percentage was a thousand times greater than he supposed, and the word "cruelty" itself was ironical understatement. It was not something they discussed, and Constantin sometimes wondered which of them was the more painfully and constantly embarrassed by the fact.

A man had just turned the corner of the Boulevard Raspail, and came up to the long queue of women in the Rue de Sèvres; they were blocking the whole pavement outside the bakery right up to the gutter. Constantin saw the pedestrian hesitate and then make his way between two housewives, pulling in his stomach and raising his hat, like a stranger passing a funeral cortege, and it made him laugh, but out there no one seemed amused. The passer-by went on, walking faster and never turning back; people all walked fast in Paris — fast but without any spring in their steps. They seemed to be escaping from something, never, as in the old days, on their way to meet someone. It was not the haste of desire one sensed now, but the headlong flight of fear.

"Didn't you sleep?" asked Romano's voice, behind him.

Constantin turned. Romano was looking at the sky beyond the rooftops and the pigeons with an expression of wonder and gratitude which touched him. The boy had the look of a child disguised, but a child all the same. Constantin ordered breakfast, and saw the unappetizing stuff which did duty for it arrive with resignation. The copy of *Paris-Soir* in the middle of the tray caught his eye. He opened it and unfolded it with a grand gesture. "Like to hear the news?" he asked, and began reading items out, with much expression. "All going well, the Wehrmacht magnificent as usual. Before taking Stalingrad, we are fleeing decisively all over Russia . . . We have been triumphantly routed in North Africa, we are successfully retreating in Sicily . . . What else? Let's see . . . Marshal Pétain is going to be eighty-six . . . they haven't found the man who killed Colbert, the militia captain murdered in the Rue des Saussaies . . . ten hostages picked at random from the population will be shot tomorrow."

Constantin raised his head. "Hear that? Ten civilians shot! You know, the people here have a funny way of showing all that sympathy for the occupying power we hear about . . . Here, what's the matter?'' he added in surprise, for Romano was in the bathroom, and Constantin heard him vomiting with a loud retching noise, very surprising in someone so reserved. Finally Romano came out, stopped in the doorway, stood there, looking aloof, and glanced at Constantin. Leaning on the door frame, he wiped his mouth on a towel — not a very aesthetic gesture, but it disturbed Constantin rather than irritating him. Why was Romano unwell? It wasn't the breakfast, revolting as that had been: he had a cast-iron digestion. It wasn't the defeats suffered by the Wehrmacht; he could only be glad of that. It wasn't that he was sorry to have forgotten Marshal Pétain's birthday. It had to be that business of the Rue des Saussaies. And yet Romano spoke of executions and the horrors of war with terrifying composure. No, for once he must be directly involved. Suddenly, Constantin was so much afraid that he felt sweat trickling down the back of his neck. It was no secret really: he knew well enough that Romano did not devote the whole of his time to the beds and the wallets of his many protectors of both sexes. What exactly did he do? Why was he so shaken all of a sudden?

Constantin decided to tackle the subject indirectly. "He must be feeling bad, don't you think, whoever did kill Colbert? Thinking of ten poor innocents being shot in his place."

"That depends," said Romano. "There are some bastards who do more harm, left alive, than there is in innocent people dying. Well, not that their innocent families would see it that way, of course."

Constantin looked up. "You don't think this man Colbert had any innocent family of his own?"

Romano began to laugh. "No, only victims," he said with certainty. "Look, Constantin, I don't know my way around your peculiar humanist ideas too well, but I do know people like him must be killed. Colbert did the interrogating of Resistance workers in the Rue des Saussaies. Some of them were women.

Quite recently. Mostly, people didn't have to be finished off after one of his interrogations. No need for it. But he'd been interrogating some Resistance women, and they forgot to finish one of them properly. Before she died, she had time to tell her friends just how Colbert had questioned her, and the story got about. So Colbert had to be killed, if only because of all the others, all those people who'd come before him in the past and the ones who risked coming before him in the future."

"And how do you know all this?" asked Constantin, in what he hoped was a tone of idle interest.

"I know because believe it or not, there are other newspapers besides *Paris-Soir*," said Romano. "And other salons besides your friend Mme Bragance's, and other people involved in the fighting besides your noble Wehrmacht officers. That's how I know!"

And he smiled a wide smile, smiled with a mixture of revulsion and anger which made him quite ugly, thought Constantin, turning his head away so as not to see it. It was with an effort that he tried to reply.

"That doesn't mean that . . . I still think those women, all those people who'll be shot in someone else's place — I think it's unjust."

"Unjust? Really?"

And Romano began to laugh with a bitter laughter Constantin had never heard from him before. It was almost an old man's laughter.

"Unjust!" said Romano. "Unjust . . . you think your fellow countrymen 'unjust'. Oh, my poor friend, it's a very long time since Germany or the Germans had any idea what 'just' and 'unjust' meant. Those are old-fashioned words, you see, 'just' and 'unjust'. But going back to Colbert's murderer, the man 'responsible' for the death of the hostages, you have to imagine what's in store for him if he does the noble thing and gives himself up. SS men selected from among the 'worst' of the SS — to go along with your theory — will torture him, and when they've pulled out his nails and cut off his balls and gouged out his eyes, they'll ask for the names and addresses of his friends so that they can do the same to them. And perhaps — I say perhaps, mark you, because one never knows what pain may do to a person — perhaps he'll talk; in fact I guess that's the reason why the wretched fellow doesn't give himself up. And then again, perhaps he wants to kill more Colberts. Because you see, Constantin, even blindly, even at enormous cost, the Colberts have got to be killed. Definitely. Because big Colberts will produce little Colberts, even more of them than we've got now. And the whole world will be covered with little Colberts, organized killers and sadists . . ."

"Oh yes, and who does the organizing? Hitler? You think a nation can be entirely changed just like that? Now you listen to me, Romano!" Constantin had exploded. "It so happens I was brought up in Germany. I lived there as a child. I know the German people very well. I know German peasants; they're rather slow, perhaps, big hands, rather a simple expression, but those are men who love their families and their country and care for their farm animals when they're hurt. And there are women too, lovely blonde women who can warm a man against their breasts, the way you see it in strip cartoons. And there are little clerks with little pince-nez on their noses, trotting along the street, the picture of honesty. And there are more prosperous people who may be a bit crazy, but they're good at heart. I don't believe what you say. Any more than I believed Uhlans cut the arms off little French babies in the '14–'18 war. It's ridiculous."

Romano began to laugh, but mirthlessly.

"Hard to imagine, isn't it, Constantin? Well, I'm telling you, I mean all Germans and not just the SS! They're all like that in your country now, can't you get that into your head? They're like hyenas, savage and contemptible and tireless. They can't be stopped unless you kill them, don't you see that? It's not just the

SS, Constantin. That's the worst of it. At this moment, in your country, there are people doing the killing and people who let them, and that's all. You can't believe me, can you? Your own country, your beloved Germany a nest of vipers, right? You absolutely won't believe me, will you? Spoils your zest for life, eh?"

And under the wide and horrified eyes of Constantin, Romano gave the breakfast tray, which was already on the floor, a kick that sent the contents of the teapot flying over the hotel's handsome plum-coloured carpet — which had already suffered considerable damage from Constantin's forgotten cigarette ends and overflowing bathtubs. Constantin did not so much as blink. He was looking Romano's way, in the direction of his voice, but apparently without seeing him.

He was listening to him, though. Was Romano telling the truth? Through the wave of horror and weariness which had overcome him like an overwhelming desire to sleep, Constantin realized he was no longer even asking that question. Confusedly, he knew it was the truth. Confusedly, he sometimes knew everything he refused to see, everything that as a German and a voluntary recruit to the German cause he refused to see or judge. He would not pass judgement on his own country, particularly if it had done indefensible things, as it had. Or so at least he told himself, forcefully, but the idea occasionally passed through his mind that this noble refusal to judge came in useful, if only as justification for his blindness. He scarcely heard what Romano was telling him as he paused in the doorway.

"Poor Constantin," he was saying, "poor Constantin — you sometimes say I don't talk enough. Well, for once you've had an earful!" And he went out. Constantin did not even hear the sound of his footsteps fade away. The vodka and its consequences did him a favour; his headache had disappeared and he let himself go, plunging into sweet, deliberate, delicious sleep.

Constantin woke at four in the afternoon, in a very good mood, and while still half asleep decided, on remembering his disagreement with Romano, to put it down to exaggeration or a mistake; he therefore made a face when he picked up the newspaper and saw the subject of their argument featured in the middle of the front page, with a black border, and nothing ambiguous about it. He was going to toss the paper aside when despite himself, his glance fell on the names, in the list of hostages, of Weil alias Petit, and lower down Schwob alias Duchez. Instead of tossing the page of newsprint away, Constantin dropped it; although crumpled, it floated in the air for a moment before falling to the floor at his feet.

Constantin's first reaction was of stupor. He knew Bremen was all-powerful, and Bremen's aide had promised him his protégés' lives. So why deny his request; why had they lied to him? The Gestapo had rounded up enough people and taken enough prisoners not to miss two men. And why lie to him into the bargain? He had believed them; Constantin trusted people, first instinctively and then because he was determined to. And when life showed him how dangerous such an attitude was, and his friends mocked him and his credulity, he would say haughtily, "I'd rather be deceived than distrustful." In point of fact, he found distrust more tiring and unattractive than its opposite. But his friends and acquaintances in general, who thought it shameful and intolerable to be deceived — his friends who could not understand the way he could console himself afterwards and who would have thought it perverse of him to mind in advance — forced him to say, "I laid a bet when very young that mankind was good!" and to act accordingly, as usual allowing his impulses to pass for decisions, and his natural character for an ethical system.

Therefore, Constantin was stunned, even shattered, but to his great shame no more so by the possible execution of his two friends than by all the trouble he was going to have to take to avert it. He wanted to lie on the floor, listen to Edith Piaf records, smoke English cigarettes and drink mint juleps. He felt overcome with indolence at the idea of going out, and with boredom at the notion of begging from Bremen. And Constantin knew boredom and indolence to be feelings as violent and uncontrollable as love or ambition. He knew it all the better because those two weaknesses had very often triumphed over the last-named passions in him: his indolence by making him miss important meetings with powerful producers, and his boredom by half sending him to sleep in the company of young women whom he had thought he loved as long as they kept their mouths shut. Yes, those pseudo-emotions had a very strong hold on him.

He must pull himself together; after all, he admired Weil and liked Schwob. He could not think without flinching of the two men at dawn, their eyes pale and their skin crawling, facing the firing squad and death. He could not think without horror of those two men, who had trusted him, whom he had tried to protect . . . oh yes, I could, though, he told himself, oh yes, I could! And he began to laugh hysterically. Yes, indeed, he could have forgotten their fate, and still could, if that kindly, amiable character the better Constantin von Meck did not come back to take the place of the other Constantin, the lazy great oaf who wanted to be left alone to read Sacha Guitry in peace. He might as well admit it to himself: the death of Weil and Schwob did not bother him in the least at this moment. He felt total indifference, calm and cynicism take root in him, and would have been disturbed had he not been as unsure of his faults as his virtues. He knew quite well that the loyal, courageous character who was horrified by this side of him would be back, the decent character whom he was not sure whether he should despise, admire or cling to for dear life; a character within Constantin who was, after all, himself, since he nearly always acted like that character and according to its standards, and that was the character who would win this little struggle between his heart and his intelligence, or rather between his duty and his indolence.

The phone rang, and Constantin jumped up, hoping it would be Romano. Romano — he must talk to Romano, explain why he had gone to Germany, what he, the liberal and democratic Constantin von Meck had gone to Nazi Germany to do. He must justify himself to Romano, and he cursed himself for having instinctively rejected the idea of doing so before, thinking, like any appalling bourgeois, that he had no need to explain himself to that young man. He sometimes hated himself for acting according to precepts he had always detested. Romano was a living human being who had seen his family robbed, destroyed and burnt by Constantin's compatriots, and who must be quite unable to understand his coming back to Germany in the cruel, dark Nazi era. By what right had he omitted to tell him, by what right had he failed to explain? The right of the strongest, or the richest, or the oldest? Constantin did not know, but he was going to put the record straight; as soon as possible he was going to apologize to that insolent, mocking boy, a young man he had both protected and maltreated. He must take him away from Paris very soon, from a place where he was in such danger, very far away; he must admit to Romano that he thought a lot of him, he both admired and liked him. It was so as not to say those things that he had never told him the rest of it, as he now realized, blaming himself as if it were courage rather than sensitivity he had lacked.

But it was not Romano on the phone; it was Maud Mérival, the concierge told him. A Maud who would have read the paper, who would be in tears, who would want to ask him, Constantin the all-powerful, to put things right as he had promised, to make good the promise the German officers had given him; she would sob, her tears would run all the way down the line, reach his room and flow into his ear. Constantin told the concierge he was out, and then went back to the window and leaned his forehead against it. All of a sudden the idea of Maud collapsing into his room in tears reminded him of her way of speaking the line, "How could I?" The memory of that "How could I?" uttered like the squawk of a toucan or a parrot's cry simultaneously revived his memory of the way Maud had looked in her crinoline, and the prettified set; he saw, as if in a still, the distressed girl suddenly turning into a fishwife. And behind her on the right, leaning over a crate, indeed with his head right in it and shedding tears of mirth, he saw Schwob. Yes, it was Schwob there; Constantin even remembered thinking he looked like a bottle upside down in a dustbin with his legs kicking, his hair a little too long and too black against the pallor of the crate. Constantin saw his designer straighten up, face flushed and puckered with laughter; he saw his eyes, his hair, his skin . . . and the idea of Schwob's possible death made his stomach turn with horror, as at some macabre obscenity.

Constantin took from his wardrobe the only conventional suit he owned: a black and grey herringbone three-piece, which made him look even thinner, and gave him the theatrical air of a Russian terrorist. Even taller, even leaner, even more nonchalant than ever, Constantin went down the stairs of the Lutetia Hotel and got into his Duisenberg to drive to Gestapo headquarters.

The Gestapo building had a sinister reputation, no doubt deserved, since Constantin knew no one who worked there, or at least no one who admitted it. He had tried to telephone Goebbels in Berlin, but in vain, which bothered him. His last film had been enormously successful in Germany and all the occupied countries, and he had had a note of congratulation from the Minister himself — although he had laid the melodrama on so thick in this latest effort, *The Violins of Destiny*, that he doubted whether Goebbels would fail to notice the fact. He went to see General Bremen, therefore, without telling anyone.

The corridors of Gestapo HQ in Paris were much the same as

the corridors of Gestapo HQ in Berlin: endless and icy, with steel-helmeted soldiers stationed every ten metres along them. Constantin was shown into a waiting room, where he let his gaze stray out of the window to the chilly chestnut trees of occupied Paris. He waited there in his dark suit, feet together, feeling restless and ill at ease like the parent of a schoolchild waiting to see the headmaster — although parents do not often have to beg a head-master to let their children live. After ten, then twenty minutes he was beginning to feel impatient, when at last an aide came to fetch him: not the same officer as the one he had already met at Boubou Bragance's. This one was fair, slim, charming, and instantly recalled to Constantin's mind what Romano had told him about the General's tastes. He was shown into a huge room, and smiled to himself at the thought that however hard he tried, General Bremen could never match the luxury of the Minister of Propaganda. His desk — which of course was placed at the far end of the room, so that any visitors had to cross an acre of floorboards to get to it — was not even half as big as the one at which Goebbels sat. The aide preceded Constantin, swaying his hips like a girl: Bremen was right not to let him out into the salons of Paris — he was too striking. On reaching the desk and Bremen, who rose very politely, the young aide turned to Constantin.

"I just wanted to say, Herr von Meck," he said, blushing prettily, "I just wanted to say how I love your films."

Constantin bowed slightly. "Thank you very much."

"You can leave us now, Captain!" interrupted Bremen, obviously impatient with these polite exchanges.

The aide blushed again, raised his arm, and shouted "Heil Hitler!" clicking his heels so violently that Constantin jumped. At Bremen's invitation, he sat down in the armchair facing the desk and laced his hands nervously together. There was a nasty atmosphere about this place; it was like being in a cake-shop and a hospital at the same time. Something in the air smelled of neither ether nor vanilla, but vaguely suggested both, and the combination was most unpleasant.

"I'm sorry to trouble you, General," Constantin began. "I ought to have sent word first, but I happened to see in the paper that the friends I mentioned to you yesterday are down to be shot tomorrow morning. And I must say I'm surprised, considering our discussion yesterday, and the assurances you gave me . . ."

He paused between phrases, hoping Bremen would interrupt, but the General said nothing. Both hands on the arms of his chair, he was looking fixedly at Constantin, mouth drooping, eyes screwed up by the effort of thought, obviously weary.

That old pansy, thought Constantin savagely. That old pansy! How could Romano go to bed with him? A horrible thought . . .

He tried to rouse himself to anger with detailed pictures of it, but couldn't: Romano seemed so distant from this little old man of fifty or so who looked a hundred. Bremen gave him a sour but ingratiating smile, like a parish priest seeking excuses for his flock during Confession.

"I expect you want to talk to me about your Jewish . . . friends?"

Bremen had paused between "Jewish" and "friends", as if the two words were incompatible. Constantin frowned.

"That's right," he said. "Schwob and Weil are to face tomorrow's firing squad under the names of Petit and Duchez."

In Constantin's optimistic imagination, things ought to happen fast now: Bremen would take a piece of paper from his desk, write the names of Petit and Duchez on it, and hand it to Constantin, who would give it to the aide, who would pass it on to God knows whom, and he would find his two assistants downstairs and take them away at once in his car, just like that. However, it did not seem to be so simple. He gave the General an amiable smile, which was not returned. Bremen had folded his hands in front of him and was examining his nails with close attention.

"You should know, Herr von Meck, that your friends may pay dearly for their false papers. It was a definite attempt to dupe the authorities . . . or a definite attempt to escape death, from their point of view. Well?"

"Well, in that case, I'm the guilty party." Constantin was beginning to lose his temper. "I was the one who got them those papers. Look, General," he said, leaning forward, "look, let's be sensible about this. Those two are very good assistants, excellent fellows, intelligent and able. I needed them during shooting, and I need them now for the editing of the film."

"Herr von Meck," said the General, in a pained voice, "Herr von Meck, we will forget all this. We will forget that *you* provided them with their false papers. In fact, we will forget the whole thing," he added firmly.

"I don't understand you," said Constantin.

He felt himself turning pale, his heart thudding between his ribs. There was something menacing, something final in the voice of this over-powerful little old man, something which sounded like a flat refusal.

"Herr von Meck, I'm afraid you must forget about your . . . your Jews. In any case, they're Aryans now. At your request, we had them taken to the prison for Aryans, as being Aryans themselves. That was the idea of your plea, wasn't it?"

Although the word "plea" made Constantin flinch, he nodded.

"Well, yes, General. But I didn't ask you to have them shot, and . . ."

"Let me finish, please, Herr von Meck!" Bremen interrupted. "At your request, my aide very kindly had your friends moved to a different prison in the middle of the night, a prison where it so happens certain civilians were picked at random this morning — your friends among them. I'll agree, it's an unfortunate coincidence."

He obviously enjoyed saying these things: he was wallowing

pleasurably in despicable callousness; presumably he thought it admirable.

Constantin stood up. "Tell me, General," he asked, "are you saying those two men are to be killed because they're Jewish, or because they're not Jewish now? Or because they said they weren't? This is getting complicated, you know!"

Bremen, who had jumped and half risen at the same time as Constantin, sat down again, but had obviously perched with his buttocks on the very edge of his chair, for his visitor's voice had changed.

"Please calm down, Herr von Meck!" he said. And he looked around in alarm for the bell.

Briefly, Constantin cherished the wild hope that the aide was going to come in: he would make short work of both him and Bremen. He would throw the pair of them into the fireplace, clamped together, like a couple of dolls! The blood was beating in his temples, at his wrists and his throat, as so often, and for a split second he felt his heart hesitate and stop. I shall die of a heart attack one of these days, he thought; Wanda used to say so often enough. I'm going to die stupidly here on this floor at the feet of a fool. How contemptible life is! And how contemptible the Germans are! Contemptible, yes, Romano's right. Whether it's the officers thrusting their chests out or the soldiers barking salutes, they're all contemptible. What the hell am I doing here? he wondered again, with a fierce pang of despair.

"Herr von Meck," said Bremen nervously, facing him, "Herr von Meck, there's nothing to be done about this."

The telephone in his office rang, and he raised the receiver, while Constantin let himself drop back in his chair, arms and legs stretched out, and flung his head back, tie loosened. As if in a dream, he heard Bremen say, "Oh, really? Look after him, will you? He's valuable, don't do him too much damage. Be careful. I'll leave him to you." A vague idea went through Constantin's mind . . . the man must have some dim notion of compassion somewhere in his heart, he thought.

"You needn't feel guilty," said Bremen. "After all, if your two friends weren't shot they'd have been sent to Auschwitz."

"Yes, well," said Constantin gloomily, "but there's still a difference between being shot and going to a labour camp, isn't there?"

And Bremen's doubtful smile and shrug of the shoulders seemed to him the ultimate dishonesty.

"General," he said, leaning forward, "General, I beg you, see what you can do. Let me call Goebbels — I'll get him to speak to you. He'll tell you that . . ." The telephone rang again, and casting up his eyes to heaven this time, Bremen picked it up. Constantin saw him suddenly turn pale.

"Good God!" said the General. "I'm coming. Do what's necessary, untie him, call the doctor, get him lying down. I'm coming." And he rose with remarkable speed and disappeared through the door at the end of the room. Bewildered, Constantin watched him leave at a gentle trot, elbows tucked in, chin in the air. Ridiculous. He was ridiculous. Twenty thousand francs was not too much. Romano had been very courageous.

Constantin stood by the desk for a moment, and then cast an eye over it at random, looking for any paper headed "Liberation Warrant", "Order of Release", "By Command Of", or something along those lines, even while he was aware of the pointlessness of his search. There was nothing of the kind: only papers dealing with trains, journeys, lorries and trucks, as if the office belonged to Paris Railways. A slight cough made him step back, caught in the act, but it was only the aide appearing in the doorway at the end of the room, still pink with emotion.

"Herr von Meck," he said, in a voice which was both sibilant and emotional, "Herr von Meck, I can't help saying how much I admire and envy you! To think you married Wanda Blessen! What a life you must have had, Herr von Meck!" he added, casting swift glances at the door through which the General had disappeared. Constantin nodded, with some irritation; it was a fact that Wanda had always fascinated homosexuals.

"Herr von Meck," the aide went on, coming closer, "Herr von Meck, I have to tell you . . . I overheard . . . do forgive me, I overheard your conversation with the General and . . . well, I really have to tell you, the hostages . . . they were executed this morning."

"What?" said Constantin. And for once he felt the cliché about one's legs giving way beneath one was real. He leaned against the desk. No — no, he was not indifferent to the fate of Schwob and Weil! What foolishness, what extraordinary foolishness had made him think so back at the hotel just now? He felt a pang at his heart.

"We pretend hostages are still alive, you see," the aide went on, "because people will often decide to talk the day or the evening before an execution, to save them — people come in and denounce someone or something, so it pays off. But the fact is they were all shot this morning. It wasn't worth your while coming to ask Heinrich . . . sorry, I mean the General," he added hastily. Even in his fury and despair, Constantin had time to notice the aide blush, smile, and stop with his mouth open, aware of what he had just said and what it implied — the use of the first name, his confusion — and aware that that confusion had not escaped Constantin.

"Might I venture to ask for your autograph?" he went on, and Constantin, his face drawn, signed his name on a piece of pale blue paper, adding, at the boy's request, "For Dieter, Constantin von Meck" — Dieter being not the aide himself but, he explained, a very dear friend of his.

The young man backed out, smiling, even forgetting his final "Heil Hitler!" Constantin was left alone, a prey to unfamiliar panic: what was he doing here? It was obvious that the boy had told the truth. He felt like murdering the General: he was choked by the sensation of powerlessness he had felt facing him just now, a sensation he had hardly ever known before. He didn't mind if Bremen killed him, he didn't mind being arrested and imprisoned, but it wasn't just himself: there was Romano too, who needed him in order to live. He had better leave. He had definitely better leave before that idiot came back and his anger got the better of him.

Constantin wiped his forehead on the sleeve of his jacket, and was surprised to see it drenched with sweat: he looked for the door, picked the wrong one, and found himself on a gallery surrounding a lift cage. He decided to bring the lift down. There was a scuffle and the sound of exclamations above him; raising his head, he saw a bleeding object topple over the gallery on the floor above, fall screaming through the open lift shaft before his eyes, and crash to the tiling on the ground floor ten metres below; it was instantly covered with blood. But as he passed, the man had shown Constantin a distorted face which was no longer a face at all, but a surface without features or eyes, above a torso covered with so many black marks and streaks of red that only the bare hands stretched out towards him in a last reflex action told Constantin this had been a white man. With an instinctive movement, Constantin first drew back; then, with a slight whistling in his ears, he stepped forward again and climbed the stairs four by four, as he was well able to do with his long legs, and jostling past shadowy shapes, he found himself facing General Bremen again. He took him by the collar and flung him against the opposite wall, while other hands clutched his arms, head and torso and tried to restrain him. All the same, he had time to strike Bremen several times with the flat of his hand — or the back or the palm, he no longer knew which — with savage energy, with a force that showed pleasure in such lack of restraint. Constantin felt all-powerful: he struck and struck at that undismayed, lying face; he struck those hard features softened with lies, false contrition and genuine cruelty. He struck what might have been his own face, though he had not known it, for the last three years.

They were separated only with great difficulty.

A week later, accompanied by his latest conquest, the young film star Maud Mérival, the hope of the French cinema, Constantin von Meck the director set off for a holiday near Aix-en-Provence in a house placed at his disposal by one of his friends, the elegant Mme Elisabeth Bragance. Nor was it to be all holiday, since the director was taking with him M. Bruno Walter and M. Jean-Pierre Danoux, an adaptor and a scriptwriter well known to the public, and also M. Romano Woltzer to find suitable locations. For the famous von Meck was planning to make a film on location, and hoped to have the great star Wanda Blessen in the lead, playing La Sanseverina in a film of *La Chartreuse de Parme*, from Stendhal's novel — a novel which M. Darius Popesku, the UFA representative on the production side, was horrified to find ran to over five hundred pages. It was all very well for Stendhal to have written those pages in three weeks, and for that brief period to excite the admiration of Constantin von Meck: Darius Popesku, as he did not conceal from the latter, feared it would take him as long as that to read them.

Part Two

I

Although Lucien Marrat, the young leading actor cast by
Constantin von Meck as Fabrice del Dongo, had much of the
beauty, character and demeanour with which Stendhal endowed
his hero when on foot, he had no charms whatever on horseback.
Once he was in the saddle, his face could be seen writhing, his
back bending, and the ease of manner required by his role left
him. UFA had searched the whole area and then Paris for a
suitable stand-in, but it seemed that forced labour service,
captivity or the Resistance had gone out of their way to stake a
prior claim on every good horseman in France. Those remaining,
at all events, were too short, too fat or too sturdy; there was not
one who really looked like the handsome young man. Constantin
von Meck started by spending some time shooting Provençal
scenes which resembled the Italian setting of Stendhal's novel;
then, when Wanda Blessen arrived, he shot those outdoor
sequences involving the Duchess of Sanseverina on her own or
with Count Mosca. Meanwhile, riding masters spent a fortnight
trying to instil a few notions of horsemanship into an increasingly
stiff Lucien Marrat.

This morning, the first of the third week's filming, the
unfortunate leading man had to mount one of those fiery and
magnificent animals which Constantin von Meck had declared
suitable for the fine horseman described by Stendhal. For if, at a
pinch, Fabrice del Dongo could ride over the field of Waterloo

on some secondhand nag, he definitely could not perform showy manoeuvres under Fausta's balcony on a docile riding-school horse. Thus the unfortunate Lucien Marrat had to approach a prancing half-bred horse, its black coat already wet with excitement. Lucien's own pearl-grey nankeen riding coat was wet with trepidation. While the riding master held the bridle, Lucien Marrat put his left foot in the stirrup and then, stimulated by everyone's attention, brought his right foot into action too; this had him momentarily sitting his horse before the animal bucked and sent him flying through the air. It was all over in a second. There followed ten minutes of cries and exclamations of great variety, since the team was a positive tower of Babel. The two young stars, Maud Mérival and Lucien Marrat, were certainly French, but the great Hollywood star Wanda Blessen was of Swedish origin, and Ludwig Lentz, playing the second male lead, was a German of Hungarian origin, a very handsome and civilized man. The rest of the cast and the technicians were a mixed bunch too. The unhappy Lucien Marrat was picked up and dusted down with great to-do. He got back into the saddle very slowly, and as swiftly as before found himself back on the grass of the meadow, which luckily was extremely soft. Faced with Constantin's curses, and piqued to find his lessons had been so ineffective, the riding master decided to tame the horse and mounted it, thus increasing the animal's fury. He just had time for a superior smile before he too bit the dust. The frantic horse was walked on a leading rein to calm it down, but when, ten minutes later, young Fabrice del Dongo mounted his horse himself under the eye of the camera, he stayed on its back just long enough to touch the saddle.

This was a source of dismay to M. Popesku, the UFA representative, for whom every lost second sounded like a death knell. The director Constantin von Meck, on the other hand, having exhausted his anger, had taken refuge in laughter and fatalism. As Darius Popesku was tearing his hair and going imploringly from actors to horse and from horse to actors, as if his mediation might bring about some silent and mysterious understanding between the animal and the bipeds surrounding it, aid came from an unexpected source: the silent, handsome and reticent Romano Woltzer, whose job it was to find locations, swung himself into the saddle with one bound, and rode the horse at an easy, graceful trot to the other end of the meadow where they were filming. The young man sat a horse wonderfully well; what was more, his combination of vigour with a slim build actually made him look like the young leading man. The situation was saved! Romano would gallop around instead of Lucien Marrat, who would be perched on a chair for close-ups and shaken vigorously up and down by the scene shifters, an old trick of the silent movies. Of course, Romano was fair, much too fair, and he refused point-blank, God knew why, to have his hair dyed black, but a shako would solve that problem.

Romano Woltzer's unexpected talent might draw admiration from the male members of the cast and film crew, but its female members had long admired the handsome, melancholy young man — as they had frequently and very discreetly shown. Such, at all events, was the impression gathered by Darius Popesku from the rather risqué comments of the ladies present; the athletic talents of M. Romano Woltzer were not, it seemed, confined to outdoor sports. Apart from that, no one knew anything about him. He was one of those followers whom Constantin von Meck took everywhere with him, like his designer, his head cameraman and his secretary. Popesku would never have noticed the retiring young man if his equestrian feats and the laughter of the women in the company had not suddenly attracted his attention. After rendering much service to German science in the capacity of ethnologist by denouncing such Jews as he knew, Popesku was now actually employed by the Gestapo as an informer. Since they had come to the South of France, unfortunately, he had not had the slightest suspicion upon which to feed, not a single suspect, and although all the payment he got for the job was to stay alive, Popesku was beginning to feel guilty towards his undercover employers.

"Well, M. Popesku," inquired a loud voice behind him, "well, M. Popesku, is UFA saved?"

Popesku turned at the voice of his real employer, his present official master Constantin von Meck, who was looming over him, casual and loose-limbed, in a startling, old-fashioned raw linen suit of the style worn at Deauville around 1930, with a blue and white silk square around his neck instead of his famous red scarf, and who was smiling happily. In spite of himself, Darius Popesku scrutinized the man. Constantin's forehead was high and curved, his eyelashes and eyebrows were as thick as his moustache and his hair, his eyes were large too, and elongated, his cheekbones were too prominent, his nose was too thrusting, too aquiline, and his teeth too white between lips that were too long and too thick above a chin with a cleft in it. There was not a single receding element or feature in that face, and Popesku, though there was nothing effeminate about him, could vaguely understand why women wanted it on their shoulders, wanted to hold it close to them in the dark — an energetic face with its primitive design civilized and even, if you looked a little, made vulnerable by life, intelligence, time and wrinkles.

"Well, yes," admitted Popesku, looking up at the shadow which had come between himself and the sun. "Well, yes, I confess I *am* relieved, M. von Meck! It must be hereditary, is it? I dare say you're a good horseman yourself?"

"Hereditary? How do you mean, hereditary?" inquired Constantin, surprised and wary.

Popesku was cast into confusion. "I only meant that elegant horsemanship must be a talent that runs in families, isn't it? I mean, your cousin M. Woltzer rides so well . . . I'm so sorry," Popesku interrupted himself, "but you see, it does say in M. Woltzer's records — I mean, he's down as a relation of yours, so that's why I ventured to say . . ."

"A distant relation, yes," said Constantin, looking both annoyed and relieved. And he walked away without turning back, leaving Popesku bewildered. It was as if Constantin had disowned that branch of his family; as if he had suddenly had an attack of some kind of snobbery, although Popesku had never detected the slightest trace of such a thing in him before.

While they took Fabrice's splendid riding coat off Lucien Marrat and put it on Romano Woltzer, Constantin von Meck crossed the clearing in which his company was milling about and went to knock on the door of his ex-wife Wanda Blessen's dressing room — or rather, her caravan. She was sitting on a chaise-longue at an open window, reading. Her sublime face, famous all over the world, did not show a superfluous line when it was thus exposed to the bright light of June. In the ten years he had known and loved her, Constantin had never seen her look any older than thirty: she was thirty for all eternity. She turned her head when he came in and smiled at him, an affectionate smile which exasperated him. For since her arrival Wanda had refused to make love with him, something that struck Constantin as odious, not to say perverse. They were natural lovers, surely made so from birth, and even if they were not married now, they belonged to each other for always. It was not as if there were any third party, and regrets involved, to account for her refusal: a refusal which robbed her presence here of any justification. He simply did not understand. America had been at war for months now, and she was American by nationality. Yes, her father's illness had brought her back to Sweden, fair enough: but the fact that she had gone straight from Sweden to occupied France to make a film for Germany, the enemy country — even if it was a part that appealed to her so much — well, it struck him as incomprehensible if not to be explained by their mutual passion. Constantin had often had difficulty in understanding his wife's behaviour, and for a long time had even taken a ridiculous pride in his inability to do so. The fame and popularity of Wanda Blessen were heightened by her whims, her flights of fancy, her follies, and Constantin had long enjoyed saying, "I really don't understand my wife at all!" as if to let his partner in conversation add, in parenthesis, "No, but she loves him!", which was flattering and indeed useful to him. And gradually he had come to consider his inability to understand and appreciate his own wife amusing, even normal; he had come to applaud her impulsive acts, just as the newspapers did, while like the rest of her court he disregarded her deeper nature. Gradually, too, Wanda, trapped by her habits, her actress's instinct and her desire to please him, had accepted the fact that he loved her for what he liked best in her: her instability and her changing moods. They both had a vague idea of all this, and each of them regretted it enough to blame it on the other.

In any case, their physical compatibility, which had been so instant and so striking, did not decrease; it remained almost incestuous. And if Wanda's refusal to make love since she arrived had at first surprised Constantin more than it hurt him, that refusal now aroused in him an unknown and confused pain which he had not known he could feel for this woman. It was something that affected his love quite as much as his vanity, though he might try to attribute it entirely to the latter. How could he have been so conceited, he asked himself, as to think that Wanda had defied the rules of war, public opinion and patriotism simply to be with him, risking her career and her life for a man she had known for years, whom she had already left of her own accord after Mexico and had not wanted to see again, a man to whom she had been as unfaithful as he had been unfaithful to her, and whose moustache she sometimes couldn't abide? No, it was for her part, it was to play La Sanseverina, a character who had fascinated her for twenty years, that Wanda was forgetting the Nazis and their war, or else adapting herself to it. It was for the sake of fame she was flirting with dishonour. But she had no use now for him, Constantin, unless perhaps as a director whom she knew to be clever, and to whom no doubt, when they got to the big scenes and the close-ups, she might find it in her heart to be accommodating. No, no, he was going too far, he was slandering her, he was out of his mind: Wanda had never sunk as low as that, he was the one who had sunk low, out of mortification. Unhappiness did not agree with Constantin, unhappiness made him coarse and mean-minded, it was only happiness that set him somewhere near heaven and all its angels. Which was not very meritorious, but at least he knew it.

Standing before her at the foot of the chaise-longue, he scrutinized her. He looked at the black hair which seemed blue in the sunlight, the face with its forceful, although gently forceful, bone structure, covered from cheekbones to chin with skin so white that it flushed pink at the least word. He looked at the long nose with its flaring nostrils, the mouth turned down at the corners that said No. The whole of the face sought love, her eyes dreamed of it, and her mouth said No to that face. Like a doting critic who had written about her, like the audiences of her films, like the producers of those films, although they were obliged to appear indifferent, Constantin could not help looking at her. He knew that when the corners of her mouth turned up in laughter, gaiety gave a childlike expression to her face, a face that was almost too moving.

Yes, she was a lovely creature, Constantin said to himself tenderly, a lovely and very complex creature. And it was a lovely face too, one of those few faces whose intelligence increases their sensuality.

And a groan of anticipatory pleasure escaped Constantin's lips. He blinked, and met the briefly concerned, briefly affectionate eyes of Wanda.

"What's the matter?" she asked in the husky, cynical voice which was famous too.

"Nothing," he said, shrugged his shoulders, and sat down at

her feet. A scent of warm grass and earth, a scent of the summer countryside wafted in to them through the small open window, and he took Wanda's hand and laid his cheek against it with ardour resurfacing from adolescence. He felt far, far away from the war when he was with her. With her, he could rediscover his past, his profession, his life, rediscover the great beaches of America, yellow or grey, strong sunlight, the smell of the wind and of petrol, excited voices, vast houses, ruffled palm trees, cars smelling of leather, bars, pianos; he rediscovered the backdrop of his existence, the tonality and odours of his life, the flesh on his skeleton. And a nostalgia for the tropics constricted his throat as he sat beside this woman, even though she herself had been born beside a colourless, lightless fjord in the middle of the night, a white night. Other things came back to him too: chewing gum, muted trumpets at dawn, the sound of dollars in cash registers, adulterated whisky, crap games, brothels, ports, all brought back to him by the hieratic profile of this lovely creature made of snow and fire, as the critics superfluously pointed out. She had let him retain her hand, and he pressed his eyes and his long eyelashes to it.

"You know," he said, low-voiced, "I miss America."

"What a curious thing to say!" remarked Wanda, flatly. "I love it here. I never knew France before, or at least I didn't know it well."

"But it isn't France you're seeing," said Constantin. "This is occupied France. It's not precisely the same thing."

"It isn't?" she said, apparently without irony, before allowing silence to fall: a silence which, however, he felt to be questioning, if not severe.

What did she want from him? What did she think he could say in answer to that? Could she imagine, even momentarily, that he would now be able to justify the dreadful mistake he had made in 1937 any better than he could justify any other, lesser stupid thing done years ago? Could she think he had aged, he had matured, he would have answers to her questions? She knew perfectly well that there had only ever been two women who could supply the answers to any questions for him, first his mother and then herself. Wanda had no business asking him questions and he had none giving her answers, particularly when she was acting in such a prudish way. Constantin was not waiting for a lawyer before he answered her; he was waiting for the two of them to be in bed. It was only in the dark, between warm sheets, beside a woman and after making love, that he could provide answers to everything. It was not emotional blackmail, but the proper way to behave.

Wanda's hand was on his hair.

"Do you know what makes Count Mosca in this book so noble?" she asked out of the blue, waving Stendhal's novel in front of him; she had been reading and rereading it since she arrived. "Any ordinary Frenchman or American of fifty in his situation would tell himself, 'So my mistress prefers that young idiot to me, does she? Then she's a whore.' But Mosca tells himself, 'How could she fail to prefer that handsome young man to me with my old hide?' He gives La Sanseverina all the liberty and aesthetic choice men still refuse women today. What it boils down to, you see, is that men think women — or at least they want to think women — are more fascinated by money and power than a man's looks, which means that at heart they see them as tarts, who can be bought and kept by money. They only actually *call* them tarts when they've stopped acting like tarts, when they abandon security and luxury to follow their natural tastes, when they'd rather have a handsome young man than money. Now Mosca doesn't think for a moment that his rank is worth as much as Fabrice's youthful cheeks and mouth. He thinks Fabrice's looks weigh more in La Sanseverina's eyes, even though he thinks more highly of her than he has ever thought of a man. And I'll tell you something else: Mosca's the character Stendhal really likes. He has no time for Fabrice del Dongo!"

Constantin looked at her in surprise. "Since when have you been thinking about Stendhal? Since when have you been thinking at all?"

"Oh, for ever," she said, fanning herself gracefully with the book.

"If you do all this thinking, then why did you come here to make the film?" Constantin could not help asking. "With America at war with Germany? It will be difficult for you when Germany's lost the war, you know . . . when *we* have lost the war," he added, with grace.

"So you think you'll lose it?" said Wanda, and she burst out laughing. "You think Germany is going to lose the war, in spite of your cooperation since 1937? By the way, can you tell me what came over you in 1937?"

"I'm talking about you. I'm worried about you," said Constantin.

She looked at him kindly. "It will be difficult for me, will it?" she said. "Oh, this little lapse will be put down to my mad passion for you."

"Whereas it's the part of La Sanseverina you're interested in, am I right?" inquired Constantin lightly, as he thought, but it made her laugh.

She ran her hand through Constantin's hair and smoothed his moustache and eyelashes in a light-hearted, possessive manner which he found very displeasing.

"You'll see," she said, "you'll see what my motives are. Anyway, you can't be sure of anyone, I promise you can't . . . Off you go, darling, they're calling for you out there. Young Lucien must have managed to stay on that horse at last."

"No, it's not him on the horse," said Constantin, gloomily. "It's Romano, the locations fellow. He's riding the horse instead."

"Ah, Romano!" said Wanda, laughter and irony in her eyes — damn her, she always knew all about Constantin's affairs of the heart! "Ah, the handsome Romano! He ought to be playing Fabrice, you know," she added, smiling, while the infuriated Constantin left the caravan.

They were indeed calling for him. Fabrice del Dongo, otherwise Romano, was in the saddle, prancing about in the middle of the grassy space. Constantin saw him at once, sitting his horse as it reared in the sunlight. He felt a surge of passion and admiration for the little gypsy under threat of death who could leap skyward from the grass with such obvious freedom and carelessness. The horse was nervous, restive, the kind of stallion that the aristocratic Fabrice del Dongo would have broken gradually over a period of time, with the help of riding masters; it was also the kind of wild horse on whose back Romano, as a poor gypsy boy with a taste for danger, would have jumped by means of some trick a few years ago, on the Hungarian plains, to the angry shouts of its owner. Whatever the privileges of one and the handicaps of the other, Fabrice and Romano were both spirited young men, physically tough and without much heart. For Fabrice del Dongo felt only mild vexation when he admitted to not loving anyone, while Romano almost congratulated himself on it. None the less, seeing him place himself at the centre of attention for the first time in his life like this, in front of the fascinated film crew, perhaps in front of startled spies, seeing this young gypsy whom no one, including himself, really knew, leaping for the sky, the tree tops and the pleasure of being alive, Constantin felt for a moment that he was on stage in the middle of some noble and lyrical opera . . . And after all, it was the first time he had seen anyone so merry in the face of death. In Hollywood, he had seen people merry in defiance of the brutal hazards of living in the glare of publicity, and sometimes doing it with great style. In Europe too, quite recently, since his return, he had seen plenty of people merry in the face of denunciation and fear and traps. But it was the first time he had seen a young man, innocent and clear-headed, prance so merrily in the face of death, defying it and obviously enjoying what he did. And in this, perhaps, Romano was more the romantic hero than Fabrice del Dongo, who risked nothing but a death in which, unlike Romano, he was unable to believe.

"Cameras roll," said Constantin, briefly.

But he had not reached the camera himself before he was being badgered by three people: the technician framing the shot, who could not get it centred properly, the chief cameraman, who was afraid the light might not last, and the wardrobe mistress Luce, a perfectionist, complaining that Fabrice's coat showed a crease from neck to waist when worn by Romano, who was thinner than Lucien Marrat. This, from a woman who had been wearing rayon and wooden shoes for the last three years, quite melted Constantin's heart again. He turned his attention to all the fiddling details which made up such a large part of the director's job, details to which he had devoted himself constantly and systematically for three years, perhaps to help him forget other, more serious matters. He supplied answers, instructions, decisions, prohibitions; in short, he was part of the game again, he entered the enchanted world of *La Chartreuse de Parme*, where people loved one another and wounded only with words, or at least not with such instruments as had sent a body he might have taken for an animal's falling from floor to floor before his eyes in the Avenue Foch, a body he had recognized as human only by its two hands stretched out to him as it fell.

Romano was therefore filmed from a distance in the part of Fabrice del Dongo all afternoon. Like Fabrice, he was swept from the saddle and lost his horse at Waterloo; he fled from the police on another horse, he galloped towards Giletti, he pranced below La Muffa's balcony and went to meet La Sanseverina. He spent nearly six hours riding the two horses, and filming did not stop until eight in the evening, when Romano took his stallion, now quiet as a lamb, to the horse box waiting for him, and dismounted under the stern gaze of Constantin, to whom he returned a sideways glance of contrition, but of pleasure too.

"What an afternoon!" he said, almost in spite of himself. "What an afternoon! That horse is fantastic. He could jump two metres if he wanted to."

He slackened the girth, picked a handful of grass and rubbed down the horse's lathered flanks with an expert hand.

"What did you do that for?" asked Constantin curtly. "Not very clever, was it, drawing attention to yourself?"

"I couldn't help it," Romano was quick to answer. "When I saw that man there, your actor — no, it was the other man on him, the riding master — when I saw he was going to use a second bit, a chain bit as well as a snaffle, I told myself he'd spoil the horse's mouth."

"And you couldn't have considered your own mouth more important than the horse's?" inquired Constantin, with good humour which he did not feel.

"Well, no," said Romano, with a little smile, "well, no, of course I couldn't! A horse is sacred to a gypsy, understand? Didn't you know that? Anyone can see you're no Romany! The only things that matter to my people are horses, the gypsy festival at Les-Saintes-Maries-de-la-Mer, and our knives!"

And he picked up his scarf, tied it round his forehead like a headband and snatched Constantin's hand, as if to read its palm, with a wild and cunning look. Constantin, annoyed, resisted; he never knew how just how much nostalgia there was mingled with the fun when he went along with Romano's gypsy fooling.

"No need to kiss my hands, young gypsy," said Constantin, shrugging his shoulders. "All I've ever done was snatch you from the jaws of certain death, thanks to my reputation and my courage. Seriously, I wish you hadn't gone prancing about like that. I wish you hadn't drawn attention to yourself. There are informers about, even here."

"Well, I do wonder," said Romano, laughing, "I do wonder if hiding away isn't more dangerous just now than drawing attention to oneself. I'm not too sure. Listen, seriously, I didn't do it on purpose. I've had a happy afternoon. Don't spoil it for me."

And without waiting for Constantin's reply, he went of his own accord to knock on Wanda's door. She opened it to him, looking lovely in a beige, gold and blue pullover which brought out the blue, black and white of her own colouring.

"Come in," said she, "come in, O handsome young man, and as for you, you noble old soul there, why not come in too and have some of that synthetic port M. Popesku kindly gave me? And would you wind up the gramophone, Romano, and put on that Edith Piaf record that makes me cry so much? Come along in."

Constantin followed Romano in, surprised and delighted to find that such an understanding existed between the two people he loved most in the world. They were looking at each other shyly but confidently, each as if tamed by the other. It gave the relationship great charm, or so at least he thought. Romano wound up the gramophone and put on a Piaf song whose words, though not very subtle, gave Constantin gooseflesh. But Wanda forgot to shed tears.

"Romano," she said, "I saw you through the window, you were marvellous. How good you look on horseback! You looked like a god. Now if you were really playing the part of Fabrice, all of it, instead of that wretched Lucien Marel, no, Marrat or whatever his name is, I can tell you it would be a great help to me. Are you listening, Constantin? Are you sure you can't send your actor packing and dye our friend's hair black? Or rather, stop dying his hair, because that peroxide must be doing dreadful things to his scalp. Show me," she told Romano, who knelt before her on one knee, as if kneeling to a queen, presenting her with his fair hair: or rather, bleached hair, bleached by Constantin a couple of days earlier.

"Frightful!" said Wanda. "It'll ruin his hair, it'll damage the roots, dry it out entirely. This really won't do!"

And she cast Constantin a reproachful glance, at which, bewildered and confused, he could only lower his eyes.

"All right," he said. "Well, are we going to have dinner? Personally, I'm dying of hunger."

"You're always hungry when people say things you don't like," said Wanda, smiling.

"What d'you want me to say?" muttered Constantin. "Well, what? So the Third Reich likes fair people better! It's not my fault."

"I've heard that they do, yes. But then how did the Germans come to elect that dark little man to lead them? Can you tell me that? No, of course you can't!" she added. "Well, do let's go and have dinner. Poor Boubou must be bored to death, all alone in her simple dwelling."

The house inherited by Boubou Bragance from her first husband was one of those ochre-coloured, vast Provençal farmhouses, built in the shape of an M around a farmyard rechristened a patio, containing a swimming pool of too blue a colour and unbleached canvas deckchairs. Inside, however, the place was full of furniture, crammed with it: Chinese, Chippendale, rustic Louis XVI pieces, with an occasional straw hat or rattan armchair among them, reminding you of the cypress trees and vines, the summer countryside surrounding the house. There was going to be chicken for dinner this evening, thanks to Romano, who was displaying his thieving, gypsy talents by regularly stealing poultry from the local henhouses, partly as a game, partly from hunger. Not all Constantin's lordly authority or Popesku's venal obsequiousness had managed to extract anything whatsoever from the greedy and suspicious peasants. Consequently, it was up to Romano to go looting and stealing by night, defying the farmers' blunderbusses and the fangs of their dogs, bringing back sometimes eggs, sometimes — more rarely — a fowl, usually caught after a desperate nocturnal chase. These birds always arrived on the table with a solitary drumstick, which surprised Romano, who remembered their fine turn of speed and communicated his surprise to the other guests. One evening, after several days of perplexity, Boubou Bragance cried, meeting all their eyes, "Yes, yes, I know there's one leg missing, darling, but if you knew who we carved it for back in the kitchen you'd approve. In fact," she concluded, instantly commandeering the bird's other leg, "you'd give me a round of applause."

This was taking cynicism rather far, for though her tone suggested the presence somewhere within her walls of an anaemic child, an old man on his deathbed or a pregnant woman, Constantin had found her a few days later busy vigorously carving the fowl herself in the kitchen and eating its leg before the bird was served. He had laughed a lot, but said nothing, thinking that here he had a wonderful tool for blackmail, something that might well come in useful with Boubou. Moreover, it was for her very ferocity and cynicism that he liked her. He could see, too, that the Occupation suited her very well indeed: for years her fortune had obliged her to live on a lavish, even a luxurious scale, but present-day rationing and privations now forced her — or rather allowed her — to follow her natural bent for parsimony. None the less, she had a natural and agreeable instinct for hospitality.

Most of the film crew were staying in small local hotels dotted around the place. Boubou had the four leading actors staying with her, as well as Constantin the director, Romano the locations assistant, and of course Popesku, the UFA representative. All the same, that made eight people counting Boubou herself, and two chickens would hardly have been enough to feed them. They were therefore rather put out on arriving back at the house — particularly Romano, who was starving after his afternoon's exertions — to find another guest present, someone else to share the meal, and a Wehrmacht officer at that, Captain von Kirschen, who jumped to his feet, beaming, on seeing the unkempt and dusty party come in, while Boubou eyes sparkling, legs bent, ran to meet them, waving her little arms like semaphore signals.

"Guess who's here! Just guess who's come from Draguignan to see us! Guess who's going to dine with us! Go on, guess! It's Captain von Kirschen."

"I couldn't very well have guessed," remarked Constantin, "since we've never met."

"Well, you have now," said Boubou, not abashed for a moment. "Captain von Kirschen is going to be kind enough to dine with us this evening — aren't you, Captain?"

The Captain, unable to contradict this, nodded his head, clicked his heels, but omitted to raise his arm and shout "Heil Hitler!" which was not a bad start, thought Constantin, despite his annoyance and fatigue. They all sat down to table with differing expressions on their faces: Romano concentrated on his plate, Constantin's manner was abstracted, Boubou was over-excited, and Wanda, as usual, was being seductive. The new arrival, of course, was the recipient of the full force of her glance, the touch of her hand, everything about her that had already fascinated millions of spectators, besides some private individuals. He too fell victim: he made conversation, he preened himself, and after dinner, when they were out on the balcony and she chided him gently for leaving them so soon, he replied that he would be passing quite close tomorrow evening, by train, and would be thinking of her.

"You won't even come in and say good evening?" inquired Wanda. She looked as if she were melting into the background of tulips and gladioli beyond the window, her face standing out against it like another and slightly paler flower.

"I'm afraid I can hardly jump off the train!" he said regretfully. "We'll be on our way south. But I promise I'll think of you at midnight on the dot."

And he was off again, delivering enthusiastic lectures on Heine, Beethoven, Rainer Maria von Rilke; and while Constantin yawned in time with the other guests, while Boubou wondered whether Wanda might not perhaps be a possible competitor in the charm stakes after all, Romano was feverishly calculating the number of hours to go before midnight tomorrow.

"I really shouldn't have told you that, my dear Mme Blessen," said the officer — persisting, as those who have committed a blunder will, in believing that to repeat the blunder cancels it out — "I really shouldn't have told you that, but then whom can one trust in this country if not you, Mme Blessen — Wanda, if I may — and you, M. von Meck, you who rejected your American past to come to the aid of our country — and you too, Mme Bragance, welcoming us here as allies, not treating us as enemies as they do in Paris."

"And fast-moving allies at that," remarked Boubou Bragance unkindly, for the defeats suffered by the German army were piling up in this month of June 1943. "All the same, I have to say there are some boors among you I wouldn't call my allies for anything in the world, though I may have been foolish enough to consider them my guests for an evening."

"What do you mean?" inquired von Kirschen, sounding much displeased.

Boubou chuckled and shook her head.

"Oh, nothing! Nothing serious! Just an exceptional case, someone in your army. One of those exceptions that prove the rule, I imagine."

At this point Constantin intervened, his fatigue instantly forgotten. "I'm very pleased to meet you, Captain; and more particularly I'm pleased to see our dear friend's ability to judge the German Army calmly is restored to her. Boubou, haven't you told Captain von Kirschen about your misadventures? Then I will, if you don't mind!"

"No, no!" cried Boubou, voice suddenly very shrill. "No, no! Be quiet, for goodness' sake, Constantin. If you insist on going over that very boring story let me do it myself!"

Constantin clicked his tongue reprovingly. "Now, now, you can't tell it properly yourself; it hurt you too much, left too much of a mark on you. Oh yes, it did! I know you, Boubou — you have so much sensitivity underneath your . . . your raffish manner!"

"No, let me do it!"

There was a gleam in Boubou's eyes which as usual arose from a combination of her taste for danger and her fear of scandal, and it was for this that Constantin liked her. Her taste for danger won the day. She shrugged her shoulders, as if defeated.

"My dear Captain, I beg you not to listen to more than half of this, and don't believe a quarter of it! You know what M. von Meck's imagination is like!"

"But I should be delighted to hear the famous Constantin von Meck tell a story!" said the Captain, bowing again and only just refraining from clicking his heels.

Constantin was already seated in his favourite rattan armchair, and spreading his hands by way of introduction, coughed to clear his throat.

"Well," he said. "Are you listening, Captain?"

Wanda began to laugh confidently, and Constantin shot her a glance of affection, that affection all husbands feel for their wives when they appear appreciative.

"Draw up your chairs, good people," he began, in the voice of a wise peasant telling tales of an evening by the fireside, "draw up your chairs and hear the sad tale of Boubou Bragance," he continued, delighted to have everyone's attention. "You cannot be unaware that our friend Boubou Bragance has always presided over one of the most brilliant salons in Paris, if not *the* most brilliant, and not only recently, in these — why, these three last years! Good Lord, how fast time goes, it's crazy, don't you think so?" But there was no reply to this question. "Well, not just for these three years, but even before that, when none of us here were around. The Parisians — those invited to Boubou's salon, I mean — were proud of it, even when reduced to their own sole company."

"Stick to the subject, would you, Constantin?" said Boubou, her voice hard.

"Yes, yes, yes, I'm getting back to it. Well, three years ago Boubou refused to leave Paris or close her doors. If there was only one small candle, one little torch of the French spirit still burning in Paris, it would be at her place on the Quai d'Anjou. She would hold it aloft, unlike those cowards and ill-disposed persons who had skulked off to the United States or elsewhere. And so I say to her again, well done, Boubou, well done!"

Constantin clapped heartily, but Boubou contented herself with shaking her head.

"Unfortunately, like everyone else, Boubou has some old friends, rather old-fashioned, rather out of touch, rather . . . rather racist, to tell you the truth, but not in the genetic sense like our Führer, oh no; racist in the sense that . . . well . . . the Boches, you see, the Uhlans who cut off children's hands in the '14-'18 war, the fathers of these people or they themselves at Verdun — anyway, these friends of hers wouldn't have liked to find themselves surrounded by people in German uniforms. So Boubou had the brilliant idea of forbidding anything that reminded people of the war in her house: no heroic tales, no political discussions, no uniforms even. The officers got into the habit of changing into dinner jackets or double-breasted suits in the cloakroom. Nobody mentioned war, unless in connection with Joan of Arc, who was burnt by the English, as you know, so no doubt she was pleased, even at this late date, to see the bombs descending on their heads. Conversation was of a truly exquisite nature, wholly conducted by persons in bow ties: Heinrich Heine was a favourite subject, as always, and the beneficial effect of music on the character, and the ability of poetry to transcend frontiers . . . all was for the best in the best of all possible little worlds. If you forgot that the women were dressed in rayon, the cakes tasted of carrot, the drinks had a medicinal flavour, and a certain accent . . . a guttural accent . . . pervaded all conversation, you'd have thought yourself back in the old pre-war days. But alas, a spoilsport was about to come on the scene. Take people like, for instance, Villeneuve and Fario — you know them, Captain? The literary critic and the film critic? Everybody here knows them. Take Villeneuve, for example, a decent, well-bred sort of man; there he is, perfectly happy, visiting his friend Boubou Bragance, droning away, exchanging spiteful remarks with Fario. All the men are in dinner jackets, of course; everything is going well. Then, all of a sudden, he sees someone, an SS man dressed in an SS uniform, a black uniform of impeccable cut which adds nothing to the gaiety of the evening! Villeneuve is surprised, he goes to see Boubou who is surprised too, and makes for the place where the intruder is to be found. She sharply requests him to go and change in the cloakroom like everyone else. So what does our stranger do? He starts carrying on in German, coldly. He even starts shouting. So far as Villeneuve can understand what he's saying, he is explaining that he is just back from Russia, his comrades are currently dying in this uniform in the cold snow, just as they're dying under the African sun, and it is out of the question for him to abandon it in order to reassure a set of cowardly little Frenchmen who have been running from that uniform as fast as they could go since '39! That uniform is his flag, he says, and it should be the same for all his comrades in arms too. Whereupon he produces a notebook and a pencil and asks for the names of all the bow-tied officers present. Panic sets in! Villeneuve is annoyed, first because he never ran from the German uniform in '39 for the very good reason that he wasn't even in the army, having been discharged, and second because he is not at all keen on finding himself surrounded by the enemy in their black or grey uniforms, or rather, by those who have now become the enemy, since it's well known that the cowl makes the monk. Fario quite agrees. When he sees the German officers, looking crestfallen, making off downstairs again in a tearing hurry to put on their warriors' outfits, he decides to leave and goes to kiss Boubou's hand. Whereupon Boubou, whose feelings I can well understand, since she is not just an excellent hostess but a great lady too, asks him drily if he is thinking of leaving her alone with the soldiery, and lets him know that if he sets foot outside her salon now he will never set foot inside it again: not during or after the war, not even very long after it. Fario is rooted to the spot, torn between the perfectly normal desire to protect the mistress of the house — who is also his friend — and the more instinctive desire to get out while the going is good! And he has every reason to feel uneasy, since the frenzied officer, having drawn his pistol from its holster, keeps on tossing it from hand to hand like a cowboy in a Western. Indeed, he does this so often that it goes off, bang, and there is a bullet in the ceiling."

Here Boubou raised her voice, in indignation and regret. "Yes, he even broke one of my Venetian chandeliers, one of the best of them, the ones my first husband brought back from Venice and which . . ."

Constantin stopped her. "Let's not get off the subject, darling. So great was the moral damage, we needn't dwell on the material sort. Well, there stands Fario, looking now at Boubou, whose prohibition alarms him, now at the SS man, whose pistol alarms him, and to tell you the truth, his teeth are chattering. Someone does try to mollify the SS man with a drink, but unfortunately it is vodka, that notorious aluminium-based vodka found only in society salons, which drives the unfortunates who drink it mad, and I know what I'm talking about. This only increases the rage of the patriotic warrior. He even manages to get the men and the women separated on either side of the salon — Boubou's guests,

I mean — and he threatens them with an execution in the near future, perhaps next morning. Just think of Villeneuve's face — he with a wife and children — and Fario's too, the editor of the paper for which he writes being very punctilious about the hours his staff keep. The difficulty is all the more painful for Villeneuve in that, knowing the house as well as he does (like any good parasite) he is aware that behind the tapestry against which he is leaning there is a door which will have him inside the service lift and then out in the street and safety, within thirty seconds. Only of course Boubou will see him. He won't get executed, but he will get ostracized. The same choice confronts all Boubou's guests: die with her or live without her. Well, what do you think they did, Captain? Which do you think won, snobbery or the instinct of self-preservation? I bet you'll never guess: it was snobbery! There wasn't one of them who left. Not a man nor a woman! Admirable, wasn't it? Better to die and be in *Comoedia* than live and never feature there again. I always knew snobbery was a violent passion. As for the sequel, that's worth hearing too, don't you think?"

"Oh, yes, that was the best part," said Boubou, who had recovered her spirits after a moment's melancholy at the mention of the chandelier. "Fario went and sat at the piano, you see, to lighten the atmosphere; everyone followed him, Villeneuve leaned his elbow on it and Fario began singing in a quavering voice, I think it was *Auprès de ma blonde* or something like that — something silly, anyway! Villeneuve struck up next, and everyone started singing, horribly out of tune, starting with folk songs — *Au jardin de mon père, les lauriers sont fleuris*, and the bells of I forget what, and then *Nearer, my God, to thee*, and hymns, and a Maurice Chevalier song, absolute nonsense, all of it, and then after a bit they started singing rounds, and . . . and . . ."

She was suddenly convulsed with laughter, and signed to Constantin to take up the tale again.

"Yes," said Constantin, his eyes shining with mingled excitement and regret at having missed this scene, "yes, they were singing old French folk songs. All of a sudden they were ... well, like patriots facing the firing squad, singing the Marseillaise. I can just see Villeneuve bawling *Paris reine du monde* with a defiant glance at the SS man. It must have been wonderful. There they all were around the piano, the old ladies in their pearls and their rayon dresses, sniffling over *Les Cloches de Corneville* and *Les Gars de la Marine*. It must have been great! And until four in the morning the unfortunate officers standing to attention in front of their evil-tempered comrade had to listen to the entire French folksong repertory, and all the old Jesuit or Sacred Heart hymns, sung by that little company of society folk, their voices husky with heroism, thinking themselves great patriots. The things you sometimes see in Paris! And to think I missed it, Boubou! I shall never get over that, never!"

"How about the SS man?" asked Maud, in a small voice.

"Well," said Constantin, "history doesn't relate if it was the choral singing that did for him or the rest of the aluminium-based vodka, but all of a sudden he collapsed on a divan and began snoring. He slept like a log. His friends took him away at arm's length, whispering their apologies to Boubou."

There was a silence.

"They were right," said von Kirschen, "they were right! I hope you kept a note of the officer's name, Mme Bragance. When I get back I shall give himself the pleasure of finding his unit and having him severely reprimanded for such an abuse of power. There is no reason why one man should bring dishonour on an army corps like that!"

"Particularly," said Constantin, perfidiously, "particularly as defeatism of that kind might infect his men too. What did he think he was about, yelping away like that, calling Stalingrad and Tunis catastrophic, maybe even fatal defeats for our forces? Good God, the Third Reich can do better than that, I should hope! We're not so close to surrender, are we?"

"Come along, children," said Boubou, suddenly feeling the mood change, "come along, children, I don't want to hurry you, we've had a good laugh, but it's time to go to bed. I want you as good-looking as Stendhal specified. Mind, I don't think there was ever anyone who liked Stendhal as much as I do; well, André Gide, perhaps, and I'm not sure who else . . . anyway, time you all went to bed. Good night, everyone."

And they all left, going down one of the corridors leading to her huge drawing room, each with a plan in his or her head, but none the less bidding each other elaborate goodnights.

II

After showering and shaving, Constantin anointed his hair with the marvellous and unobtainable toilet water Wanda had thoughtfully brought him from America; he opened the bottle, put three drops on his neck, and America at once came back to him. The memories he retained of it — cut up and arranged in his mind as if in dummy drawers by resentment, this absurd war and these bewildering times — these lifeless snapshots, these dead postcards suddenly connected up and became the living, feeling, pleasantly melancholy film of his past life. America was no longer that geographical entity which his liking for happiness had vaguely situated somewhere very far away; once again it became a continent cradled by sun and water, a place where he could live, from which he could be exiled and suffer for it, since Wanda had come from America and might go back again, leaving him here. It was enough of a miracle that she had reached him at all, what with all these storms of metal, these cloudbursts of bombs, and her own responsibilities! When she had turned up at Boubou Bragance's, wrapped in furs despite the mild weather, her dark glasses on her nose, in the style of a true star, when he had taken her in his arms, Constantin had secretly trembled with happiness and incredulity; his face buried in the long fur of that luxurious coat, his nose in her scented hair, his cheek against her soft, powdered one, his lips against her smooth, warm neck, he had quite forgotten La Sanseverina, he could not have cared less about La Sanseverina. Wanda, his own Wanda, had come back. He had asked UFA to get her for the part, but without believing for a moment that they could do it, and he had been astonished to hear a fortnight later that she had agreed and was coming from Sweden, where she had been for the last six months with her sick father.

But now Wanda had been rejecting his advances for a week, and although her rejection had not yet made inroads into the capital of happiness created by her arrival, Constantin was beginning to get annoyed. He knocked on her door and walked in without waiting for her to reply. She was lying in bed, still reading *La Chartreuse de Parme*; she raised to him eyes exaggeratedly widened in what had to be feigned surprise.

"Good evening," he said. "I mean good night. I came to see if you needed anything," he added with a touch of sarcasm, which caused his ex-wife to shrug her shoulders slightly.

"No," she said in a weary tone, "no, I don't. Oh, sit down, do!" And she indicated the armchair beside her bed, but at once rose prudently, hiding her legs as if the situation were a delicate one, and began putting away the clothes lying about everywhere — a task in which Constantin automatically assisted. They had shared so many ship's cabins, hotel bedrooms, apartments in New York, Venice and London, so many rooms (where each always put away the other's things, partly out of affection and partly out of annoyance), in short, so many boltholes that it seemed unthinkable to Constantin, even indecent, not to lie down on the bed beside her afterwards. She was his possession, his wife, his mistress, his friend. And for her to go on rejecting his advances after a week struck him now as a childish and grotesque whim. He indicated as much when she was in bed again by lying back not in the armchair but against her knees, at the foot of the bed and across it, commandeering a pillow and lighting a cigarette without even looking at Wanda, like a Caliph in his harem.

"Really, how pretentious and vulgar you are!" she said, unruffled. "Where do you think you are? We're not married now, my dear!"

"Don't tell me," said Constantin, in bored tones, "don't tell me you've left some great, constant love in New York or Sweden. You've never believed in anything but the present, darling."

"And apparently you've never believed in anything but the past," she replied. "Let me tell you little Clelia Conti, your Maud, is mad about you, and entirely at your disposal. As for me, I am READING, Constantin. I'm WORKING, and I am READING!"

"Darling," said Constantin, sitting up and taking his wife's knees in his arms. "Listen, Wanda. This is me. This is you. This is us. Stop and think. Are you crazy? Look at me!"

Wanda smiled at him, and leaned so close that her mouth touched Constantin's. He instinctively closed his eyes, as if at an unexpected blow. Wanda's face, which had become milky, formless, unreal, moved away and regained its precision. She really was arrogant and vicious, he thought.

"You're vicious!"

"Now that really is the limit," said Wanda. "I'm vicious because I don't want to sleep with you, is that it?"

"Yes," said Constantin firmly. "For heaven's sake, you're mine. Just as I'm yours. It's idiotic."

"No," she said, "I'm not anyone's, and I don't know who you are. You're a good lover, you're a good director, no doubt about that. But what kind of man are you? What sort of hornet's nest have you got yourself into? I'm sometimes afraid in this country, Constantin. I get the impression of constant danger. What do you think of the place? Well, what *do* you think of it? What are you doing here?"

He had left his head on her knees, but he raised his eyes and saw in his wife's blue ones a shrewd, hard gleam which surprised him. What had the crazy woman thought up this time?

"Wanda," he said, "please, not you, not you. When I'm with you it's America I see, and the Atlantic, and ships. Ships! I beg you, don't talk to me about Europe. I've been here too long. Six years, do you realize?"

"But what about your dear friend Goebbels?" she asked. "I thought he was mad about you?"

"I don't know," said Constantin, "and I don't care. Or at least, I do care, because as long as he's mad about me, as you put it, I stay alive."

There was a silence; she looked at him, she put her hands to his face as she used to do, as he remembered, and he abandoned himself to her and let her run her large, long, soft hands over his own big head, stroking every part of his face, relaxing it, giving it back a human shape. Only my wife's hands can give me a human face, he thought, and he began to laugh at himself and his lyrical flights, magnified by fatigue. Directing a film was tiring, in spite of everything, particularly when you were trying to film a book you admired.

"Tell me, Constantin," Wanda went on, "why did you come back here, why did you leave America in such a hurry? Everybody asked me that, and as your former wife I looked damn silly not knowing the answer. I was very upset, Constantin!"

"It was because . . ." he began, "it was because . . ." Struck by sudden inspiration, he sat up. "It was because . . . oh, listen, it's such a boring, stupid story . . ."

"Then tell it," said Wanda. "Tell it or leave me!"

Stretched out on the bed, Constantin closed his eyes and assumed his musing, secret voice, the voice he used for lying. It was so long since he had not lied, so long since he hadn't had to lie to a woman, he couldn't remember just how long it was. He told the tale of his visit to his old school after the '14–'18 war. He spoke of the survivor who struck him, and his own remorse and his obsession afterwards, blessing Goebbels and his inspiration all the time. He made a brief, sober, manly story of it, and finished on a serious note, rather pleased with himself. Thus Wanda's peals of laughter came as a shock, as if they were blasphemy. He sat up. She was saying, "Oh, really, Constantin, honestly!" and she had tears of laughter in her eyes, like Boubou Bragance's just now. She wrapped her own arms round her own chest, and Constantin, first surprised and then amused, saw that Wanda Blessen, the Duse of her time, the star of stars, the enigmatic *femme fatale* Wanda Blessen was splitting her sides with laughter. He couldn't help laughing too, and without more ado renounced the character of the patriotic adolescent tormented by remorse over the years, a character which he had, however, played with enthusiasm for some moments.

"Oh, good heavens, Constantin!" groaned Wanda, "oh, good heavens! Oh, what a story! How on earth do you expect me to believe you? I know you inside out, my dear. No one but you could be so sure of my credulity. Oh, really, Constantin! I've known you so long, I've known you for years, I know you've never been ashamed of anything, or not of yourself anyway, you simply forget anything that upsets you. And I know you've never been able to stand money troubles or set-backs or people leaving you. Constantin, my dear, if I left you after Mexico in spite of our long love affair, it was because of your cowardice and weakness and cruelty. Do think for a moment, Constantin! How could you possibly, possibly ever hope I'd believe you? That story of your old school is just so silly!"

There was a note of distress in her voice for the first time since he had entered her room; it caught his attention and made him want to apologize. Of course, he could have said firstly, that the story was true, and secondly, that Goebbels himself would confirm it. But there would still be a wide gap between the bare facts and the real truth.

It was true that the melodramatic tale he had just told could appeal only to Prussian souls. Turning his head away, he muttered, between his teeth, "What do you want me to tell you, if you know all the answers?"

There was a silence. Wanda went on, wearily, "And what have you been doing here, in all this mess? Was it that they wouldn't let you go?"

"No, I've been filming," he said, low-voiced. "I've been from set to set, script to script, production to production. I've tried to help people here and there, and well, I've kept alive . . . and that's not such a small achievement here, you know. It's difficult when you're not an out-and-out Nazi."

He turned to her, put his face on her shoulder, and added in a voice that was at last sincere, "And I've been loving you and waiting for you, Wanda, I've been waiting for you. I'm sorry I told you that stupid story. Forgive me."

She said nothing, but thoughtfully stroked his hair. Only the French window was open to the garden and the stars; a breeze laden with the fragrance of the night wafted over them. Eyes wide open, Constantin was reproaching himself. It was high time someone came along, high time someone free-spirited, unencumbered by heroism or the warrior's cast of mind, took charge of him, someone whose motivating principle was neither fear nor hatred. How could he have thought she would believe him? In telling her his tale he himself had almost slipped into an absurd sentiment of remorse, shame and false masculinity, into the idiotic and deadly gallantry he had tremulously extolled, and he was ashamed of himself. Left to himself, would he have succumbed to the call of Nazi trumpets and bugles — supposing he had stayed in Berlin, lived with his father, supposing his mother, that high-spirited Russian, had not taken him away so fast, before he quite reached adolescence, to the fabulous liberty of America? And suddenly his mother's Russian blood, that Slav inheritance of which he had never thought much, appeared to Constantin like some huge and miraculous present: that Russian blood had counteracted the heavy, thick blood of the von Mecks,

Prussian landed gentry whose pride and discipline would easily have drawn them into the Nazi net. Had his dear, bird-brained mother, whom he had always supposed to have left a solid, Germanic husband for an amusing Californian lover, had she sensed all this? Yes, she must have done, since she had taken him with her despite the fierce opposition of his father and the von Meck family; the few duties and prohibitions he had had to observe during her lifetime now appeared to him in a much clearer light than he had imagined. It was not from boredom but hatred she had fled, not from dullness but from violence, and he should have known it; yet again, he had failed to understand. Obviously he never understood anything.

"Wanda," he groaned, "Wanda, you're right not to want me, I'm an idiot, I have no blood in my veins, or if I do it's diluted, watered-down blood. I've got watercolour blood."

She smiled at him. "I'll see if that's so tomorrow," she said, pushing him away with her finger-tips. "Tomorrow I'll see if you have any blood worth the name."

And he found himself, bewildered, in the corridor outside her door. He shook himself. After all, it had not been a useless visit; Wanda was going to surrender to him, she was going to come back to him, perhaps out of pity, perhaps out of fear, perhaps out of compassion; she had just told him so, and despite all her whims Wanda was not the woman to go back on her word, or at least not over this kind of thing.

Bitterly regretting Wanda and the big four-poster bed with its gossamer draperies assigned to the great Hollywood star by Boubou, Constantin walked off down the corridor, dragging his feet. He stopped at the open window looking on to the patio, and leaned out. The tiling around the swimming pool was white, and the deckchairs seemed to be mounting guard beside the clear water. Constantin told himself that only Boubou could manage to reconstruct a Hollywood set in an old Provençal farmhouse. The moon too seemed to be trying to perform as an extra; it was too round, too fat, too yellow, with a shadow on one side which made it look like a badly shaved face. Instinctively Constantin put his hand to his own cheek, was surprised to find it so smooth, and felt vexed to have spent half an hour titivating, shaving and wasting his precious toilet water, and now to find himself, at his age, hanging about corridors like an adolescent, like young Werther. He heaved a deep sigh, and wondered at the same time why he was acting such a part for his own benefit. Why do I heave sighs when there's no audience, he wondered, who do I feel melancholy when I am actually very happy? I shall have Wanda in my bed tomorrow, and anyway I'm sleepy tonight. But no, he was not sleepy, and he briefly hesitated, wondering whether to go and see Romano. A pity to waste all his preparations. But poor Romano must be lying on his bed exhausted, dead to the world after eight hours on horseback. It was Constantin's sensuality rather than his scruples that held him back. He wanted a woman tonight; he wanted a woman's body, the pleasure a woman gave. He went back to his own room, and before he could see anything he heard through his own French window — which looked out on the hills — the loud music of the cicadas; it was quite deafening, and bothered him until he saw Maud Mérival in the middle of his bed in her nightdress, her hair tousled, looking like a trembling little girl. To his own surprise, although he had not given her a moment's thought, Constantin was delighted to see her.

"Hullo, darling!" he said cheerfully. "What are you doing here?"

And instinctively, before crossing the room to his bed, he locked the door. He was definitely in luck, he told himself. He had one woman, the woman most desired in the free world, who would be his tomorrow, and another, the woman most desired in the Nazi world, who was going to be his now. He, the grandson of a small Prussian landowner. And the two women were sleeping within fifty metres of each other, which much to his shame excited him even more. Treading softly, he went up to the bed, sat down on the foot of it, looked at Maud with affection and then took her in his arms. He was surprised, whenever he did it, that he could make love to this little blonde of whom he thought so little, whom he desired so little. He was surprised, whenever he did it, by his enthusiasm; he did not stop to think that all the walking he was doing, the fresh air and country food might be invigorating him, for Constantin had always been apt to put his few mortifications down to physiological causes, and his moments of happiness down to psychological causes.

"My pet!" he said, affectionately kissing her cheek. "My little darling! I adore you. What are you doing here?"

He kissed her fair hair, her small and too delicate nose, her little throat, with a strong feeling of pity, affection, and a vague but rising desire.

"I've tried, but I can't live without you," moaned Maud into his shoulder, "I just can't! Will I ever be able to, do you think, Constantin?"

"Now, now!" he murmured. "Don't keep talking to me in questions! That's all over, it was in *The Violins*, darling. You're Clelia Conti now."

"So I am," she said seriously. "You know, your Fabrice really is ridiculous," she added, before going back to harp on her former theme. "Seriously," she said, "seriously, Constantin, I've tried to respect our pact, but I can't, I just can't!" she repeated.

It was true that if she had been in charge of their love affair it would rapidly have come to resemble a tornado. Mercifully, Wanda's arrival, and the passionate, feverish, desperate love with which Constantin, as of old, tried to surround her, put the brakes on it. On the day Wanda arrived, Maud put on a great demonstration of delicacy, dignity and generosity, which surprised Constantin as much as it delighted him.

"No," she had told him, all the more fervently in that he had not asked her any question. "No, Constantin. When you're free, if you do free yourself some day, I'll always be there for you — as your mistress, God willing, or as your friend. Always."

None the less, she had spent the night with him, a night he had expected to be painful and which turned out very pleasant. Delighted to see Wanda, Constantin had displayed a gaiety and lasciviousness which she had never seen him take to quite such lengths before. And if Maud had wept, her tears had been of laughter and — or so she claimed — sensual pleasure. After that, apart from a slight incident in a barn a few days ago, there had been nothing between them but chaste glances; tortured glances too on Maud's part . . . when she thought of it, of course.

And if she had thought of it harder this evening, that was because since the film crew working on this movie was almost the same as its counterpart on *The Violins of Destiny*, she had long ago gone the rounds of its members, and because Constantin had made her laugh at table like everyone else, so she had taken the natural path from laughter to pleasure.

"Do you think I'm very shameless?" she began, none the less.

But Constantin instantly silenced her.

Contrary to appearances, and in spite of the shutters, open or closed on the house's dark bedrooms, no one was asleep yet.

In the room where Boubou Bragance's first husband, the late owner of the house, used to sleep, Captain von Kirschen was pacing nervously up and down, fully clothed.

The suggestion made by Boubou Bragance as she showed him along the corridors to his room had been all too clear. Kirschen dared not get undressed, and he was seeking and failing to find arguments to help him avoid advances from a lady who, he guessed, would not take no for an answer. Here he was wrong. Lying in her bed, calm and solitary, Boubou was reverently eating some chocolates she had miraculously discovered that very afternoon in the bedside table once used by her husband — a man discerning enough to like chocolates and hide some in his room before the war.

A little way off, the two actors playing the parts of Fabrice and Mosca were both awake, each in his own bedroom. The former, young Lucien Marrat, was standing in front of the mirror feeling a pimple which looked like turning into a boil; it was red and fiery. Lucien was devouring himself with his own eyes, although he was relatively unnarcissistic for a young man of his reputation and profession. As for Count Mosca, otherwise Ludwig Lenz, he was reading and rereading the German newspaper he had brought back from Draguignan: it seemed bombs were falling on Hamburg night and day. Ludwig Lentz had a house in Hamburg, and his wife was in that house with their two children, who were too young for the army but not, unfortunately, too young to be bombed. Ludwig Lentz was pacing up and down as well. He was no longer the handsome Ludwig Lentz, no longer Count Mosca, he of the fine feelings, only a man of fifty-five on the brink of tears, whom his female admirers would not have recognized.

And finally, still further off, practically at the other end of the house, the ineffable Popesku was writing in his notebook, where he carefully kept a diary: "Today Romano Woltzer, the location finder, acted as stand-in for Lucien Marrat in the horse-riding scenes. Constantin von Meck doesn't seem to value their relationship much. Telephoned the Wehrmacht in Draguignan to let them know. Spoke to a very pleasant captain called Steinhauer. He promised me to pass on this detail, which may or may not be interesting, to General Bremen, whom I have not yet had the honour of meeting. We shall see. May God protects us and the war end soon!"

Romano's room was a little further off again. Its shutters too were open, shutters to windows looking out on the countryside, and its door was locked.

Anxious to lend substance to his report for the Draguignan Gestapo, who seemed to him more interested in the gossip columns of film magazines than Abwehr intelligence, Popesku had told them that the UFA offices in Paris had several photographs he himself had sent last seek; they were photographs of that same Romano Woltzer who was too good a horseman and too distant a cousin. He had taken them himself during shooting, surreptitiously, since Constantin strictly forbade the taking of any pictures; they showed Wanda facing the camera, standing beside Constantin, and behind them, very clearly but only in profile, on account of Popesku's poor talent as a photographer, stood the aforementioned Romano.

These photographs had an electrifying effect on General Bremen when he saw them, but also, and first, on former Lieutenant-Colonel Schultert, who had risen to the rank of full colonel in less than two months at the Russian front. Indeed, during the two months following his grotesque difference of opinion with Constantin von Meck in the Lutetia Hotel, Schultert had acquired much gold braid and many medals, thanks to his great determination, a totally neutral quality on the moral plane, but one which the official reports showed had brought him his military decorations and his rank. The term "determination" also had to cover certain excesses; it was whispered in other divisions, at all events, that his own determination had been so pronounced as to weaken his men's, although they were hardened SS members; it had been pronounced enough, too, for him to accept survival at the cost of his left arm and leg and severe burns to half of his face. Back in Paris, covered with military honours for this warlike determination and with public glory by Goering, the newly promoted Colonel Schultert had a career choice between a post in the Todt organization and shared command of the Paris Gestapo with General Bremen, and he had chosen the latter, since he judged his opposite number's character colourless enough not to bother him. Besides his arm, his leg and one profile

Schultert had lost the red notebook containing the list of his feminine conquests, which was now redundant. He had kept only the little black notebook listing his enemies, among which the name of Constantin von Meck had figured large since the incident of the bathtub. It was thus Schultert who, delving into innumerable Gestapo reports and innumerable denunciations made by French civilians, came upon the little note from Draguignan in which Popesku hinted at the presence of a possibly doubtful element among the director's film crew. The reasons given were tenuous, and at first Schultert feared that Bremen would think them insufficient to warrant an inquiry. The tale of Constantin's thrashing of Bremen in the Avenue Foch three months earlier slightly reassured him. Nor did he know anything about the incursion into Bremen's life of a genuine layabout and a fake Dufy, of that fair-haired and extremely young man shown in the background of the photograph. The surge of anger which suddenly reddened Bremen's increasingly pale and parchment-like cheeks was a pleasant surprise to him.

"This man von Meck certainly keeps bad company," sneered Bremen, brandishing the photograph, in which, bending a little closer to it, Schultert in his own turn recognized von Meck's young companion, the aggressor of the Lutetia Hotel.

"Why, I know the man too," he cried, flushing with retrospective mortification, for the young villain in question had held him immobile against a door for a good three minutes.

Bremen, who had been trying to conceal his own leanings from Schultert since the latter came on the scene, and thought he was succeeding, cast him a glance of curiosity mingled with surprise, hope, and that fierce scorn homosexuals ashamed of their tastes feel for their own kind when they think they have detected them.

"Really? You know this young man Romano?" inquired Bremen, smiling, but without too much complicity in his tone, for Schultert still frightened him, both by force of character and physically.

"Yes, I bumped into him in the corridors of the Lutetia," said Schultert drily. "Just as he was going into von Meck's suite."

"Von Meck's suite?" Bremen was as surprised as he was horrified. "Von Meck's suite? And you bumped into him, that was all?"

Schultert's startled and icy gaze made him cough as if he were giving up the ghost.

"That was all. Should I be sorry?"

Oh yes, Bremen thought suddenly, emerging for a moment from his alarm and confusion, oh yes, you should be sorry, you poor perverse, sadistic swine; you should be sorry, because no one ever made love like that boy.

"No, no, of course not, but it would have gained us some time," he stammered. "Von Meck has this unfortunate way of protecting his colleagues to a quite outrageous extent. In fact that was the cause of the little argument he and I had three months ago. What's more, that little guttersnipe robbed a friend of mine."

Argument indeed — you were beaten up and never said a word, Schultert said sardonically to himself. Your officers had to rescue you from him. In your place I'd have killed that bastard von Meck with my own hands. I shall kill him very soon, too.

"The fellow stole my revolver before he ran for it," he said, untruthfully.

Bremen was muttering something, echoing his thoughts. "We shall have to be careful. Von Meck is Goebbels' protégé, and just now Goebbels is the Minister who has our Führer's ear."

This reminder, like any obstacle in his path, had the effect of infuriating Schultert.

"I know," he said, "and it's very surprising. I've seen von Meck, as clear as I see you now, wearing a silk shirt. Ridiculous! Effeminate! Disgusting! Positively grotesque! Obscene, like all men of that kind!" he added savagely. This was the last straw for Bremen, whose capacity for hatred was at that moment equally divided between Schultert and Constantin.

However, the General made a superhuman effort. "I fear," he said, "I fear that debauchery is not necessarily incompatible with intelligence, and since Goebbels is a man of remarkable intelligence, as you know, it's possible that he is on terms with Constantin von Meck which neither you nor I, my dear fellow, would be able to appreciate or understand."

Got you there, he thought, seeing Schultert stiffen. Bremen was not displeased with himself. In point of fact, he was putting up his own defence. He would not admit to having been thrashed by a Constantin von Meck who was merely decadent and ridiculous. The hiding he had received was to be borne only if administered by a man of superior intelligence.

"Besides," he continued, to complete his victory, "besides, if Wanda Blessen's left America and Sweden to join him he can't be entirely decadent."

"She left America and Sweden for financial reasons," said Schulter roughly. "You must know what she's costing UFA."

"And you must know what she was costing the Americans too," said Bremen, becoming increasingly polite as he felt himself consolidating his position and saw Schultert turn pale with anger. "No, she's in love with her husband. That doesn't mean she may not have pro-Nazi sympathies known only to the Gestapo which have been urging her to leave America from the start. There are a great many more things you can't know, my dear Schultert," he added almost affectionately, so livid had the sound side of the other man's face become. "But as we have to go to Marseilles we may as well make a little detour to Draguignan by car — both of us, if you like; there may be something we ought to look into there."

Schultert glanced at him, and for the first time in their acquaintance they exchanged a smile of some sympathy. Bremen's aide was much struck by it, even if that smile —

on both their faces — was the smile of a jackal.

At four in the morning Constantin courteously escorted Maud to her door. She was in a state of blissful fulfilment, or at least she said so, and he himself did not try too hard to work out the distinction, Maud's sensuality being much inferior to her imagination. He was not smitten with her enough to want to tell the cries of love she uttered deliberately from those she perhaps should or could have uttered instinctively, and the latter sort might have seemed less aesthetic or less disturbing to him than those with which she actually accompanied their frolics.

What was more, he had to be up in two hours' time; he was getting either too much or too little sleep these days, and crossing the drawing room, where the furniture looked like so many toppled statues or idols in the half-light, he went out on the terrace. Day was hardly dawning; it was still night, the sky was grey, and only a milky white gap as yet separated the hills above Draguignan from the persistently leaden sky. All that was really left of the night was its smell, that secret, earthy smell that was already evaporating under the touch of a wind that swept away the owls and other nocturnal creatures. Already a bird somewhere over in the still trees, invisible, was uttering its cry of greeting of the day, a surprised and plaintive cry that made one tremble with fear and pleasure as certain promises do. Constantin standing there in his dressing gown, slowly and with relish breathed in the universal, never-changing smell of the soil, damp and chilly with dew at dawn; with a sudden sense of happiness he leaned down and put his mouth to the already warm stone of the terrace. "Thank you, stone; thank you, earth; thank you trees; thank you, sky and thank you, life!" he said, low-voiced. And thus, bending down, mingling with the shadows on the ground, he was not noticed by the man climbing over the little garden wall and coming up the path with furtive tread. He collided with

Constantin just as the latter was straightening up; they both sketched the same step backwards and the same gesture of putting up their fists before they recognized each other.

"What on earth are you doing here at this time of night?" exclaimed Constantin, before remembering that it was very early and there were still people asleep inside the house.

Romano did not reply; he looked exhausted and pale, and even in the half-light he was panting like a hunted dog. Constantin put a hand on his shoulder despite himself. Where had the boy been? There was no fortune to be sought or mischief to be made in this remote country area, particularly not on foot!

"I've been for a walk," said Romano, in an undertone. "I thought I'd go out. I couldn't get to sleep."

"So that's how you've got your legs grazed, blood on your hands and hair in your eyes?" inquired Constantin with a smile. "Don't tell me you've found a local shepherdess — I've seen them all and they're hideous. Toothless, too."

"No," said Romano, relaxing slightly, "no. Anyway, if I wanted that kind of thing, there's enough to satisfy a man here, isn't there?"

"Who are you thinking of?" asked Constantin, still smiling, but it was a forced smile now, for a wave of affection, tenderness and alarm had swept over him, enveloping the trees, the stone, the terrace and the sky as well as this boy standing in front of him, lean and cunning, this boy who looked like the adolescent he had no doubt been before the storm came, before hell.

"Romano," he said, "listen, will you, Romano? Tell me . . ." And instinctively he put out his hand and placed it on the boy's shoulder, in so unequivocal a gesture that it made him feel awkward himself, and he went no further.

Much to his surprise, Romano did not pull away; he even relaxed against him. Constantin, again involuntarily, put his arm around Romano's shoulders, and with his other hand, the stupid, useless hand hanging by his left side, he touched the boy's rough hair and his straight, slim neck. They stayed like that for a little while, leaning against each other, stubbled cheek against stubbled cheek, eyes closed, utterly absorbed in their absence of desire, their great weariness, their immense relief, and above all by a shared and very distinct impression that their lives were beginning and ending there, at that moment. Or so Constantin thought, at least, and no doubt Romano thought so too, for he uttered a hoarse little cry, like a dog's yelp, before letting himself slump entirely against his friend's body and putting both arms around his chest.

"Constantin," he said. "Yes, I'm listening, Constantin."

Day was dawning now, and they looked at each other, making one another's shape out. They did not even feel ridiculous thus intertwined in the fragrance of dawn: one coming from a woman's bed, the other from the bed of night itself, and both knowing themselves incapable of putting a question. They dared not even separate, for fear of having to look at each other's faces.

"Romano," said Constantin, "do be careful, I beg you! Be careful — you know I'd hate it if ... I couldn't bear it if you ..."

"Don't worry," said Romano, and he moved his head slightly, so that his mouth was resting on Constantin's neck; Constantin lowered his eyelids. "Don't worry," he said, against that familiar yet unfamiliar skin, "don't worry, I wouldn't want to live without you."

They slowly detached themselves, turned their backs on each other and walked away, without looking at one another, both of them calm and surprised and strangely happy. Constantin von Meck had surely never felt himself so close to love. Nor, of course, had Romano, but at his age that was more natural.

III

At two in the afternoon that day, Constantin von Meck, having left his actors and camera crew behind, was striding down a sunken lane alone. He put his head back, and the trees and then the sky flew to meet him at every step he took. And that vast and beautiful sky, menacing, indifferent to his existence, seemed to him a gift as magnificent and undeserved as his present happiness; he loved and was loved, and he wondered, as his boots flung up the soil, why he felt so happy in thinking of love while he was alone, and why he was so distraught when actually with the beloved. He wondered why he had needed to see Wanda look at Romano, by way of endorsement, before he could admit to loving Romano, and why he had needed to see Romano look at Wanda, also by way of endorsement, before he could admit to respecting Wanda as well as loving her; why did he feel his gestures of love were so natural and his words of love so conventional, why had Proust's definition of love become his own: that awkwardness, that hastiness, that wish for something more that deprives one of the sensation of loving when one is actually with the person one loves? For he would have died for Wanda, and now for Romano, but he knew himself incapable of telling them so. If he tried, he would hear himself stumbling through his declarations of love like a bad script, no doubt because his love seemed to him not much to offer, no doubt because he did not love himself enough, though after all, why not? After all, he had done nothing wrong! But there had always been someone behind him, someone perched on his shoulder sneering at him, judging him, an ironic, condescending, sometimes savage character, who yawned when he thought deeply and burst out laughing when he was moved, his master and his double leaning towards his ear like an eagle or a crow, never letting go, unable to allow Constantin to forget it, and above all, always there; it was like a cruel bird, even if it was what might be called the intelligence, and was in fact that aspect of the intelligence with which Constantin von Meck was most familiar. Thanks to it, he now knew he would never do anything much, he would never make a film he himself could admire wholly or for long, and the proof was that he had never been carried away himself except in his moments of excess and dissipation, in things which in fact went totally beyond the bounds of intelligence.

Luckily for him, there was Stendhal and *La Chartreuse de Parme*, and when Constantin admired someone he could heighten his personal and professional talents. He looked at his watch; he had been walking for only ten minutes. The technicians had not yet had time to put up the rail for the dolly, while on the other hand the actors *had* had time to become fidgety, like flies in a glass jar; they were going to ask him how to interpret Stendhal's sentiments, when he himself was unable to feel any personal sentiments properly. They were going to shoot the scene in which La Sanseverina and Fabrice's mother say goodbye to him before Waterloo. He would put Romano on horseback and film him from behind, facing the two women; then, later, he would shoot close-ups of Lucien Marrat's face. The camera would have to approach the horse's ears, as if showing Fabrice's view, pass between them and come in on the two women who loved him more than anything and who were watching him go, perhaps to his death, with tears in their eyes. Then the carefree Fabrice must see the gaze of the two women as an entity, and understand the cruelty of their parting; he must understand the real bereavement his own death would be to them. Even on foot, Lucien Marrat would convey all this very well, better than Romano, whose face had remained expressionless this morning on the terrace when they had met and stupidly, imprudently, rather ridiculously but irresistibly embraced. He smiled at the memory of himself in pyjamas, like a solid citizen just tumbling out of bed, and Romano like a guttersnipe just tumbling in from the night. Life was certainly very strange, but none the less he had gleaned a genuine certainty from that moment; he now knew that Romano would never stay in anyone else's arms, he was Constantin's son, his brother, his lover, and above all, above all, Romano himself now knew it. It was strange to think of the number of composite parts they had managed to play since they met: the benefactor and the protégé, the elder and the younger, the blind man and the one who saw clearly, the irresolute and the decided, the one who compromised and the rebel. This morning, however, they had played a real part which he could not yet define.

And there were all the parts he had played with Wanda, too: the wise director and the flighty star, the peaceable husband and the unfaithful wife, the erring lover and the star sitting at home! Could one love two people at the same time without loving oneself a little? Constantin stopped, leaned against a tree and examined the lines on the palm of his hand; he thought the lifeline looked very short, and started to laugh. Shrugging his shoulders, he set off back to the place where they were shooting, whistling. He had never had anything much in the way of ideas about himself: a few memories, a few plans, a few impressions, but that was all; his imagination really functioned only in relation to his work. Now, however, he was happy to redefine himself in relation to two human beings; for three years he had regarded himself only in relation to Germany, to a threat, to obligations, not in relation to a human face, a human body or a human mind, and he had missed that more than he thought.

He reached the far end of the clearing, went to Wanda's caravan, knocked and went straight in. Even in the doorway, he caught the fragrance of that sandalwood perfume which so vividly reminded him of Hollywood and peacetime, the sun and the sea; they would all three live there, and gradually he would become happy and calm again; he would have no more nightmares, he would not see human cannonballs hurtling past with bleeding heads and striped bodies any more, he would stop thinking of Schwob and Weil. As he turned, his eyes fell on the telegram lying open on the table. "Father very ill. Stop. End probably near. Stop. Love, Mother." Constantin stood there quite still, his eyes looking for Wanda as if she were hiding, as if her sorrow had hidden her from him. She must be prostrate with grief. Constantin had once spent a fortnight fishing with his father-in-law in the Baltic, and even if he had never been so bored in his life, even if Wanda still burst out laughing when she remembered the expression on his face as they sat at table with their Swedish friends, he remembered how fond of her father she was.

Coming out again, he was much surprised to hear Wanda's laugh: that deep, throaty laugh which excited schoolboys and ancients, not forgetting the adults in between, a laugh which never trailed away and grew less, but stopped short. He took several steps in its direction, and found her with Maud, Ludwig Lentz and Lucien Marrat, sitting there laughing in the carefully restored tilbury over which the inevitable Popesku was mounting guard. All five cast him cheerful and well-disposed glances.

"Ah, there you are," said Wanda. "Have you been roaming the woods? In search of inspiration or shepherdesses?"

"Not shepherdesses!" said Maud, in the manner of the mistress addressing the wife. "He never even looked at them."

She had employed a frank and knowing tone which won her a kindly but rather condescending smile from Wanda Blessen, every inch the star at that moment.

"How lucky," said Wanda. "It would have been very un-gallant of him, with such a pretty woman here!"

Maud looked at her open-mouthed, wriggled, and uttered a small, shrill laugh, putting her head back as if Wanda's remark had been most amusing.

"Oh, come on, Wanda, you must be joking!" she said. "As if Constantin von Meck could be interested in a beginner like me! I assure you, he thinks I'm just a silly goose!"

"Very likely," agreed Wanda, with a small smile of apology for her husband's stern clarity of vision. "He always did like feathers, particularly pretty ones . . . did you want to speak to me, Constantin?"

"Yes, I did. Indeed, I did," said he, twirling his moustache. "Yes, I certainly do want to speak to you! Come with me."

He turned and strode off towards the caravan. Tottering in her long skirts, but still graceful, Wanda followed him, looking much cheered by her own treachery.

"Was that really necessary?" inquired Constantin, frowning. "Poor Maud!"

"Poor Maud is a charming girl," said Wanda, "but I don't like being spoken to in that pitying tone. Oh, dear me!"

She began to laugh, causing Constantin to frown yet again.

"You're laughing?" he said. "I don't see how you can laugh. I went into your caravan; I couldn't help seeing that telegram. Your father, your poor father . . . it sounds as if he doesn't have long?"

Wanda looked at him with some bewilderment, and then lightly slapped her forehead. "My God!" she said. "The telegram, you're right! No, no, my dear, don't worry, it's . . . it's a fake telegram. It's a code."

"A code?" said Constantin. "What do you mean, a code?"

"Well," said Wanda — unconsciously and in her own turn assuming the voice in which she told lies, a voice Constantin recognized at once, both reasonable and over-sweet — "well, you see, my father was making a transaction on the Stock Exchange, and so was I, and seeing telegrams can't be sent from one country to another, unless they're very important, we agreed that a message about being gravely ill meant the transaction had gone through, so there you are! I'm rich!" she added, with a satisfied intonation for which the merest novice would have blushed on stage.

"Since when have you been playing the Stock Exchange?" inquired Constantin, sternly and sarcastically. "Besides, in case you'd forgotten, this is wartime, and there aren't any transactions on the Stock Exchange just now," he added haughtily.

"Oh, there are in Sweden!" said the brazen Wanda. "There are just a few, in Sweden. Well, anyway, in short, I've made money. So that's it! You're not going to be angry with me, are you?" she asked in insincere tones. And shaking off the hand the irritated Constantin had placed on her arm, she left him standing there.

Constantin's next words halted her half way to the tilbury.

"You're a lying woman," he shouted at her back.

She turned, pink in the face. "So you don't like lying women?" she shouted back.

"No!" he yelled.

"Not even at night?"

Not two seconds later, Constantin's reply reached her loud and clear. "Yes, I do!" he said. "In the day too, come to that!"

Then he stood there for a moment quite still, feeling slightly peevish, vaguely irritated, all the same; what with Romano's silences, Boubou Bragance's intriguing, Maud's fantasies, Popesku's mimicry and now Wanda's lies, he himself must be the most sincere and honest person around, something that he had to admit could seldom be said of him. Wanda's laughter, that throaty laughter which stopped short instead of trailing away, mocked him. She would be his that very evening; he was going to get her back. He felt both relieved and vaguely disappointed; he would not have to put himself out to charm her any more. But an hour later, when he shot the farewell scene and La Sanseverina watched the departure of her handsome nephew, young Fabrice, with whom she was already deeply in love without knowing it, Constantin's disappointment evaporated. Wanda Blessen acted it wonderfully well; she was so right in that scene, so gay and so touching that the camera crew were as fascinated as Constantin, and applauded her. Wanda — La Sanseverina — involuntarily put out a hand to her nephew, then withdrew it to remove an invisible speck of dust from her cloak; she opened her umbrella and turned her head to the hills to hide her tears, she tried to laugh and managed so poorly that she was coughing desperately into her handkershief. And Constantin, as he shot the scene and watched her, smiled with pride; he was mad about her. The idea of holding her in his arms that evening, the mere idea that he used to hold her in his arms before, that she had been his for so long, struck him as improbable; he admired her as a man admires a woman and a director admires an actress, all the more so because in the close-up, the last close-up of her shot at the end of the day, in which she watched young Fabrice, now a grown man, riding away, he or rather the camera saw a new, unfamiliar little line at the corner of her mouth. It was the mark left by their separation, he thought tenderly, and he promised himself to kiss it in secret later that night. Curiously, it was behind that motionless close-up, very fine but lacking in mystery, that Constantin saw certain images resurface, images that were much more hazily focused but of a very precise nature, certain memories of Wanda's body and Wanda's movements on certain evenings, and he felt the strongest desire for them he had known since her arrival.

After a while the German fighters streaking across the sky amidst an infernal din forced them to stop work for the day. Wanda, in high good humour, invited everyone to have an aperitif in the little square of Salerne, a village they passed as they went back to Boubou Bragance's house.

"Starting to squander your profits already?" Constantin whispered to her sarcastically, but she pretended not to hear him.

IV

The Café de la Poste, where they all went to take their ease at seven in the evening, faced a small square surrounded by handsome ochre-coloured houses and containing four plane trees, whose thick, pale bark was scarred with the initials and hearts of known or supposed lovers. Among these four trees with their trunks that were almost white, the white of a hazel nut, a pretty little fountain disgorged a thin trickle of water. A fallen plane leaf, broad, greenish, and flattened like a hand rocked in the basin of the fountain. Seated beside one of the plane trees, eyes narrowed behind her dark glasses, Wanda was trying to decipher the intertwined hearts and letters crudely, cruelly hacked into its trunk with a knife by supposedly tender-hearted young people. However, the tree had taken vengeance; pale blood had seeped from its wounds, filling in the spaces between the letters. Swollen by sap, they had closed up again, so that an "e" became an "1", and a "c" became an "o". Which was only to be expected, said Wanda, since the tree was still green and white, as before, while the lovers had surely either parted or were unhappily married by now. Wanda's cynicism or dis-illusionment seemed dreadful to Maud, who was now sipping a *citron pressé*, which was amazingly good even though sweetened with saccharine.

A bell rang in the distance, a country bell, and something in the warm air, the rosy and golden rays of the sun, the silken, timeless softness of the evening, something or other — perhaps an angel — immobilized and fixed that scene, that square, that light permanently, like an immutable picture, in the minds of the people who happened to be sharing a table. Constantin, Wanda and Romano were ensconced at this table, and the atmosphere did not seem very promising, at least to Maud. Constantin was gazing like a beggar or a man obsessed at his wife's brown hand as it rested on the scarred wood; Romano was preserving his usual silence; only Maud did not go along with all this indolence. That afternoon, in fact, she had made the rounds — figuratively speaking, for once — of all the men working on the film. After last night Constantin, whose lack of interest she could sense quite well, was not going to promote her happiness, let alone her career. This was all the more distressing in that, as she would hardly admit even to herself, she really did like him, she was ready to love Constantin, and with feminine intuition unfortunately unaccompanied by any insight she had decided to set her sights on Romano. Such a strategy — in the absence of a whole army — was, she felt, the only way of touching Constantin von Meck. But Romano, sad to say, was not looking at her; he too was looking at Wanda Blessen, that woman whose arrival had wrecked Maud's love life — her past love life because of Constantin and her future love life because of Romano, who was quite clearly looking at Wanda with an admiration and affection that hid something else. There was obvious complicity between those two. Perhaps poor Constantin was already being deceived himself.

Wanda, totally unaware of the tortuous stratagems attributed to her by Maud's jealous eyes, turned her own affectionately, even lovingly on Romano; she was trying to draw conclusions from the interlaced initials.

"Let's see," she was saying, "I can see a C there — C for Constantin. What else is there inside that heart? Oh, wait, that's an R! Romano, Constantin — well, well, did you two come to this café to vow eternal love while our backs were turned?"

She laughed, putting her head back, but her laughter was not echoed. The two men maintained their slightly weary, slightly irritated expressions, and she turned to Maud, rather as if she were the last resort.

"Dear me, Maud, what's to be left for you and me?"

"That's not a C," said Maud, leaning forward, still anxious to display her loyalty. "That's not a C! And that's not an R either! Those initials are old ones, you know, it's all to do with some old love affair!"

There was something like a note of aggression in her voice which made Constantin and Romano look up, intrigued. Wanda, on the other hand, gave her that brilliant smile she kept for disagreeable women.

"But how can you tell that, my child? You don't mind my calling you that, do you, Maud? I could be your mother — well, in Africa, anyway!"

Caught unprepared, Maud blushed, stammered, and muttered, "No, no, of course not. I only said it was some old love affair because — well, the marks aren't bleeding any more."

"Goodness, what a very poetic thing to say!" cried Wanda. "Did you hear that, Constantin? Botany and human nature have this much in common: love's over when you stop bleeding."

Attracted in spite of herself, Maud had risen and was examining the tree marked with the supposed R for Romano and C for Constantin, which she knew for certain, thank God, could not really be their own initials.

"The R . . ." she began. But Wanda's laugh interrupted her.

"I didn't really believe in my idyll," said she. "Can you imagine these two fine upstanding fellows carving a heart on this tree? Can you imagine Constantin swearing eternal love to anyone at all? No, really!"

Despite herself, Maud began to laugh. "Well, no. But they thought you thought so!" she said, patting Wanda on the shoulder. Wanda might be a vamp, but she was an extraordinarily good actress, even in real life, and she had some amusing ideas too, Maud recognized, once again showing that she had a sense of fair play.

Meanwhile, Popesku had gone to see the local postmistress at home, and by lavishing many entreaties and a number of tips on her had succeeded in getting her to go back to the post office and open the back door. He had telephoned the Gestapo in Draguignan and asked to speak to the man he had talked to the previous day; feeling rather worried at the idea of having bothered the Third Reich over some unknown's aptitude for horsemanship, Popesku had been surprised and delighted by the interest he had aroused. He had been told to watch very closely, in the greatest of detail, and they had even emphasized the possibly dangerous importance of Constantin von Meck himself. This had disconcerted and indeed worried Popesku, for after all, leaving the Gestapo aside, his present masters were UFA and Constantin von Meck. Did he have less of a duty towards them than towards the SS? Well, no! But the SS men had more claim on him. He was given very precise instructions; he was to send word of any disturbance or change in the routine of the company working on the film, while waiting for staff officers from Paris to come and check on the spot. (Check what, Popesku wondered? The way Romano Woltzer mounted a horse or his family relationship with von Meck?) In any case, proud of all this excitement and the fervour he was setting in motion, Popesku left the postmistress with a tip larger than she had expected, which increased her goodwill. Could Popesku tell her, she inquired, how Mme Blessen the great star took it when she got the telegram? Even a film star still had a father and a mother.

"What?" asked Popesku. "What telegram?"

"The second telegram!"

And the postmistress, proud of knowing something that this man from the world of films did not know, told him she had received a telegram that very afternoon, a telegram she had given the telegraph boy to deliver, telling Wanda her father had died and would be buried in a few days' time.

"Good God!" said Popesku. "Good God!"

He was both delighted to be at the centre of a family drama, and much upset to think that Wanda might leave and disrupt shooting.

"Please tell poor Mme Blessen how sorry I am," said the postmistress. "What a sad thing! And she hasn't even been back to the house yet, poor dear! Her father died this morning, and she doesn't even know it — and as for going back to Sweden, with the war and all . . ."

"She's in the Café de la Poste," said Popesku, confusedly. "I'll tell her."

"Break it gently, won't you?" said the postmistress, rather cheered by this conversation, since she had not understood one treacherous word of the exchanges between Popesku and the Germans in Draguignan.

But once in the square, and under the spell of that dreamy peacetime atmosphere that reigned there, impressed by Wanda's happy and trusting expression, Popesku, a sensitive man, did not feel brave enough to carry out his mission. He liked Wanda very much; he had had such feelings, such fears on her account! He had been afraid that this great star would wreck his work and make life difficult for him, whereas Wanda was exquisite, punctual, charming to everyone and kind, even over details; she was a happy woman who was making Constantin von Meck happy, since it was obvious that they were made for one another. And Popesku sincerely hoped that the accusations against

Constantin were not of anything worse than imprudence. He sat down discreetly at a small table and ordered his favourite pre-dinner drink, an aperitif wine called "Home from the Fields" with a label showing a farmer's wife holding a baby in one hand and a bottle in the other, looking down the road at a farmer with his back bent who could be assumed to have a right to this comforting wine with its sugary aftertaste, so fatal to the liver. Greeted by Constantin and invited to join his table, Popesku took aboard enough "Home from the Fields" to lose his reserve and start telling funny but not very witty stories, which made first Maud and then Wanda and Constantin laugh. Romano did not laugh at all, and was probably thinking of something else; he roused himself only when a village boy, a lad on a bike, rode across the square ringing his bell and signed to Romano to join him. Romano rose, excusing himself; he was going to play a game of *pétanque* with his friends from the village, boys of his own age, and to be that age, as Popesku philosophically reflected, was like living in another country.

Romano went, and with him the warmth of the evening, and hunger, that persistent guest who had not left them for three years, made the rest of the party rise too. There was no one outside the café now but Constantin and Wanda. They were going to drive back together in Constantin's old Talbot, a car which overtook all others thanks to the high-grade petrol the Wehrmacht allowed him, a privilege Constantin felt unable to renounce. Privileged as he was, however, his eyes and voice were suddenly sad.

"Look," he said, "look, Wanda, look at the square and those trees and the fountain, the shadows growing taller, the peace of the evening — look, because we shall never see it again, or at least, I shall never see it again, it's something that won't come back, all that happiness and peace, it's an anachronism now."

Wanda reached out her hand and laid it in Constantin's. His

fingers and palm were larger than hers in every direction. That big, masculine hand, both too large and too young, gave her a curious sensation of pain.

"Let's go back, shall we? Come on," she said gently.

V

Everyone heard the explosion at one in the morning: Wanda and Constantin, talking quietly in the dark, heard it, and so did Popesku, who made up for his daytime bleatings by roaring and snoring like a tiger at night.

The first explosion was followed by three more, at fifty-second intervals, which gave the guests time to run to their windows and see the livid sky turn crimson with separate fires. Doors were opened, and the corridors filled with a small crowd, in which Boubou Bragance's guests could be told from her domestic staff only by their untidy hair. Remarks uttered by people who looked haggard but were very sure of themselves flew about. "It's the police!" "No, it comes from Draguignan, the wind's carrying the noise here." "It's the Resistance!" "It's the Gestapo!" "It won't last long." "It'll go on all night". And so on, and so forth. In the middle of the crowd, above which he towered by a head, Constantin von Meck, wearing a red dressing gown of Wanda's which came only to his knees, presented a picture of conjugal affection, though only Boubou had the courage to point it out to him. The other sleepers noticed nothing; all throats were constricted with alarm. For days the war had been far off, at least for the Parisians; it featured only in the newspapers, or in the person of a visiting German officer, like Captain von Kirschen of the day before yesterday; only a few of them had tried listening to the crackling radio set in the big drawing room, and as for the others, apart from Ludwig Lentz, the war might not have been going on. All anyone knew was that it was not really far off, that the Maquis were on the prowl, and now and then some hot-headed young man got himself executed. Life here was different, lived on common ground, on terms of the amazing indifference of a team of film-makers to everything that was not their film, of the actors' obsession with entering into their parts, of the director's schizophrenia at the moment of shooting, everything, in short, that could cut these people off from the cruel and dangerous reality around them. Boubou Bragance's house, the mild weather, Constantin's laughter had been like so many defensive walls preserving them, walls which that explosion had just knocked down.

Confusion reigned in the corridors of the house now, and Boubou, who was prouder of her efficiency than her parsimony, sent for a bottle of very strong plum brandy which either stunned or cheered her guests and her staff. They went back to their rooms with a variety of feelings, but they kept those feelings to themselves. All of them except for Romano, who had not been seen, who seemed to be sleeping so soundly that the noise did not disturb him. Once all was dark again, Constantin went on tiptoe to his bedroom door and knocked. There was no reply, which did not surprise him. He knew Romano was out there somewhere; he had known all along. He stole back to lie down beside Wanda, as if beside someone who would protect him, and only by leaning over her mouth and smothering it with kisses could he regain his calm. He had found his real life again in her arms, his real happiness in life and love; it seemed as if nothing had really happened to him since they parted, nothing but the slow discovery of a nightmare in which he would be entangled whatever happened, nothing else; there had been nothing new in his life between Wanda past and Wanda present. It was he who had endured these last few years of lies, threats and remorse. It was he who could no longer manage to shake them off, he who had always wanted to avoid this bloody and confused chaos, and now he felt imprisoned on the horrible film set where he found himself. Wanda still existed, so did America, so did his profession, but there was something fatal and final, something of death in their tenderest, happiest kisses. Constantin had never been able to admit that there was any rift between his sentiments and his sensations, and so, in order to recover that harmony between them, he slowly, passionately, sorrowfully kissed his wife's mouth as one drinks water when thirsty. Here at least his nerves, his heart and his body all came together as one.

"I saw any number of pairs of pyjamas," said Wanda a little later, "but not Romano's. Did you?"

"Yes, I think so," he muttered. "Yes, I think I saw him."

They had closed the shutters to make love, opened them again at the moment of the explosion, and then left them as they were. Wanda had put out the light, and the sounds of night were gradually returning after all the noise. The bird he had heard the day before would soon be singing, in an hour or so's time, flinging its strange cry into this new dawn, thought Constantin. And perhaps I shall go out on the terrace and see that young man come in again, the guttersnipe, the gypsy, my orphan.

"No," he said at last, sighing. "No. As a matter of fact, I didn't see him."

"That's a pity," said Wanda in a sharp tone which aroused Constantin all of a sudden. "It might perhaps mean that your friend Romano is one of those . . . those French Forces of the Interior bastards they're talking about everywhere, mightn't it?"

The drowsiness which had been coming over Constantin was gone. He stiffened.

"Why bastards?"

"I only said that out of politeness, my dear," she said. "After all, they're your countrymen who are killing the Resistance workers, aren't they?"

"My countrymen are killing their own people too," he said roughly.

Wanda's laughter took him unawares. "Well, since you're so tolerant, Constantin, I think you'd better make plans to take that young man back to Los Angeles with us. Because they'll pretty soon kill him here, gypsy or not, Jewish or not, Resistance worker or not. Believe you me, that boy is as good as dead."

"Take him to Los Angeles?" Constantin exclaimed in surprise. "You must be joking! I'd be . . . I'd be lynched in Los Angeles! Constantin von Meck, the complete Nazi, who's been working for UFA since 1937 . . ."

In her turn, Wanda sat up and leaned her back against the wall. Her voice was serious. "No, you're wrong there, Constantin. You've forgotten that since you left Hollywood Karl Werner has arrived there, and Tania and Erica have arrived, and the Schirers and Buntag have arrived, and the Paryses, and the Ernsts and the Pauls, they've all arrived in Hollywood, all those people you helped to leave, and hid, and gave papers to, those people you saved. They remember that very, very well, you see; you're spoken of as a hero in Hollywood, my dear! As for your films for UFA, the producers think they're the best comic satire on Viennese sentimentality made since Lubitsch, as far as I can gather. They're only shown privately, so as not to do you any harm, but I can assure you you'll have offers from everyone, not to mention a triumphant welcome from your friends and the people you saved. I promise you I'm not joking, Constantin," she said.

She too had been looking at the sky and the shooting stars as she spoke. As he did not reply, she turned to Constantin and saw his black, shadowy shape lying motionless on the bed, as if turned to stone.

"Constantin," she said, and nudged him with her elbow, but still he did not move. Suddenly worried, she shook him furiously. "Constantin, I'm talking to you! Say something!"

Then he turned towards her. He looked at her with that dull, lacklustre gaze she had seen in the eyes of certain animals, and in his own too when there was something he did not understand.

"Are you saying that now, now after what I've done, I can go back to Hollywood with the honours of war?"

He spoke in a clear and straightforward voice, the voice of a young man; it surprised Wanda, but it did not make her want to laugh in the least. Indeed, it frightened her a little.

"Yes," she said, "that's what I'm saying. I may not have got every detail right, but that's how it is. You won't receive congratulations for going back to Nazi Germany, but you certainly will for having got so many people out at risk to yourself."

"At risk to myself," repeated Constantin. "Now you *are* joking. Take the Ernsts, for instance; they were broke, I helped them out. I've always come by money easily, as you know . . . And as for the others, it was just chance I hid them at my place; I knew the Nazis wouldn't think very much of that, but there was always my good friend Goebbels to get me out of a hole."

"Listen," said Wanda, who was becoming impatient, "listen, will you? Whether you did it on purpose or not, there are a dozen people in Hollywood who claim to owe your their lives. That's something. What's more, as far as I'm aware you never positively wanted to assassinate a Jew, did you? Do you mean anyone harm?"

Constantin shrugged his shoulders. His face was now creased by a thousand little laughter lines, and wore a sardonic expression. He turned to Wanda and took her by the shoulders.

"Do you realize what my life is like, Wanda? Whatever I do, it turns out well for me, things go my way. All the same . . . I join up in the German army, I spend five years with the Nazis . . . I ought to be ostracized everywhere. People ought to be spitting on me. But no! I'm about to return to Hollywood in triumph, I'll be welcomed as a saviour of the Jews and the oppressed, even a spy, a double agent!"

She watched him talk, saying nothing, looking down, and for a moment he put his cheek against her hair with a kind of compassion, as if he pitied her for loving and being loved by a man like himself.

"And that being said," he added, with ironic affection, "that being said, my darling isn't ashamed of me. I resisted at heart, you know, I did resist! I spoke English on the set in front of the Germans, I made fun of the Nazi salute in front of Goebbels. I was insolence itself, I assure you, to all those generals and those swastikas. Why, I even got a German officer killed in the middle of the war . . .!"

1940 Constantin's French Campaign

The peasants, when they ran away, had left behind them a double rampart of standing corn, an undulating yellow sea into which Constantin's side-car ploughed. His copper-coloured head barely came above it. Wedged in his unsteady, grey-green vehicle at the head of a convoy of lorries, cannon and various items of warlike machinery, Constantin saw himself, to his own astonishment, invading French soil. The armoured vehicles were well ahead of them, and Constantin, who had at first been furious not to be part of the assault wave, had then imagined himself cramped and doubled up inside one of those tanks, bathing in their smell of oil and the deafening racket they made, and in addition training guns on the French people he loved. He had therefore gradually calmed down. After all, this was an excursion he was on, a splendid excursion which didn't entail the spilling of even a drop of blood. When he thought about it, he couldn't really see himself shouldering a gun, aiming it at an unknown man and shooting him.

All the same, he was supposed to be making war. Promoted to captain overnight by means of the scandalously direct intervention of Goebbels, Constantin von Meck now found himself going through the north of France as an invader, having gone all over the south of the country a thousand times as a tourist in the old days.

It had all happened so fast! As if Hitler had just been waiting for him to finish the holiday he took after shooting *Medea* to declare war on France and invade the country all at once, in a vast movement, a flow of aggression which left the French obviously crippled and probably defeated. Constantin, called up at once, had had a fortnight's intensive training, was then given an aide who was also his chauffeur, and equipped with an enormous motorbike and side-car, in which he installed himself, surprised and pleased with this new venture. And gradually his military discipline had relaxed. He had rested his flat cap on his knee, lit a Lucky Strike, perched his own sunglasses on his large nose and adopted the nonchalant attitude of a tourist, which obviously horrified his companion. The German motorbikes riding up and down the length of the convoy like fierce, yapping sheepdogs began, in view of his curious attitude, by making straight for him, but then, taking into consideration his windscreen, which was covered with rosettes whose purport no one understood, least of all himself, they saluted him respectfully before turning away, much to the annoyance of his motorcyclist, who was now muttering uninteresting recriminations between his teeth. Constantin himself had been feeling increasingly bored for the last three days; he was surrounded by soldiers who stood to attention when they spoke to him, despite his amiable manner, their eyes fixed on a point behind his shoulder and their heels together, and by officers who talked to him of nothing but tactics, military equipment and comparative military strength. In short, subjects of which he knew nothing and in which he was not interested. What was he doing here, if he wasn't ultimately going to have to fight? Once again, as in his film work, he was surrounded by people who took themselves very seriously: all these tanned, athletic young men in their grey-green uniforms reminded him of over-zealous assistants on the set. The future masters of France and the world were not even dreaming of the Place de Pigalle, the French can-can or Montparnasse. And they translated the fine-sounding verb "conquer" into "invade" or "possess"; in this, they were of a generation not his own.

It seemed to Constantin that they had been crossing this great plain for ever; all the villages through which they passed were deserted, shutters closed, uninhabited except for a few stray dogs in distress, for whom he felt very sorry. There were a few cows too, mooing because they needed to be milked, and already the pale, misty sun of spring was drawing out the shadows of the trees, laying them over the ditches, making them into an army of felled trees, trees on the ground, dead trees, dead as the men of the French army must surely be . . . No, this was not a good war. It was not a war at all. It was a visit, a visit of condolence! Constantin crossly smoked cigarette after cigarette, throwing the ends over his shoulder without a thought for those who were following behind him. They would soon arrive at Bourgneboul, a village marked with a cross on the staff officer's map, where they were to fill up with petrol, check the vehicles over, and stretch their legs. Constantin hoped there would be birds at Bourgneboul; for the last forty-eight hours he had not heard a swallow cry, not heard a bird of any kind so much as cheep. It was true that the noise they were making and their warlike appearance sent all wild creatures into refuge underground or in the air, and the threat they represented had brought about a change in Constantin's bearing: he walked with his head down and his arms hanging, looking nothing like the symbol of the perfect warrior he had so idiotically dreamed of being.

As soon as this expedition was over, he was going to go back to Berlin. He would go post-haste to Tempelhof and catch a plane back to Hollywood. He was going to bring his war to an end as soon as possible, without once firing a gun or coming under fire himself; after this masquerade, this lugubrious joke, he would be more than happy to breathe the smell of newly sawn wood in the studios again, and the sophisticated perfumes worn by the actresses, all the delights of Hollywood. Even if Goebbels had been correct, Constantin could not have felt guilty for very long towards this powerful Germany, teeming with men and armaments, a country about to invade the beautiful plains of Europe, perhaps even trample them underfoot. No, it had not been a very good idea he had on that September evening in Los Angeles in 1937, when he caught his plane for Berlin . . .

Then something or other — something which was not a bird — whistled in his ears, and he was surprised to see his placid and surly companion slam the brakes on their motorbike combination, leap off it and hurl himself into the ditch. These imitation birds were making a peculiar sound that was shrill and dull at the same time. But even though Constantin had shot or watched the shooting of so many war films, thrillers and Westerns over the last twenty years, it took him several seconds to realize that the birds were guns, and that the objects whistling around his ears were bullets, calibrated to destroy anything in their path.

His first reaction was purely egocentric. Who on earth can be firing at me, he wondered as he extracted himself with difficulty from the side-car, his head full of the ridiculous idea of a jealous rival pursuing him even as far as a military campaign. Then he found himself beside his aide at the bottom of the ditch, heart thudding; he was not afraid, but he was surprised, irritated, almost offended. He turned; the entire convoy was immobilized, not a man was seen stirring, and there was a moment of perfect silence amidst the golden, peaceful landscape before raucous shouting was heard, accompanied again by small whistling sounds and detonations from farther off, up in front. He raised his head and saw something moving, over in the trees. Constantin felt mingled admiration and pity for these poor soldiers, these idiots trying to halt the vast might of the German army at Bourgneboul, a little village which according to the guide had a population of just two hundred. They were heroes, and madmen too, for they had not even been firing a machine-gun; the bullets came from rifles, perhaps two or three of them in the cover of the trees over there, where something gleamed: two magnificent, welcoming beeches planted at the entrance of the village, and gleaming with steely glints in the light of the setting sun. Constantin could now make out the silent, low-built white houses behind those trees, and for the first time in two days he heard the cry of a genuine bird and raised his head. He saw a black, graceful shape, perhaps a tit or more likely a swallow, fly overhead, calling and wheeling as if it too were under fire. And the cry of that solitary bird, dancing in the gathering dusk above the wheatfields and among the men senselessly about to kill each other, the cry of that bird momentarily pierced Constantin's heart. Its cry spoke of other things: it spoke of the seasons, of human gestures, happiness, dates, childhood, chance encounters, it spoke of the sweetness of summer evenings, it spoke of established customs, of harvests, it spoke of life past and life to come, it had nothing to do with death or with the machine-gun behind it, already beginning to sputter and chop up the trees which guarded Bourgneboul, the trees where a few men were going to die stupidly, most likely not out of heroism but out of exasperation and fury at having to run away again. They would fall on the field of honour in the course of a defeat too long-drawn-out, too widespread for their death or suicide to be considered anything but folly. And it was folly too, when you looked at that sky promising a fruitful summer, when you smelled the fragrance of the warm earth opening to the sun again.

Keeping under cover of the lorries and the guns, three soldiers carrying a heavy machine-gun arrived almost at Constantin's side, and from their position behind the lorry that had been following him they began frantically spraying Bourgneboul with fire. Constantin turned his head; the results were all too obvious. The few bullets that still sent gravel flying up from the road above his ditch did not seem to concern him, anyway.

"Don't worry, we'll get the swine!"

There was nothing very startling, thought Constantin, about this prophecy from Captain Müller, who had come up beside them on all fours. Müller was one of the few short, fat soldiers in this magnificent army. Constantin, who was not at all sure which of the two of them was under the other's orders, thought, however, that Müller had the look of a subordinate — and an arrogant subordinate at that, a contradiction in terms which his experience as a director told him was generally disastrous. Eyes even beadier and skin even damper than usual, Captain Müller seemed to be in a state of great excitement; whether because of the smell of blood or not, he kept licking his lips. Repulsive, he is really repulsive, thought Constantin with satisfaction, for it was rare to see an adjective so well illustrated. Not just rare but reassuring, at a time when the latest theory said that people who trampled all over you did it only to hide their timidity, whereas those who crawled to you were actually bursting with pride.

"They're deserters for sure," remarked Müller, eyes glued to his binoculars, which evidently had psychological as well as optical qualities.

"If so, they're deserting from the wrong side," said Constantin jokingly. "Maybe we ought to tell them."

Müller cast him an irritated glance before returning to his surveillance. "We'll get 'em out of there, believe you me! This is your baptism of fire, isn't it, Dr von Meck?"

The irony of the phrase amused Constantin. "Well, yes," he said. "Isn't it yours too?"

Müller flushed, and did his best to get around this fact, so unfair to a man who had been training to fire on his neighbour since adolescence. "I have been in the army for four years," he proudly pointed out.

"High time you were baptized, then! Hasn't this moment seemed a long time coming?" inquired Constantin amiably, and the nape of Müller's neck turned from red to purple.

"No, military training has never bored me," he said firmly. "Though I'm afraid I didn't have time to go to the cinema, if you'll forgive my saying so, Captain von Meck!"

"Oh, that's quite all right!" Constantin smiled. "Just now there are too many people wanting to see films and not enough cinemas to show them in." He smiled, thinking how ridiculous this schoolboy argument was at the very moment when they were encountering real war, even the possibility, slight as it was, of dying. Captain Müller was now leaning on his elbows, head between his shoulders, moving one hip forward after the other as specified in the perfect soldier's manual.

"You there!" he shouted, turning to the men with the machine-gun. "You there, get your line of fire parallel to my body, will you?" he yelled at them, before creeping on. His crimson face had already passed Constantin's. Constantin, his cheek on the grass, was looking for ants or anything else to distract his eye. Unfortunately, Captain Müller's head and torso were followed by his plump buttocks, outlined by the uniform stretched too tightly over them as they came into Constantin's field of vision. Having firmly made up his mind to curb his impulse — and to his surprise failing to do so — Constantin was horrified to see his own hand descend with a suggestive, a Breughelian gesture on that odalisque-like rump, while his own lips uttered an appreciative little smacking sound. It was disastrous. For a moment Müller, Constantin and Constantin's aide all lay there stunned by the madness of the gesture.

"Mein Gott!" yelled Müller, in a different, a shrill but feeble voice, and jumping to his feet melodramatically, he put his hand to his knife. Constantin, seeing himself about to be drawn into a knife fight, was already standing up too when a loud and very close burst of gunfire sounded just behind him. One of the men with the machine-gun, over-nervous and distracted by the appearance of Müller in his field of vision, had instinctively fired it, and bullets were spraying into the wheat, mowing down grain and chopped stalks around Constantin and his aide, who were lying flat on their faces as Captain Müller collapsed without even a sigh on top of the aide, a dozen new red buttonholes drilled into the back of his uniform.

"But I . . . but I . . . but I . . ." said Constantin three times, in tones of regret and reproach, for it was a fact that none of this corresponded to his idea of a battle, or a battlefield, or the death of a fellow countryman on a battlefield. He was feeling increasingly doubtful, quite apart from questions of prestige, as to whether his presence was really an asset to the Wehrmacht in this war. Constantin had imagined himself in various roles: as an Uhlan galloping with drawn sword to meet the enemy cavalry, or else, less grandly, struggling against cold in a trench with men of his own race; finally, he had seen himself reassuring civilians who were terrified, but whose language he spoke, and drinking cool wine with them. However, this war was turning out to be a noisy, ludicrous picnic, with all the fighting too one-sided and too far away. Constantin did not feel a moment's remorse towards the unfortunate Müller's family: he had revealed him, he decided, swift as ever to shake off remorse, or at least had guessed him to be a brutal executioner, and a lucky chance seemed to have confirmed this intuition. Hated and despised by his men, Captain Müller would not have stayed at the head of his troops for long in any case; he wouldn't have reached Paris alive. The brief inquest Constantin held, his conversations with the machine-gunners, reassured him. He need feel no more remorse than he felt like feeling.

Painting in Blood

The three Frenchmen waiting in ambush at Bourgneboul sold their lives quite cheaply; the first shell fired by a tank sent the barn where they had been hiding sky-high, together with their heroic spirits. Nothing was found of them but some unrecognizable debris, and looking at it Constantin did, at last, feel something like remorse.

VI

It was the postman, of course, who brought the first news to Boubou Bragance's house at eight next morning. The French Forces of the Interior had blown up a convoy of German troops going south in a remote place three kilometres from the small hamlet of Vassieux. The incident had happened at one in the morning, and at six two German detachments from Draguignan had set off into the mountains in search of the Resistance forces: two regular Wehrmacht detachments.

That day there was shooting in a small valley over towards Vassieux itself. On their way, at eight in the morning, Constantin's motley collection of vans, cars and assorted gas-powered vehicles met the Wehrmacht detachments: some thirty men coming back downhill dragging their feet and singing none of their usual songs, but in silence. As a matter of fact, their penetrating but sometimes rather fine singing, which had appealed to the local French inhabitants at first, was now inclined to give them gooseflesh instead; accordingly, Popesku was the only one disappointed by the silence and disorder of that small troop of uniformed men.

Popesku's troubles were not yet over. In his capacity as a collaborator he already felt a failure, and he was to suffer even more severely soon in his capacity as the producers' representative. They were shooting the scene in which young Fabrice del Dongo has to defend himself against Giletti and his knife, watched by Clelia Conti, who has not yet met him. Seated beside her father at the door of her carriage, Clelia Conti was to cast glances of surprise, astonishment, and dawning emotion at the handsome young man: but if there was emotion in her eyes they must also display alarm and modesty. Doe's eyes were called for. Maud could make doe's eyes easily enough; she had none of the plumpness which suggests a bovine eye, or the flightiness suitable to a goat's eye; however, unfortunately she did sometimes display a total blankness of mind which meant that she made melting, docile sheep's eyes. The unfortunate Lucien Marrat raced past her, followed by the actor playing Giletti, to no avail; the small cluster of extras standing by showed every sign of alarm and interest, also to no avail. The camera, trained on Maud at the door of her carriage, revealed the ravishing but lacklustre profile of a drowsy sheep. In front of his sarcastic team, Constantin tried coaxing, irony, anger and threats, but all in vain, and meanwhile Lucien Marrat, playing Fabrice, was starting to sulk, feeling worn out with racing round and round that carriage and making no impression on the actresses playing opposite him. Popesku was in despair: it was nearly ten o'clock, they had been here since eight, and for two hours he had been watching UFA's money and his own reputation evaporate in this unpleasant atmosphere. In his despair, Popesku made his way to the front of those extras standing and watching who were not on camera at the moment, attracted Maud Mérival's attention and tried to prompt her — as a clever pupil at school prompts a dunce. Using every feature in his fat face, he mimed what he thought indicated an innocent young girl's interest, concern, even a touch of erotic attraction, and to set Maud an example he turned his two little piggy eyes, now glowing ardently, on young Lucien Marrat. On catching that look Lucien Marrat, who was just finishing yet another circuit of the carriage, stopped in his tracks, first alarmed and

then indignant, and not without reason: making his female lead
yawn and then getting a production assistant so worked up was
more than the handsome young star could take. He strode in a
very virile way towards his director, who did not appear to see
him. Heels apart, head back and looking at the sky, Constantin
von Meck was twirling his moustache with both hands while
tears flowed slowly from the corners of his eyes; he had been in a
position to observe Popesku's lesson in acting to Maud Mérival
from the start, and wouldn't have had anything interrupt it for
the world. He therefore seized Lucien Marrat by the back of the
neck, like a good swimmer saving a man on the point of
drowning by half strangling him and paying no attention to his
cries or struggles — for the unfortunate Lucien Marrat did
struggle. Constantin did not let go until he was out of earshot of
the film crew.

"I may be disfigured," said the young man gravely, "but that's
no reason for Mlle Mérival to think she can just ignore me and
behave so — so brutally! I mean, Mme Blessen is as polite to me
as ever, and . . ."

"What on earth are you talking about?" said the bewildered
Constantin.

"I'm talking about this . . . this thing here on my face!" said
Lucien Marrat, crossly. "I can't help it; it must be something I
ate, one of those picnics M. Popesku keeps feeding us — if I can
still call him *Monsieur* Popesku, that is!"

Here Constantin's mirth burst out. He had some difficulty in
explaining to the young man the reasons for his howls of
laughter, and the professional rather than licentious feelings
which had motivated Popesku. This wasted another quarter
of an hour's shooting time. After that, Constantin asked
young Marrat, who was feeling better now, to send Maud over
to him. She arrived looking a little pale beneath her hooded
cloak — since Constantin was able to frighten her — and said
in her sweetest voice, "You're cross with me, aren't you?

Oh dear, I'm sure you are!"

As this was the voice she employed for melting the hearts of idiots at the Conservatoire or in Maxim's, Constantin really did lose his temper now.

"Why would I be cross with you? It's only ten o'clock, or nearly. We've only lost half the morning because you'd rather sleep than act. Why the hell would you think I'm cross with you?"

"I didn't sleep well last night," she began, voice quavering.

"Nor did I," shouted Constantin. "Nor did I! As a matter of fact, I thought I heard an explosion."

And he stationed himself in front of her, looking her up and down with his most ferocious expression — his Russian expression, as Maud called it, and at present, she thought, it was singularly lacking in warmth.

"There's a war on, didn't you know?" he continued. "If you're not going to be able to act next day whenever a train's derailed, we shall never get this film made! About to cry now, are you? Oh, calm down," he added more gently, for she was thrusting out her lower lip, narrowing her eyes, crinkling her nose, and again she looked ugly enough for her grief to be credible.

"It wasn't the noise kept me awake," she wailed, "it wasn't the noise, it was you."

"Me?" exclaimed Constantin, bewildered. "Me? But I didn't say a thing to you . . . I didn't do anything to you . . . I didn't so much as set eyes on you! I wasn't even in my bedroom!"

"Exactly," she said, weeping in good earnest, "exactly! You weren't there, and then I saw you in the corridor with Wanda."

He was holding her away from him at arm's length, but she persisted in keeping her head bent, and now resembled an obstinate goat rather than a drowsy sheep.

"Well, so what? I was with my wife, believe it or not," he said with dignity. But even as he spoke, he heard his own intonation, and the ridiculous aspect of that dignity, the absurdity of their conversation took the wind out of his sails and his anger.

"So what are we going to do about it?" he said. "If you can't act any time I don't sleep in my own bed, I'll have to find another Clelia Conti, and fast. Whether it's my wife I'm going to see or someone else."

"I don't mind you deceiving me," said Maud (very firmly and also, Constantin thought, totally irrationally), "I don't mind you deceiving me, but I don't want to know about it!"

"And how did you know about it?" he asked, annoyed. "Who told you?"

She raised her eyes to him, their expression calm and logical. "Nobody told me, but when I saw you in the corridor wearing Wanda's red dressing gown I knew. I'm not as stupid as all that, you know!"

"I was only out in the corridor because there had been an explosion," said Constantin, gently and slowly. "I doubt if there's going to be an explosion every night — I hope not, anyway. So there's a good chance that if I sleep with someone else you won't know every time. There, is that settled? If there's no explosion you'll work?"

And as she blew her nose and nodded, smiling, Constantin wondered whether he had not underestimated her: perhaps she really was either utterly crazy or utterly stupid. Perhaps Popesku had been right to try teaching her her part after all.

"Did you see your friend Popesku helping out just now, miming Clelia Conti?" he inquired.

"Yes," said Maud, thoughtfully, "but it's a funny thing, I don't see Clelia Conti exactly like that, do you? Myself, I see her more . . . oh, I don't know . . . more artful, maybe. What do you say?"

But without saying anything, striding out and pulling her along by the hand, Constantin von Meck took her back to the carriage. She acted the scene to perfection, she was charming and convincing, and if anyone could have been more seductive than

La Sanseverina that morning, it would have been Maud.

The morning was thus a long one for everyone, particularly
Wanda, who was ready, costumed and perfumed at nine-thirty,
as required by the shooting schedule; a scene between herself and
Mosca was to be shot after the sequence with Clelia in the
carriage. So she stayed in her caravan, playing endless games of
patience, much to the admiration and alarm of Popesku. His
small store of experience had taught him that great stars do not
like hanging about at the whim of beginners, and this was one of
the reasons that had induced him to put on his pantomime in
front of Maud, hoping to speed her up. As has been seen, there
was no immediate reaction, and when he saw Wanda come out of
her caravan in her own clothes and with a decided look about
her, and get into Constantin's Talbot, he could only give her a
small, understanding smile. After all, the poor woman had just
lost her father, and now she had been kept waiting for an hour, all
by herself, in very hot weather and laced into voluminous skirts.
The cruelty of it all filled poor Popesku's heart with anger and
compassion. Accordingly he leaned in at the car door, as if drawn
by a magnet, just as Wanda was about to start. He was the only
person so far to have noticed her departure, which she wanted to
pass unobserved, and she waited for him to move, her face
expressionless. In fact, she found Popesku repulsive; every pore
of his fat face seemed to her to ooze hypocrisy, cowardice,
contemptibility, indifference to others and servility; few men had
made her feel quite so disgusted with the human race.

"I'll be back in a little while, M. Popesku," she said. "I have to
make an urgent telephone call."

Popesku hesitated, going a little redder in the face: not easy in
view of the crimson shade inflicted on him by the sun over the last
two days.

"Oh, I know," he said, "I know . . . I beg your pardon, Mme

Blessen, but I heard yesterday . . . forgive me, I don't know how to put it . . . I'm so very sorry about your father, Mme Blessen. Please accept my deepest sympathy. I value your discretion and your courage for more reasons than one. I'm not speaking to you as a producer now, I mean a production assistant, but as a man — a friend, if you'll let me call myself that!"

He was stammering, and could not meet her eyes; despite himself, he glanced inside the car as if looking for some weapon or some suspicious item there; he was the very picture of a spy, even that debonair side of him which amused Constantin and horrified her, Wanda, like an invisible form of leprosy.

"Thank you," she said in the same neutral tone, "thank you. It certainly has been distressing, and I felt I'd rather not talk about it. I can't go to Sweden, can I, M. Popesku, you couldn't get me there? We theatrical folk are like a family, you know, but I don't like to upset the others. And anyway, the show must go on, mustn't it? You know that too," she added with a small, ironic laugh at the threadbare nature of these two platitudes. Popesku, however, took her laughter for courage, and bending down all of a sudden, he put his lips to Wanda's hand where she was leaning her arm on the car door.

The movement she made to pull her hand away, her instinctive recoil, was so violent that as her fingers passed Popesku's cheek she almost crushed her cigarette out against it. Letting out a yelp of pain, he stood up abruptly. Standing there in front of her, he put his hand to his cheek; his eyes were popping, he was the very image of reproach.

"Oh, my God!" said Wanda, horrified. "Oh, my God, I'm so sorry! Did I hurt you? How silly of me! But you scared me — I really am sorry . . . show me, M. Popesku, show me the damage, do! I feel terrible, really terrible. You scared me . . ."

She was stammering and agitated, but she stopped short when she saw two large tears well out of Popesku's eyes and roll down his cheeks. She sat there, open-mouthed, until he told her, calmly, "Excuse me, Mme Blessen, those are tears of pain. I just can't stand pain, you see — I suppose it's because of my nerves, but I never could . . ." he continued, as calmly as ever, and spreading his hands as if confessing or explaining something inadmissible or inexplicable.

The two of them looked at each other with wholly objective attention and interest, divested of the slightest sentiment, without hatred or suspicion. They considered each other, but like two inhabitants of two different planets.

"And how did you know about my father?" asked Wanda at last, in a very youthful voice which surprised even herself.

"Oh, from the postmistress," said Popesku. "The postmistress at Salerne. You remember — we had a drink there yesterday evening."

And in an access of emotion and generosity which survived the horrible pain of his burnt cheek, he added, leaning down again, but keeping at a respectful distance, "Mme Blessen, if I may say so, you ought to tell M. von Meck his little cousin isn't a reponsible young man. He could make trouble for M. von Meck. He really could — you should point that out, believe me, Mme Blessen."

And stepping back, he turned and went away with that expression of mingled cunning and satisfaction on his face which it wore at moments of euphoria. He had returned good for evil, given advice in exchange for his burn, and he was not sure that in the obvious bewilderment that had spread over the star's face he had not seen a slight, very slight, trace of admiration in her eye.

But when Wanda Blessen came back an hour later, Popesku did not think for a moment of looking for a trace of anything in her eye — nor did the rest of the film crew either. Everyone was anxious to avoid it. Wanda drove up fast, braked suddenly, and brought the Talbot to a halt outside her caravan, in full view of the camera. She slammed the door, went into her caravan, slammed its door too, and three minutes later her dresser was seen to come out shaking, her face bright red. After another three minutes Wanda herself emerged, impeccable, in the character of La Sanseverina, costumed and made up to perfection, just as if she had not been at the wheel of a car five minutes earlier. She scrutinized the startled company from the top of the three steps of her caravan, and finally turned an icy glare on Constantin.

"Are we eventually going to shoot something?" she asked. "I thought I saw the shooting schedule mention that M. Lentz and I were to exchange a few trifling remarks, in costume, about nine-thirty. Perhaps the idea doesn't seem like much fun to any of you now?"

She had assumed her famous flat-toned voice, so slow and biting and above all so calm that it made strong men tremble. The stoutest scene-shifters in the crew took a sudden interest in their feet, while the thinner ones got behind them. Only Constantin remained standing upright and facing her. They were on about the same level, and they looked at each other, suspicion in Constantin's eyes and indifference in Wanda's, such indifference that they soon moved on from Constantin as if he were some inanimate object.

"M. Lentz?" she said, in her flat voice. Ludwig Lentz instantly appeared.

The company moved aside for him; he went to the bottom of the steps, raising his hat and bowing as if he really were Count Mosca. Everyone present subconsciously admired his courage.

"I'm glad to see you're ready," said Wanda, giving him her hand and gracefully coming down the steps. "Heaven knows we've both had time enough."

And glancing all around, she saw Maud, who was not yet out of costume and was vainly trying to hide behind Popesku.

"Have you quite finished your scene? Or perhaps I should say your *appearance* at the carriage window?" asked Wanda, with formidable graciousness. "We both thought it delightful . . . Where do you want us now, Constantin, please?"

Two assistants rushed forward, and Wanda, on Ludwig Lentz's arm, went to sit in the small gig where she was supposed to hear Mosca's declaration of love. Fortunately, the delay meant that everything was ready, and no sooner was she seated beside a Count Mosca even more nervous than his lines demanded than she nodded her head and dismissed the make-up girl with an authoritative wave of the hand, and an arrogant "It's not worth bothering." Arrogant but correct: not an eyelash was out of place. Anger gave her face an immovable look, as if the powder and make-up themselves were clinging to her skin in terror.

Mosca's gig was to go along the same road as Clelia Conti's carriage, the road from Parma which led without a bend to Modena, a straight, dusty road lined with tall, light, airy poplars. In fact Popesku had thought that this scene, which consisted of close-ups, could quite well have been shot in the studio. Constantin von Meck, however, as always a perfectionist, claimed that fresh air made a difference to an actor's face and voice.

Seated in their horseless gig, whose wheels the scene-shifters were to shake slightly, Mosca and La Sanseverina had a camera trained on them in close-up and passing from one to the other, never lingering long on either; it moved forward or back to suit the lines. The light was the bright light of noon now, and when Constantin, of whom nothing could be seen behind the camera but his red hair and big hands, emerged again, his shirt was drenched with sweat. The wardrobe mistress brought him another, and he changed into it unselfconsciously, while little Maud turned her eyes modestly away from his naked torso, to the great delectation of several ill-disposed persons. "Silence!" shouted an assistant, and Constantin said, "Take!" as Ludwig Lentz turned to Wanda.

"I am no longer twenty," said Lentz, in the part of Mosca. "Age does away with one's liking for intrigue, as you know, Duchess, and heightens one's doubts of oneself."

"Cut," said Constantin, and leaned on the gig. He turned his whole attention to Ludwig Lentz. "Listen, Ludwig, don't you think that line is rather like a proverb, some old saying? Do you see what I'm getting at? You seem to be resolute and wise, but in fact you're committing an act of folly; you're telling a woman you love, a woman you're beginning to love, that you are old; you're telling her things which will do you no good; in fact, you're telling her you're afraid of ageing. Do you see what I mean?"

"Yes, you're right," said Ludwig Lentz, who spoke French laboriously but with a flawless accent. "I'm sorry, Constantin," he added, "I sometimes get into a muddle over the Count. When I make him speak drily, my heart's supposed to be breaking, and when I make him speak gently it works even worse. At least I hope I'm not annoying the divine Wanda."

"The divine Wanda loves a muddle," said that lady, looking at him with sudden affection. "It's not your fault if Stendhal gave his hero silly things to say. I mean, losing one's liking for intrigue and one's self confidence at fifty . . . do you know any fifty-year-olds like that, my dear Ludwig? Perhaps they don't exist outside Germany. Personally, I've never seen any in France or America."

"Would you like to start again?" asked Constantin, standing his ground. "Look at Wanda, please."

Ludwig Lentz nodded; he looked a little awkward.

"Yes, of course," he said. "Let's get on with it."

"Silence, cameras roll, take." The fateful words were spoken again; Ludwig Lentz leaned forward. "Alas, I am no longer twenty! Age does away with one's doubts of oneself and — oh, damn it all," he said with total sincerity, "oh, damn it all! I'm so sorry, I'm getting muddled up myself now! I do apologize, Wanda, and to you, Constantin."

The film crew looked at him sympathetically. Putting themselves in his place, they were sorry for him. None of them would have been able speak straight with such a stormy atmosphere hovering around Wanda and Constantin. The scene-shifters themselves were giving the gig only the feeblest of shakes now, and soon stopped entirely.

"Well," said Wanda, with good humour so artificial that it was worse than anything that had gone before, "well, that was really bothering me; I don't think you'd better say that line, my dear Ludwig, I really don't. Men of fifty — men of fifty these days, anyway — aren't like Stendhal's fifty-year-olds any more. A poor man of fifty would like money to make women love him, and a rich man of fifty would like women to love him for something other than his money . . . it's simple, really! Moreover, men of fifty are arrogant, bad-tempered, self-indulgent, liars and vindictive. Well, I mean . . . I mean in America, of course."

"Ludwig," suggested Constantin from behind his camera, "shall we take that scene again?"

But here Wanda Blessen rose in a single movement, stood there on her long legs and pointed her hand at Constantin, with her parasol like an extension at the end of it.

"Leave poor Ludwig alone, why don't you? Why are you trying to make him say lines he can't speak with any conviction? What's the matter with you, boring everyone? This is a disastrous day, it's a disastrous film, Stendhal's *Chartreuse de Parme* might as well be a hospital, we're all so bored here, we're bored to death, let me tell you, Constantin! People will be yawning their heads off at your film. Anyway, I'm leaving, I've had enough, I'm going back to my caravan, which is about the pleasantest place around here, and I'm going to play cards. Anyone here know how to play gin rummy?"

And her eyes swept the entire cast and crew, seeming to weigh them up in search of whoever was most likely to amuse her. Some hunched their shoulders, but a number of the men thrust out their chests and gave her an engaging smile.

Wanda's eyes fastened on Romano. "You," she said, "you. Come with me. Leave those stage tricks and come with me. Yes, all right, I know, I know, it's not the done thing to talk about stage tricks when you're on the set, I'll buy everyone a drink soon to make up."

And like a Fury, abandoning the gig, Ludwig Lentz and Constantin von Meck, she crossed the clearing and went back to her caravan. Romano, abandoning his electric cables and casting an amused and fatalistic glance at Constantin, followed her, whistling. He seemed neither surprised nor alarmed. And indeed, he was more envied than pitied, at least by the men. Constantin, smiling, turned to the horror-stricken Popesku and slapped him on the back.

"Don't worry, old fellow. Wanda will be in a better mood in a couple of hours, or even just one hour. Anyway, it's almost lunchtime, isn't it? Eleven forty-five. Come on, everyone stop for lunch. Personally, I'm going for a drive," he said, to the company at large. "I think I'll go up and have a look at Vassieux."

"You can't get right up there by car," said one of the scene-shifters.

"Then I'll walk the last part of the way," said Constantin, getting into his Talbot.

He needed air himself, and more particularly, he was afraid Wanda had ruined his gearbox. He hated anyone to borrow his car; it was the one thing in the world he didn't like lending. Popesku watched him go, and on turning round saw that he was not alone. Maud too was watching the car drive off down the dusty road, looking tragic. Popesku laughed coarsely.

"So the little cousin's not good enough now?" he inquired.

Maud looked at him, baffled. "Little cousin? What little cousin?"

"Why, Romano," said Popesku. "He told me . . . that is, I thought . . ."

He suddenly stopped short. He had met Romano that morning, and laughing, actually laughing, without the slightest suspicion, had congratulated him on sleeping so deeply the night before. He was the only person, Popesku had said admiringly, not to have been milling around in Boubou Bragance's corridors "after the explosion".

"Oh, I was awake," had said Romano at once, "I was awake, but I was with Maud and then . . . well, I didn't like to come out . . ."

And Popesku had been surprised, not by the fact that Romano had been sleeping with Maud, since the entire cast and crew had done that at one time or another, but by the fact that he admitted it. In the normal way, Romano would have given him an icy glance, looking straight through him, Popesku, as if he were transparent; this was the first time he had deigned to give him an explanation, a reply, even a few words, and the alibi in itself struck Popesku as something of a confession, especially now that it turned out to be false.

"Ah," he said slowly, "ah, I see! You and little Romano . . ."

"Oh, that was ages ago," said Maud, "ages ago! It's all old history! When we were filming *The Violins*, yes, at the start, but not since then. If you ask me, he's got a girl-friend in the country somewhere."

And knowing that Maud had no unnecessary modesty, in fact, knowing that like Spitfire pilots notching up the number of hits scored in the air on their fuselages, Maud would happily have notched up the number of lovers who passed through her bed for all to see — knowing, therefore, that she was not lying, Popesku was baffled. For not only had Romano Woltzer taken the trouble to answer his question; he had gone to the additional trouble of answering with a lie.

VII

"Can you by any chance play gin rummy?" asked Wanda as she walked into the caravan. Thanks to the closed shutters it was dark in there, dark and cool.

"I can play any card game," said Romano, smiling and raising his eyes to her. His glance was questioning, but calm.

"I need to talk to you," said Wanda. "Wait a minute while I take off my make-up and wig and these skirts."

She went behind the screen and undressed rapidly, with surprising modesty for an actress with such a beautiful body. All Romano saw of her was a shoulder and a bare breast, and to do that he had to lean craftily forward. She caught his eye in the mirror and frowned, but there was so much admiration and pleasure in those ingenuous eyes that then she could not help smiling at him.

"Do you know you're rather good-looking too?" she asked. "Very good-looking, in fact. I told Constantin yesterday, and I'm telling you now, you ought to come to Los Angeles with us afterwards. You'd be a great hit there."

She had emerged from behind the screen in a blue cotton dressing-gown which brought out the blue of her eyes, and went to sit in her usual rocking chair. She patted the stool standing a little way away from it, and Romano obediently sat down.

"What do you say?" she asked.

"Why not?" said the boy. "Why not? If we get out of this . . ."

"You don't think we will?"

"You will, yes, I hope so," said Romano. "Yes, I'm sure you will, there's no reason why you shouldn't . . ."

"Oh yes," said Wanda. "Oh yes, there is a reason." And suddenly she looked forty, and tired. "There are reasons, you know there are. They're all over the place, and very well informed. And Popesku is an informer. You do know that, don't you?"

Romano was indignant. "Popesku? Constantin wouldn't have an informer on his set!" And then he stopped short.

"Constantin never suspects anyone," said Wanda, smiling. "How about you? Are you sure no one suspects you over that train?"

"Train? What train?" repeated Romano slowly, as if she were setting him an arithmetical problem.

Wanda shook her head, irritated. "The train you derailed last night," she said in an undertone, glancing at the door. "When you'd heard what time it would be passing from von Kirschen, at dear Boubou Bragance's. Oh, how angry I am with myself for getting him to say that," she added.

Romano shrugged his shoulders. "Look, that train was full of men and equipment to prevent landings in the south of the country," he said. "Don't tell me you're a Nazi! I've been watching you since you arrived."

"Well, of course I'm not," said Wanda, with renewed irritation. "As it happens, I'm working for British Intelligence. I'm here on a mission, a very precise mission which did not call for all this to-do: not the explosion, nor the train, nor the inquiry it's all going to set off. That's why I'm angry with myself, that's the only reason. I'm not angry with you, of course."

Romano whistled quietly through his teeth: it was a whistle of surprise rather than admiration, and Wanda did not catch it. "So you're working for the British," he said. "Since when? Since the start?"

"Yes," said Wanda, stretching gracefully, "since the start — since before the start. My father himself . . . well, in short, I came here on a mission, a mission more important than your train, my poor dear. And I need you to help me bring it off. We've had a setback, a bad setback. I had a telegram telling me about it yesterday, and you're the only person who can help me. I can't get away from the location here; I'm filming the whole time. I want you to go and find someone for me, he's a hundred kilometres away, someone who's needed — needed urgently — in America, in Arizona, to be precise. He's a scientist, a physicist. His escort were fools enough to get picked up in a raid. They won't have talked, I'm sure, but meanwhile our man is stuck where he is; he doesn't know anyone. You, or somebody else, has to go and find him and bring him here, where a plane is going to pick him up — pick us up," she added, "because this is going to attract a lot of attention; it will pick up the four of us, him, you, me and Constantin, and the whole thing is timed for tomorrow, because we're living on top of a volcano, my dear."

Romano looked fixedly at her. "And why are you trusting me?" he asked.

"I'm quite well informed," said Wanda. "There's a radio transmitter not far from here. You don't think I'd have come here but for all this, do you? I wouldn't — not for Stendhal or Constantin."

"Not even for Constantin?" asked Romano, eyebrows raised doubtfully. Wanda shrugged her shoulders and looked away.

"Well, yes, partly for him, of course. Anyway, I'm here. Now listen: we are leaving tomorrow, and you must go and find our man tonight. In Draguignan. Can you do it? If you don't go, if you don't bring him back, if you get captured we're lost. The war itself may be lost. And if you give us away, if you let our man down, we shall kill you before the Germans even touch you. Understand?"

Romano had drawn his stool closer. He leaned towards the

rocking chair. They looked calmly at one another for some ten seconds. She could see the dark roots of his fair hair, and tried to imagine him entirely dark, but he looked quite hard enough as it was; he looked older and more dangerous than he should have done. He was twenty-two, and already self-controlled and dangerous; he had to be. For once, Constantin had chosen well; he was right to value this young man, and if Wanda could have been jealous of Constantin she would have been jealous on Romano's account, but she was too sure of him for that; even in the midst of his infidelities he had given her too much proof of a love that would stand the test of time for her to have the least fear.

"You heard what I said? If you agree to do it and you let us down, we'll kill you. I may not be the one who does it, but if I die first others will do it for me."

"Are you sure the Nazis won't be before you?" he asked calmly.

And suddenly Wanda felt furious with herself for the stupid cruelty of threatening this young man, who had kept alive only by a miracle for almost four years.

"I'm sorry," she said, "but it's so important! This man is the most brilliant physicist in Europe. His name is Otting, and they need him in America to finish making their bomb — the A-bomb. If Hitler gets it first it will a disaster for everyone, Romano, for the whole world."

"What is this A-bomb?" he asked, smiling. "Even bigger than the usual sort, is it? Will it need an air freighter to carry it?"

"No, it's smaller," said Wanda, "but it's the most effective — or it would be the most effective, devastating bomb you can imagine. Or rather that you can't imagine. Nobody will ever use it: no American or European would use it, perhaps even a German wouldn't use it, nobody would but Hitler. And that's why we need to have it first, and we need him to know it!"

"I'll go and find you your scientist," said Romano, "I'll go and find him for you tonight and bring him here, I promise. But that doesn't mean we'll all be leaving tomorrow . . . can you imagine Constantin abandoning his film?"

And he smiled, leaned a little further forward and rested his head on Wanda's shoulder.

"You know," he murmured, "if you weren't Constantin's wife and if you didn't love him, I . . ."

"And if you weren't Constantin's friend . . ." she said, and both felt their faces relax into a smile.

"Well, we can fix that up in Los Angeles," said Wanda. "One day when Constantin's chasing someone else over the sands of Santa Monica. We'll act Phaedra and Hippolytus."

"Don't know them," said Romano, regretfully.

Wanda put her hand gently against his cheek. "That's a pity, but I'll teach you," she said. "I've always dreamed of introducing Racine to a young man . . . particularly such a good-looking one . . . Ah, well, shuffle the cards, will you?"

Obediently, Romano picked up the pack and shuffled it. "And where exactly am I to go tonight?"

She looked at him with eyes that were suddenly cold. "I won't tell you until the very last moment, when you're about to leave. Oh no, what a terrible hand you've dealt me . . ."

"By the way," said Romano, amused, "you were only pretending to be in a rage just now, weren't you? So as to talk to me?"

"Yes, and you see, Constantin believed me; he believed me at once. He always believes me when I act stupidly. Ah, here's a good spade for a start. Tell me, Romano, do you think you might talk if someone pulled your little finger or your ear rather hard? Personally, I think you'd tell all."

Romano began to laugh. "You're right. One must never trust oneself."

That afternoon Romano, who had never lost a card game in his life, found himself losing four games of gin rummy in an hour.

Then he realized that Wanda was cheating, started cheating too, and won back all the pebbles she had stolen from him. They enjoyed themselves very much, until the moment when they began to worry about Constantin's absence. For it was over an hour and a half since he had left.

VIII

Setting off at speed, to show his anger, Constantin von Meck soon took his foot off the accelerator to show his maturity; then he found himself frequently changing gear as he drove along in the dust of the steep road leading to Vassieux, a place mentioned in the Guide Michelin as having a ravine apparently little visited by tourists; ever since they had arrived in the area, small fires in the grass of this ravine had been sending up their smoke into the sky. The road climbed precipitously, and then became so narrow that he had to stop the car. He got out; climbing was hard going under this leaden sun, and he nearly gave up. Indeed, he would have given up if he had not been attracted by some indefinable odour, an odour which grew stronger as he climbed on, a smell of burning. In his memory, however, such a smell was usually accompanied by excited voices, the sound of water and of running, hasty footsteps, instead of the total silence that now surrounded him. The smell and the silence did not go together. This rift between his senses of smell and hearing made him go on, feeling annoyance and a vague kind of worry. It was not something arousing his curious imagination that sent him on up the steep path, but a source of irritation to his memory.

The sign with the name of Vassieux on it shone in the sun at the top of the rise, and no sooner had Constantin passed it than he found himself in the middle of Vassieux itself, a place consisting of a dozen farms and a kind of general store in a small square, with the local big house on the left and a communal barn on the right. Or rather, he was in the middle of what had been Vassieux, for it was now only charred and smoking rubble, with a few fires still burning. Constantin stood still for a moment, as if viewing some spectacle, and then took a few paces towards the big house, which had been boarded up with new planks. And as he walked forward he also saw that the strange black objects arranged vertically against its wall like beads on a rosary were corpses, the corpses of ten men who had been shot and whose clotted blood now scarcely seeped through their clothes, blackened by the fire. Ten bodies arranged in so symmetrical a fashion that initially they struck Constantin von Meck, as a director, as being those of ten bad actors, or rather those of ten actors placed in position by a bad director, who had also let two of them get away, since two corpses spoiled this awful harmony by lying as if crawling towards the house, perhaps for shelter. Or at least it was the idea of shelter that occurred to Constantin before he saw an arm sticking through a gap in the planks that boarded up the house, an arm which was not an adult's. He took three more steps, kicked the charred planks, and they gave way at once, crumbling to powder. Behind that crumbling barrier, the sun shone on burnt and twisted bodies, some of them very small.

There was still no noise, nor was there any smell now. The birds and the smoke were fleeing with the wind, fleeing from Vassieux. Constantin turned round and vomited; he vomited over something that looked like a man's body, flinched back, moved away, and vomited again on a black, charred plank; finally he retreated step by step, as if the burnt objects at his feet were threatening him. Retreating slowly like this, it seemed to him as if he took an hour to cover the ten metres separating him from the turn in the road where he no longer saw that sight, and could sit down heavily on a white, warm, intact stone wall. A lizard was sleeping there uneasily, swaying its little green head from side to side, eyes closed, and seeing the lizard Constantin was grateful to it for being alive and moving. He was shivering and suffocating with heat at the same time in the blazing sunlight; now he knew why the Wehrmacht men he had met that morning on their way down from Vassieux were not singing any songs in praise of the Fatherland. Constantin straightened up, felt dry, harsh nausea, and leaned over again. And when for once we had cherry jam for breakfast, he thought, real cherry jam! The incongruous ineptitude of this thought did not make him feel shame; he had gone beyond shame now, he had sunk much lower than that.

He stood up and leaned over the wall, and through a gap in the leaves he saw the clearing far below where his cast and film crew were waiting for him; he saw tiny white, red, blue and green people, people moving actively, caravans, horses — Fabrice's horses running in the sunlight. But there was that charnel-house behind him, and the two images could not be superimposed on each other. Constantin sat down again on the wall, his legs weak; the lizard had run away when he got up, and he felt horribly alone. Above all, he felt cut off for always from the German nation, cut off from his native country, his language, his roots. He felt an orphan for ever, an orphan filled with hatred, which was the last kind of role to suit him. And all that time, which seemed to him to be hours, he heard his own voice saying *Non, non, non, no, né*, but never *nein*, he who had always cheerfully mixed all the languages he knew. He would never say *nein* or *ja* again, he would never let anyone call him Herr von Meck again.

And when, hearing someone shout his name far away and looking at his watch, he saw the time, he thought he must have gone mad; he seemed to have been away from his film crew for days. He rose and went down towards the voice, swaying on his feet. It was the voice of Romano, who was riding up on horseback, face tanned, shirt open, hair shining in the sun,

Romano trotting towards him smiling, smiling when there was nothing to smile about, when he was crazy to smile, when he should be forbidden to smile! Constantin caught him round the waist and practically dragged him off his horse. Romano was not smiling any more now; he had seen Constantin's face, and it was he who was supporting Constantin.

"What's the matter?" he asked. "What's going on?"

"Go back," said Constantin, painfully, gulping again, "go back. Don't go any further. Please."

Romano had put his head back and was sniffing, sniffing the air like a hound; his body stiffened against Constantin's.

"I know that smell," he said in an expressionless voice.

And with one light, extraordinarily active movement, he escaped Constantin, who was trying to hold him back, mounted his horse and rode off towards Vassieux. Constantin stood there motionless, hands hanging by his sides, and saw him disappear before he himself turned, ran to his car, and drove away.

He could take no more. He should have picked up the German army knife one of the soldiers had left up there, shining among all the bodies, he should have picked it up and cut his throat with it. He was going towards dreadful disasters, he was going to be horribly punished, because he had at last seen something which he should not have seen, which he had always refused to see, and which he had always been wrong to refuse to see.

1913 In Prussia

The von Meck estate in Prussia comprised, besides the manor house and two hundred hectares of land, certain features of historical family interest: a lodge which was theoretically a hunting lodge but might be used for assignations too, depending on the inclinations of the current heir, a small, steep mountain which climbers could scale in summer with the family's permission, a forest chapel where it was said that Ludwig of Bavaria had been present (showing obvious regret) at the marriage of Constantin's grandfather. The land was a great expanse of yellow, green and rose, with wheat, barley and maize growing in fields bordered with oaks, poplars and elms, with thoroughbred horses meeting plough oxen along the forest paths, with fat geese staring stupidly at hooded falcons. In the house you would find guns and rakes, boar spears and pruning shears, four-poster beds and straw mattresses, old men and children, the legal heirs and the bastards, Steinways and shepherd's pipes; at least, that was the impression Constantin gleaned from birth to adolescence in his constant explorations, but he was the only one to view everything with equal admiration: his father drew strict distinctions.

There were also the times, particularly in late summer, when the grain slid down a wide, wooden chute all the way to the cellar, where men would put it in sacks. The children used to go down the chute too, when no one was looking, sliding slowly and surely from the corn loft to the cellar, where they landed drowning in the grain — white wheat, yellow maize, dark rye — suffocating in the smell and the dust of it, and went on sliding and sliding, exuberant, private, for whole afternoons. Once down, you had to climb the ladders again, and Reinhardt the tenant farmer's son, their best friend, used to climb up first and give the red-headed children of the house a hand, hauling them along and laughing at their clumsiness. With his elder sister Stephanie, Constantin used to spend a third of the summer there in a strange mood of intoxication; Stephanie in particular never tired of the game. Older, taller and heavier than Constantin, she would go racing round the bend of the chute clutching Reinhardt and laughing too loud. They disappeared from view as Constantin, in a panic, pushed off hard, accelerated, and landed upside down and submerged in the grain at their feet. Stephanie cheered him up, Stephanie hugged him; she hugged him particularly hard the evening when she took to calling him "Reinhardt" for fun. That was before he was eleven and went to school in Essen. But there were still the holidays, away from the harsh and noisy school where he had to fight. Sliding down the chute in the summer was balm to little Constantin's bruises.

And then there was the summer when he was thirteen, and came home so proud of the twenty centimetres he had grown during the winter, but Stephanie was not there. She had been ill since autumn, and was going to stay with Aunt Britt near Dortmund to convalesce. There was Reinhardt too, a Reinhardt who had become silent and fat, Reinhardt who had a silly, high voice and was the butt of the farmhands' jokes. Reinhardt who would not talk to him any more. And then, like lightning striking the house, came news of Stephanie's accident, the rat poison she had swallowed by mistake and which killed her. And then, then, there was their mother's face — his mother alone now, not theirs — a face suddenly devoid of make-up and laughter, a face which was keeping something from him. Finally there came the evening when she had led him by the hand to a car, and then a train, and then a ship, and they had gone to America. She had never once mentioned that time again: that strange, cruel time. And with a pang of the heart Constantin suddenly realized, understood for the first time, that young Reinhardt had been castrated, actually castrated by his father, the proud country landowner von Meck, because he and little Stephanie were sleeping together. Yes, even his childhood, his delightful, green and silken childhood had been drenched in blood, Reinhardt's blood. His sister had killed herself for it and his mother had gone into exile, while he, Constantin, had not understood at the time and had not wanted to understand later. Once again he was a man who did not understand things, as he had better admit to himself once and for all. He was a happy man, and determined to stay happy with all the forces of cowardice and compromise at his command.

IX

No sooner was Constantin von Meck back from his long lunch-time expedition than he declared shooting over for the day and had all the equipment packed up, on the grounds that the light was not right any more. It was true that the wind had changed, and was now blowing up big black clouds; it also carried a strange, indefinable odour which made the horses restless. The few suggestions Popesku allowed himself, as representing the production side, were received with so cold a glance that he soon gave up.

Constantin had got back behind the wheel of his Talbot, taking with him those few actors who moved fast enough to be ready. Only Wanda, who had put her period costume on again, had firmly refused to go with him, saying she had no intention of getting that beautiful dress all creased up on the old seat of the Talbot. If everyone else was in such a hurry, she would come back to Boubou Bragance's house standing in the back of the lorry, surrounded by the spotlights and the camera platforms.

"Just watch me," she told the amused crew, "just watch me on the lorry — I'd make a prizewinning statue, don't you think? Marie Antoinette on her way to the scaffold in her gas-powered tumbril . . ."

Whether because he did not hear her or because he was still angry with her for making a scene that morning, Constantin did not even smile. He had left without a word, taking Maud, who was only too happy, she said, wrinkling her nose, to get away from that horrible smell. The smell, she pronounced, as one laying claim to occult powers, was a smell of burning.

Wanda was thus on her way home in the back of the lorry, joking with two of the scene-shifters, when the sound of horse's hoofs made them all turn to look. What they saw was a pale and dishevelled horseman whom they did not recognize for a moment. It was Romano, but Romano with his eyes dilated, and like his horse drenched and gleaming with rivers of sweat.

"Why, if it isn't the Comte de Fersen himself!" cried Wanda gaily.

But this pleasantry, uttered from the back of the lorry, drew only a brief smile from Romano. He was holding his horse on a tight rein, and the animal was restive, kicking, rolling its eyes and putting back its quivering ears.

"Your horse is frightened of something," said Wanda severely. "What's the matter with you? Calm it down and then try a little elegant prancing around this lorry and my crinoline, so that I don't feel so lonely if we pass through any large towns on our way back."

And as Romano did not reply, but was fighting his horse, in a manner quite unlike himself, Wanda leaned a little further forward.

"What *has* been going on?" she asked roughly, but in a voice the very roughness of which implied intimacy, and made the two scene-shifters turn round.

"The Germans have burnt the village up there," replied Romano, getting control of his horse at last. "They burnt the women and children inside a house and shot the men. It's all black and charred . . ." he finished, with a vague gesture.

"My God," said the head scene shifter, standing next to Wanda, "my God, the bastards, the bloody bastards! Excuse me," he added, looking coldly around him, but the German members of the film crew had already left. "Well, the bloody bastards! So that was the smell, was it?"

He went as pale as Romano already was, and as Wanda now turned. She was standing very upright on the platform at the back of the lorry in her violet crinoline, with the two scene-shifters in their dungarees beside her and Romano riding along behind them, controlling his horse. How odd we must look, she thought for a moment, abstractedly, how odd we must look against the background of that fire, that horrible background. But it was a horror which she could not yet quite envisage. She leaned yet a little further towards Romano, she saw the nerve beating in his jaw, the small blue vein throbbing at his temple, and realized that the boy was exhausted. She felt a surge of tenderness and affection for him, as if he were her son or her much younger lover; she would have liked to take his head between her hands and kiss his mouth lingeringly, sadly, as if in farewell. But she pulled herself together.

"I'll see you back at the house," she said. "You must leave at once, in the Talbot. I'll speak to Constantin."

"I met Constantin up at Vassieux," said Romano. "He'd been there already."

Wanda put her hand to her forehead. "I see," she said. "Oh, poor, poor Constantin!" Then, looking at Romano again, she added, "And poor, poor Romano!" in a tender voice which made Romano turn his head away, and then drop the reins and gallop off along the road ahead of them.

"Poor lad," said the scene-shifter, "poor fellow, he was in tears. He's only young, poor lad."

Wanda nodded without replying. She looked at the pale ears of wheat, shining silvery in the breeze which sent them swaying to right and left. She saw the fruit trees, the white road and the peaceful houses a little way off, basking in the afternoon sun, houses the clouds had not yet reached and extinguished with their shadow.

Constantin von Meck could not be found until dinner-time.

Romano set off in the Talbot "to look for another location", and Ludwig Lentz and Lucien Marrat spent the afternoon playing games of patience which, judging by their faces, never seemed to work out. Wanda played the piano in an absent-minded way, and Boubou fretted, while Maud did her nails interminably.

It was not raining yet. There was something softly violent in the light which seemed to be a forerunner of the storm, or to be summoning it, and which in any case put everyone on edge — although no one seemed, to outward appearance, aware of the fate of Vassieux.

This dinner is not going to be very cheerful, said Boubou Bragance to herself as she sat down, glancing at her guests, or rather her customers, since UFA were paying her a handsome fee to accommodate part of their film crew and cast. Boubou had of course protested at this simple notion, saying it was unthinkable, her friends treated her house as their own, her friends' friends were her friends too, so they too must treat her house as their own, etc., etc., and in spite of all this dreadful rationing she would manage to feed them somehow, if it took her all day to do it. But a little later, once her hospitable outburst had passed over, she had come to an agreement with Popesku whereby half of the very sizable fee was to be paid to her at once, and the second half at the end of shooting, with telephone expenses, service, heating, etc. extra, of course. Thus she could play the munificent mistress of the house with enthusiasm, and retain all the advantages of that role while doing away with any inconveniences; she was the one who fixed timetables, gave orders, invited whoever she pleased, and in all circumstances wore a most convincing expression of kindness, attentiveness and generosity.

She had worked out a seating plan according to principles of her own as follows: Constantin, taking the place of the master of the house, was facing her, with Wanda on his right and Maud on his left; Boubou herself was ensconced between Ludwig Lentz and young Lucien Marrat; Romano and Popesku naturally sat at the two ends of the table, and it was always the same unless an extra visitor upset the immutable order of this seating.

But that night, sitting with her guests, who had suddenly become so gloomy, goodness knew why, and waiting for a gratin of vegetables, which was to be washed down with her neighbour's rough red wine — for she was keeping her husband's Bordeaux in the cellar until her entertaining was genuinely free — she reflected that it looked like being a dismal evening. Constantin's eyes and mouth, which usually held amusement, were hidden behind his eyebrows and moustache; Romano was not back yet; Maud was looking like a violated virgin, Popesku like a bureaucrat out of a job, and Ludwig Lentz, after listening to the radio, looked like a widower already; as for the young leading man Lucien Marrat, he could not manage to get rid of his pimple, which visibly absorbed all his attention. Only Wanda Blessen displayed that composure, vivacity and Olympian carriage of the head which any hostess should be able to expect of her guests. To make matters worse, the vegetable broth was oversalted.

"I suggest," said Boubou Bragance, in the same way as she would have said, "I order", "I suggest we all try to act like civilized beings, for the length of this meal anyway. We all know that dreadful things have happened quite close to here," she added — for the news had finally, at about six o'clock, found its way to her house — "but there's nothing we can do about it." And passing a finger over her upper lip, she added, "One must learn to rise above reality. Futility can sometimes be extremely elegant."

She cast a glance at Constantin, who had always liked her axioms, but he did not even raise his eyes. Wanda looked approving, but Maud and Ludwig sighed in chorus, with their usual lack of understanding, while Lucien was fingering his pimple under cover of his napkin. Popesku stared at her in bewilderment. Boubou raised her fork to her lips and put a fibrous and flavourless morsel into her mouth, chewing it first with disgust and then with anger. Her round dark eyes rolled in their sockets, her cheeks turned from bright red to deep brick colour, her bellicose chin took on the appearance of a nut-cracker, and her skin, already stretched tight as it joined these various features to each other, seemed to tighten a little more, so that it was surprising to find she could still open her mouth.

"Some people," she exclaimed, "when dining in the company of civilized persons, well-mannered persons, have the good breeding to leave their own troubles in the cloakroom. I myself saw men and women in fits of laughter in the Pré Catalan in 1914, even though some of those men were off to the front next morning and some of the women, myself included, were already weeping for their departure."

There was a startled and awkward silence abruptly broken by Constantin.

"Let me just point out," he said, in his most lordly Russian manner, "let me just point out that judging by your age — well, the age to which you admit — you can't have been laughing to hide your tears in the Pré Catalan in 1914, you were still playing in the park at the time."

This unexpected lightning attack silenced Boubou for a moment. Wanda saw her suddenly counting and recounting in her head all the years she had glossed over since the 1914 war, a process which unfortunately meant that she had to keep folding and unfolding the fingers of her right hand, for she was as bad at arithmetic as she was good at business.

"Oh, you'd say anything!" she cried at last, leaning so far towards Constantin that her breasts rested full on the table. "You'd say anything!" she repeated firmly, so that the slowness of her reactions might be attributed to indignation. But she said no more, since she had not yet finished her calculations, and her hand went on tapping the tablecloth. It even moved to a spot above Ludwig Lentz's plate — he was surprised, but calm — and her forefinger began tracing little circles in the air, like a Spitfire, concentrated and furious little circles above the salsify which lay on the plate. Before she finally gave up her sums and thus the hope of finding a more elegant way to change the subject, she let her finger come down right on the vegetable and brought it up again covered with white sauce, to the bewilderment of everyone, and without any comment.

"You'd say just anything," she repeated, wiping her finger on her napkin and glancing severely at Popesku, for he too, no doubt out of professional habit, seemed to be devoting himself to mathematical operations as useless as they were ill-mannered, since he had not the shadow of a chance of knowing her age.

"And you're not being fair, Constantin," she went on, in a broken voice, "you're not being fair, because you know the truth quite well. You know I wasn't old enough to be married in 1914, or to be in the Pré Catalan, or playing in the park either!" she said firmly, with the emphasis of mendacity. "Now, Constantin, no one knows that better than you," she added with the melancholy of ancient rancour, "and you can't tell me I ever told you otherwise."

"Well, well!" said Constantin, who should have enjoyed her mendacity, but who was being very stupid this evening. "Were you weeping or were you not weeping in the Pré Catalan in 1914, then?"

Boubou cast him a pitying glance. She had recovered her spirits. "I was *watching* people cry, *watching* them," she said, emphasizing the word. "I wasn't old enough to be crying myself, but I was of an age to understand other people's tears. Thank God, I have never grown beyond *that* age, and I never will!" she added, in a voice that was suddenly both rejuvenated and furious, "for compassion and understanding are something you are either born with or you never acquire at all, my dear Constantin!"

All the guests looked down at their plates, except, of course, for Constantin and Wanda, who seemed to be enjoying herself.

"I don't know if it's just what our friend means," she put in, in a clear voice, "but the fact is, Constantin, you've never been particularly good at understanding other people."

And she winked at the disconcerted Boubou at the same time as she made a remarkably vulgar and puerile gesture, which made Popesku suddenly burst out laughing, to the astonishment of everyone, for no one had seen the colour of his teeth in over two years. In any case, the result was that Constantin rose and left without so much as a "Good night", quite contrary to his usual excellent manners. They sat there stunned, until Boubou, aware that if she had not won on points she had at least avoided a technical knockout, clapped her hands briskly and rose. The vegetable dish was uneatable.

"Children," she said, "children, there's nothing else except some figs and nuts, not very good ones, which I'll leave here on the dining room sideboard in case you feel hungry in the night, until such time as the Arsène Lupin of the henhouse feels like returning to the scene of his crimes . . ."

And she let her sentence trail away, to no avail, since Romano was still not back yet.

Dinner had seemed to Constantin interminable, apart from his argument with Boubou and her fine show of mendacity, when for a few brief moments he had felt he was back with his own familiar war, in the happy time when, for him, it took place in salons, on sets, in front of his camera, when he refused to see that there was another kind of war going on just outside his door. That other war which he had kept out of range of his own personal camera, like a conscientious director and an equally conscientious bastard.

His bedroom door was gently opened, with a nasty squeal

which instantly stopped. Torn between wanting someone to relieve his solitude, and the impossibility of keeping a conversation going with anyone at all, Constantin froze. The door opened a little wider, making the same horrible noise again, and despite himself he smiled slightly: if someone was spying on him it was very inexpertly done. Then the door opened entirely to let in a hairy whirlwind wagging its tail: Azor, the dog of the house, who had developed a passion for Constantin and never left him from the time he came back in the evening until he left again next morning. Suddenly Constantin remembered all those photographs in the German press of Hitler smiling, in sentimental mood, flanked by a fair-haired little girl and an Alsatian dog. Azor bounded up to him, covered him with kisses and then, discovering that for once there was no other biped lying beside Constantin, jumped up on the bed and lay down on his friend's stomach, growling happily. Only animals really love you, thought Constantin automatically, with that leaning to platitude which came over him when he found himself in rather too intense a situation, and he abstractedly patted the dog's head. He had just remembered the thoughts that occurred to him while he was vomiting with horror at Vassieux that morning; he remembered thinking of that cherry jam while his breakfast landed in the charred grass. He had pushed the thought away at the time, he believed he had not even registered it, and now it came back to him like shattering proof of his insensitivity. Perhaps there actually was an unconscious and fatal displacement between thoughts and feelings, as there was between ideas and feelings. But he felt unable to tell anyone at all about his stupid, childish reaction, his appalling reaction over that jam, not even Wanda or Romano. They would have accused him of cynicism, or rather of going along with cynicism. And yet, yet, Constantin had always found that in the most extreme situations small thoughts of that nature shot through his mind, cold and swift as fish, whatever his feelings were at the time. He had not thought until that morning that anything could really compromise a man: it had taken the worst to make him believe in the bad, and the bad to make him believe in the good — and the sight he had seen today to show him that the good was absolutely necessary.

The dog went to sleep beside Constantin, his head heavy against Constantin's side; he dared not move, although he would have liked to get up, take off the clothes which still seemed to him to retain the dreadful odour of Vassieux, and wash his face in front of the mirror. He would have liked to see another face in that mirror, a young man's face, perhaps, or the face of a man, a real man. What crime had he not committed against himself? For though he had worn the uniform of the Wehrmacht and not the SS, he had seen that morning how slight the difference was. He had covered up for extortion. He had compromised his name, his reputation, what confidence people still had in his intelligence and his integrity; he had lent it all, like a mask, to a perverted power. He had dishonoured himself, as they would have said in the last century, and it seemed that such a thing was still possible. Perhaps, somewhere, young people had said, "If von Meck is going along with the Nazis, von Meck who hates injustice so much, von Meck who is so independent, then perhaps we can follow him." Perhaps he was responsible for even one man's joining that army he now hated, he, von Meck the independent. Oh yes, he had played at independence all right, with the support of Goebbels behind him! He had put it well enough to Wanda last night: he had been a man of straw, straw that concealed blood and tears.

In any case, he, Constantin von Meck, was finished now. Finished, because he had been a cheat and a liar, even if not on purpose. He was not dead in his own eyes, as in the eyes of the world. And suddenly Constantin von Meck, who was well over six foot tall and weighed over thirteen stone, Constantin von Meck with his big moustache, laughing eyes, and his once athletic body covered with reddish fair hair, Constantin von Meck curled up in the foetal position and began to sob spasmodically and childishly into his pillow. He wept: tears flowed from his eyes, ran down into his moustache, trickled over his temples. He wept as he had never wept in his life, as he could never remember having wept in his life before. He had not wept such tears for the death of Michael, his best friend and his lover; he had not wept such tears when his mother died either; he had not wept such tears when Wanda left him for good, or at least, for the last time . . . He had not wept such tears for anyone, and now he was weeping them for himself, for the image of a self now in distress, and the idea that it was for himself, for his own person, that he felt such intolerable grief increased his shame, his despair and his sobs.

Azor, roused, tried to lick his face through his fingers; Azor sought a face that Constantin hid from him, as much ashamed before the dog as he would have been before a human being.

The first person to enter his room was Boubou Bragance. Boubou had many faults, but some virtues too, and it was one of the latter that caused her to withdraw and close the door quietly behind her, without the slightest sound, and without the slightest sign of surprise on her face either. The second person was Wanda.

She had lain down beside him, she had put his hirsute, tearful head on her right shoulder and caressed his face with her own right hand, tracing his features in a slow, leisurely manner, as she used to do, knowing he liked it. She liked it too; she had never seen such skin as Constantin's, so taut, so warm, so dry. She seemed to feel the veins through his skin where she had seen them throbbing blue; she sensed the throbbing of them with her eyes, with her wandering fingers, at the corners of his mouth and his eyes, on his temples, at the nape of his neck; her fingers saw them where her eyes could not.

"Speak to me," she said, whispering in the dark. "Say something!"

But he said nothing; he abandoned himself, head thrown back, from time to time giving a convulsive spasm which both alarmed and pleased Wanda: never since she had known and loved him had she seen Constantin weep, except for once when he wept with anger, and she saw his slanting, cat's eyes shed round, well-defined tears, fat transparent tears which might have been an owl's and made her laugh in spite of herself. But this time he was weeping in earnest, weeping just as he laughed, as he did everything — weeping to excess.

"Say something," she whispered. "Say something."

"It wasn't real," he said at last, making a great effort, in a husky and affected voice, a voice which tried to suggest the voice of an English gentleman shocked by some social misdemeanour, but which failed, swollen and broken as it was by a horror he still could hardly believe. "What I saw wasn't real," he repeated, and glanced wildly at her before letting his head drop on her shoulder again. If it was the first time he had really wept, it was also the first time he had made Wanda feel a protective, even respectful compassion, something hitherto unknown in their relationship.

"Come now," she said, lowering her own voice instinctively, "it wasn't you who did all that. You were never German, Constantin, my old lion, oh, you poor bastard, my Constantinoff!"

And she heard the silly, loving pet names of their early days as lovers coming from her mouth, revived by herself. She felt very calm, very sad, indefinably happy.

"How do you mean, never German?" said Constantin. "I wore their uniform. I may have got other people to wear it, young men, pushed them into doing it. People everywhere must hate me, and they're right, don't you see?"

"But . . ." she said, "but you never harmed anyone, you helped people to escape; I told you, there are people alive because of you now. You never harmed anyone at all!"

"Yes, I did," he said. "I refused to see people were being harmed. I wouldn't see it, I told lies, I've always told lies. I've always been pretending, I've always let things drift. I ought never to have kept quiet, Wanda. I ought to have shouted, denounced them, got myself killed. I'm my country's accomplice, I'm responsible for my actions this time, Wanda. There have been too many deaths . . ."

"They weren't actions," she said. "It was a blindness, it was . . ."

But Constantin was not listening to her. For once in his life, he was telling the truth, and he heard himself tell the truth with interest and curiosity: it was a truth, he thought briefly, no truer than the rest of his life. Truth, like everything else, was only an option for him, even if at this moment he was intent upon making it unbearable. He made one more effort to wound himself further, but the cynical bird on his shoulder was already laughing at him.

"I'm responsible for my silence. My silence ought to have been shouting in my ears for the last three years, Wanda, and you know it. You talk about the future, you talk about a future in colour, but I've been seeing in black and white for the last three years! I can't imagine the future. My future's out of date, Wanda . . ."

And he stopped, because she was weeping. Weeping broken-heartedly, and he could think of nothing but comforting her, for she too seldom wept, and her tears were so slow, so warm, so unsalty, of such an exquisite flavour. It was the Constantin of the past, the future, of always who took her in his arms, apologized, made her laugh and made love to her. But it was an unfamiliar and subdued Constantin who listened to her afterwards.

To this unfamiliar Constantin, Wanda told her story of the scientist Otting whom she must bring to London, of how it was absolutely necessary for all four of them to leave for London the next night: him, herself, Romano and the scientist. And it was an abstracted Constantin who agreed to everything: agreed without hesitation to abandon La Sanseverina, his film, Europe, his equivocal role, everything that had made up his own life for the last four years. He would be taking with him only what he loved and admired; he was ready, it seemed, for anything, he would agree to it all.

This was the one moment when Wanda Blessen felt that she was making a sacrifice, for she had often dreamed of the moment when she would tell Constantin the truth, and see in his eyes, after his first surprise, the awakening of retrospective alarm, of love and admiration; she had dreamed of seeing Constantin's eyes show respect for her inspired by something other than her beauty or her acting talent. That night, however, Constantin was unable to feel any surprise at anything; it must be enough that he would agree to go, leave his past life, those last four years which might have proved fatal to him.

In fact Constantin, in his weariness, anger and disgust, and in the sense of relief that was beginning to surface in him too, was reassured by only one thing: the imminent danger of the hours ahead. As a director, he could not help relishing the complexity of the way they must now behave, the manoeuvres they had to perform, the parts they must play, all those precise operations, all that timing. It restored him to a world he knew. The plan Wanda and Romano had made was simple: Constantin and Wanda would go out for dinner together the next night, carefully mentioning this fact as if by chance to the cast and crew. They would fetch Otting, bring him to the place where the plane was to land, and where Romano would join them. This called for a considerable amount of play-acting, of coming and going, to-ing and fro-ing, while Popesku had to be watched at the same time: in short, it called for various manoeuvres which Constantin, as a man of action, was already working out, and enjoying it. After that they would get into their plane, and never mind what happened next! Whether he was shot or hailed as a hero in London was all one to Constantin. And the relief he felt at putting his future life into other hands, hands he did not know, was a sign of extreme fatigue in him. Anyway, he had deceived himself, and now others were going to be deceived about him, all of which was only to be expected.

Meanwhile, he was going to set the record straight with that gypsy who had just come back with his Talbot, that gypsy who had lied and concealed the truth from him. He was going to have things out with Romano. Wanda was asleep, exhausted and lovely, lying back dishevelled on the pillow. Constantin strode off to Romano's room and flung the door dramatically open, to find himself in the shadows beyond the dim yellow light of a small lamp in which he saw his lover, his friend, lying stretched half-naked on the bed, the sheet over his legs, barely decent, his body relaxed and his head back as if he were already dead. He seemed calm in his sleep. But Constantin could see that despite his tan he was exhausted under that youthful skin; he saw that he was alone in his great beauty, just as he remained intact and kept his integrity even in debauchery. It was impossible to imagine that General Bremen in Paris had been able to touch that body for twenty thousand francs, impossible to imagine that he, Constantin, had been able to change the quality of that profile in any way at all. There was something insane, not of a demonic but of an angelic nature, in this boy rejected by the world, who was condemned to death and knew it, who was sleeping despite himself, and must be sleeping dreamlessly, so motionless was his face. Constantin bent down and laid his head slowly on Romano's shoulder. Romano scarcely moved, but groaned and brought his right hand round to the nape of Constantin's neck. For a moment Constantin rested his mouth on the boy's neck, and then lay quietly down beside him like a brother. He did not desire him any more, or rather he desired him so much that it was no longer a distinct desire: he loved something other than love in

Romano, something other than friendship, something other than pleasure, he loved someone who was himself and whom he did not know. He slowly dropped off to sleep, lulled by that breath which was unaware of his presence, lulled by that happy sleep, by oblivion of everything, by a sweetness whose nature he could not recall.

In going to sleep, of course, Constantin relaxed and let his weight fall on Romano, who woke and struggled under it, opened his eyes and recognized Constantin; seeing him there, lying across him, he thought some carnal impulse had brought him. Laying his hands on Constantin, he was able to reawaken the man of pleasure in him and satisfy him as one boy satisfies another. But Constantin, opening his eyes and seeing Romano's dark eyes over him, ironic, mocking, tender and weary, his sensual mouth and sharp, triangular teeth, Constantin, closing his own eyes again but unable to abandon himself entirely to a pleasure he had not asked for, had to admit that this was not what he wanted, that he wanted a great deal more and a great deal less, and one day this boy would give him all the love he had not yet given — unless it was he, Constantin, who paid it back to him with interest.

Constantin disengaged himself and smiled, but there was faint resentment in that smile. "What right do you have to make love to me?" Meaning, "What right do you have to give me pleasure, and what sort of pleasure?" This was one of those questions Constantin did not work out in his own mind, any more than he wondered why he had risen from Wanda's bed to go to Romano's, and was not planning to do the opposite, or why he felt he had arrived at his journey's end, although he had never entertained any ideas of what his journey's end was, any more than he had for a moment envisaged their future life in Hollywood or elsewhere, whatever Wanda thought.

"Something wrong?" asked Romano, in a tired but light-hearted voice which suddenly got on Constantin's nerves.

"Why didn't you tell me?" he asked out loud, and then abruptly lowered his voice to a whisper, as if in a comedy thriller. "Why didn't you tell me about it?"

"Ah." Romano sat up in bed, looked for a cigarette, found one, of poor quality, and lit it carefully. "Wanda's been talking to you?"

"Yes, Wanda's been talking to me," said Constantin. "Indeed she has."

They glanced at each other in the lamplight with sudden friendship, a kind of fraternity very different from their usual feeling.

"I'm in real trouble now," said Constantin, with a brief laugh, "or rather, we are! And you've been in this for a long time, haven't you?"

Romano shrugged his shoulders. "Well, for a while . . . when I think of the risks people have taken for that idiot! Otting, I mean . . . I brought him back here this evening. Wanda and her missions! The man's a hopeless fool — and a redhead, it's a wonder he hasn't been arrested ten times over with that red hair. He stands out a mile in the street. And as for his conceit . . . so yes, he's going to America to make this A-bomb, but you get the impression that makes him master of the universe inside his little head. It's crazy."

There was a silence. Constantin's voice was suddenly horrified.

"The A-bomb?" he said. "The atomic bomb? Are you joking? In America? It's going to be made in America?"

"Why, yes," said Romano, taken aback. "Apparently it's some bomb that's more powerful than other bombs."

Constantin smiled. "Oh, this is marvellous!" he said. "This really puts the lid on it! I have a friend called Borg, Nathan Borg, one of the best scientists of his time, he's told me about it. You don't know just what it is. It's great stuff, the A-bomb. We're quite right to be helping this charming fellow of yours to finish it! Oh, it will be worth it, believe you me . . ."

"Well, worth it or not, Otting's supposed to join his fellow countrymen at Los Alamos," said Romano, "and we're the ones who are going to get him there."

"Amazing," said Constantin, still thoughtful. "An amazing bomb . . . not much is known about its qualities except that it's certainly ten times more devastating than any other . . . I doubt if the Americans would dare drop it on anyone. Or even the Germans, Romano, if you ask me, no, even a German wouldn't!" And he lay down again before repeating, "No American would dare drop it, even a German wouldn't, believe me, Romano!"

There was a certain challenge in his tone which roused Romano to reply wearily, in Wanda's words, "Maybe even a German wouldn't, Constantin. But Hitler would!"

However, Constantin's head was drooping; he was clearly exhausted. He went to sleep, and slept curled up, knees bent towards his chin while his guardian angel, his Romano, his gypsy lay full length beside him, making sure neither of them fell out of bed.

A quarter of an hour later, for the first time since they had come to the house, for the first time in two months of a torrid summer, rain began to fall. It was the first rain of autumn, the first rain of September, and it went on and on, cool and silent, reviving all the fragrance of the earth.

X

They had not been able to begin shooting until early in the afternoon, and the cast and crew, as if refreshed like the soil by that long downpour, were crowding around Constantin, who seemed rejuvenated himself, animated and smiling. The light had literally changed overnight; it was no longer a pale, white light, but yellow and rosy, an autumn light that softened contours and features but brought out colours. Everyone looked more sun-burnt, more attractive, gentler, livelier (even Popesku, Maud noticed, looked almost tolerable; only almost, of course, but that was still a great gain where Popesku was concerned). As for Constantin von Meck, the great Constantin von Meck with his engagingly awkward gait, he was more seductive than ever with his sunburn, his red hair and moutache, and his light green eyes, full today of an unexpected tenderness which made him lay a hand on a man's shoulder here, caress a woman's neck here, even pet the camera as if it were an animal with his clumsy and over-large hands. There was a kind of affectionate excitement in him, a kind of rather melancholy attention which restored him to his film crew as they had known him before at his best, at the height of his happiness, his talent, his freedom from care, at the height of everything they had all lacked so sadly for years. As a director, he had never before been so much in love with his heroine, La Sanseverina, or made her so enchanting.

"Now then," said Constantin, "now then, here comes the

worst bit, children! Thanks to La Sanseverina, Fabrice has escaped from prison and perhaps death; he is back with her, but he is pining, pining for little Clelia Conti whom he hardly knows. And she feels he is pining, she guesses, and it hurts her. So we are now going to shoot the sad state of mind of a young man who wishes he were back in prison. They go to the end of the path there, he is walking beside her, she laughs, or tries to laugh. We hear her laughter in the distance, but as she approaches us it trails away, and by the time she's right here in front of us she isn't laughing at all. Fabrice, however, has been walking along with his head bent, not joining in her laughter, and as it dies away and falls silent he raises his head so that in the end he is looking at her, intrigued, perhaps rather irritated. They change, they reverse their attitudes as they come up the path towards us, understand? Right, let's go.''

The head scene-shifter, who along with Maud represented the less imaginative part of the company, shrugged his shoulders and kicked a pebble before turning to Constantin. "I don't mind what you say, the man's a fool!" he said in a carrying voice. "Given a choice between her and her," he continued, pointing first to Wanda's caravan and then to Maud, "well, a man who could choose . . . er . . .''

And he stopped short, rather late in the day and somewhat embarrassed, while the rest of the film crew hurriedly looked for something to do. Maud's clear voice, however, was heard next moment.

"Well, I say, you nearly dropped a brick there!" she remarked. "What a good thing Lucien's busy in his caravan dealing with that pimple . . . I can tell you, he wouldn't have liked to hear you call him a fool!''

A general laugh of relief greeted this observation. Constantin looked at the sky once more, and Wanda emerged from her caravan, but was intercepted en route by young Lucien Marrat, in his handsome costume and his cloak. Constantin raised an imperious hand.

"Cameras roll!" he said. "Take!"

The camera began its familiar whirr. Constantin was concentrating entirely on the path and the trees from which it emerged. He was not really thinking of anything but the take, of the moment when La Sanseverina would laugh, and the way Fabrice del Dongo must first look down and then gradually up. Nothing else was real or interesting, nothing else was important. The idea of abandoning this film in the middle of shooting, cancelling *La Chartreuse de Parme* just like that for political or moral reasons, whatever they were, suddenly struck him as wicked, absurd, ridiculous. He was a director and this was his film. He had a film crew here waiting on his word, and actors who needed him, and somewhere or other Stendhal must be turning in his grave. There was only one absolute essential for a man who had signed a contract to make a masterpiece, and that was to shoot the film and finish the job as well as he could. The obligation of a director to a film always came first. It was not so much Stendhal who mattered, either, as the idea of these whirring cameras, these technicians, this formidable combination of money, talent, expectations and efforts which was assembled under his command, for which he was responsible. The Wehrmacht, the war, fires, massacres, all seemed very far away: all of that was fiction. Reality was here.

He was shaking so much that he saw the beige, lilac and brown of the couple slowly approaching hop about in the viewfinder of the camera, as if in some nonsensical dream. La Sanseverina lowered her head slowly, and Fabrice raised his own much faster than he should have done and glanced uneasily at his aunt — yes, far too fast. It was then that Constantin realized there was no sound at all, that the film crew itself was motionless, intrigued, almost embarrassed: La Sanseverina had not laughed. She had arrived at the point where they were to stop, she was standing beside the handsome young man she loved, but she was looking at him, Constantin, with panic in her eyes. She was pale and silent. Constantin came down to earth abruptly.

"What on earth is going on?" he thundered, in a hoarse voice that surprised even himself. "What's going on? Are we making a silent film now? Wanda!" he said, and in speaking her name, her familiar name, he remembered where he was, who he was, and what was happening.

"I couldn't laugh," she breathed. "I'm really sorry, forgive me, but I just couldn't laugh."

And she abruptly turned her face away, gestured from him to the camera, and then walked off to her caravan, the door of which could be heard slamming next moment. Reality exploded inside Constantin's head: this was only a film, and she was his wife. She was afraid; they were caught up in a dark tale of war and murder. In eight hours' time they would be airborne on the way to England and then perhaps America. In eight hours' time, the whole film crew would be left behind in this little French town, and *La Chartreuse de Parme* would be over; as for himself, he, Constantin von Meck would be genuinely discredited this time, as a diretor. Discredited, he tried to tell himself forcefully, discredited! But he knew now that the real dishonour did not lie there. Constantin passed a hand over his forehead, and then before the eyes of his alarmed film crew, waved that hand in a carefree manner, attempted a smile, and said, "I'll be back," with rather too obvious a wink. He went to Wanda's door, knocked and went straight in. She had her back to him; she was in La Sanseverina's costume, with its voluminous skirts, her beautiful head was bent, and he felt his heart breaking.

"Duchess?" was all he said.

Wanda turned, took a couple of steps forward and flung herself into his arms. She was weeping, nervous little tears this time, cold tears, and he held her tight and was closer to her than he had been last night even when they wept together. For once, they were feeling exactly the same grief, suffering the same humiliation, and their remorse was identical: it was professionally that they were affected, in their own respect for themselves, and perhaps nothing could have made either of them feel quite so bad. For once they were truly united, for once they really understood each other, and this time they were both slightly ashamed of it.

"Don't worry," said Constantin, patting her on the back. "Don't worry, Aline de Dema will replace you; she'll be wonderful!"

He had named the worst actress of the period, and she responded at once. "And Jeannot Sentier will finish shooting your film!" she replied quickly.

They both began to laugh, nervously, like children quarrelling. She shook her head, looked at herself in the mirror, picked up a powder puff and repaired the damage caused by her attack of nerves.

"After all this," she said, as if to herself, "after all this silliness, I wonder if I'll be able to act even reasonably well again?"

And so saying, she stepped past him like a queen and went back to the wood in search of Fabrice del Dongo and his pimple. Her laugh sounded like the cooing of a dove in the little wood, and she appeared, trimphant, at the end of the path. As they walked down it that laugh re-echoed, and trailed away of its own accord at just the right moment, in front of the entire, fascinated film crew, Constantin included. He was not the first to applaud the fine little performance, but directly afterwards he extemporized, bowing, hand on heart: "My dear Duchess, may I thank you for your acting talent by inviting you to dine privately with me on a turnip or so at La Gentilhommière this evening? Would you be kind enough to book a table for two in my name, M. Popesku?"

He felt very proud of his presence of mind.

EPILOGUE

It had been a good day's work: so Popesku thought, anyway. He was all the more surprised when the voice of the captain in Draguignan undeceived him.

"Are you out of your mind?" he yelled at the other end of he line. "Where? When? You should have phoned me at once! You stupid idiot . . . I've received very precise orders . . ."

And he started shouting down the ebonite phone so loud that the unfortunate Popesku, sitting in the café at the far end of the village of Salerne, covered the receiver with his hand and glanced uneasily around him, but unnecessarily, since there was no one there. The staff of the café were out on the doorstep staring at a house among the vines where there had just been an explosion. Apparently a group of German soldiers had broken into it and found a radio transmitter. Popesku was not well enough informed to know that this was Wanda's relay transmitter. In any case, she and Constantin had already left to dine at La Gentilhommière, one of those provincial restaurants of dubiously manorial atmosphere. Moreover, the agent working the transmitter had been blown to bits as the SS went in.

Popesku learned, with mingled surprise, pride and concern, that the movements of a whole SS detachment which had been hastily recalled from the Var depended on his information. He was to stick to Romano like his shadow, wait for Constantin and Wanda to come back, and send word at once if there were any newcomers at Boubou Bragance's. He was also to phone at nine to give the latest news of what appeared to be some affair of state.

On arriving at the manorial restaurant in question, Constantin and Wanda sat down, ordered aperitifs, and drank them with relish until the moment when Wanda announced in a carrying voice that this was a frightful place, Constantin was frightful too, and she for one wasn't going to spend the evening here, though he, Constantin, could stay if he wanted. She marched out past the bewildered diners and the disconsolate waiters; Constantin followed her (that at least could be checked later). They got into the car and drove to pick Otting up at the farmhouse where he was hiding. He did not utter a word. The landing strip was ten kilometres away; they reached it without hindrance. It was then ten o'clock, and the plane would arrive within an hour at the latest.

Unfortunately, it was only nine o'clock when dinner at Boubou Bragance's came to an end; a dinner which had been a gloomy meal in the absence of the famous couple, a dinner which Maud had tried to enliven in her sugary-sweet voice, with the support, for once, of Ludwig Lentz, who told several anecdotes about the Côte d'Azur, where it seemed he had taken swimming lessons at the age of seven. Poor Lucien Marrat's pimple was no better, however, and Boubou was beginning to think that Constantin might be a capricious guest, but was indispensable too. As for Popesku, he was watching every move Romano made, as Romano noticed. He realized that he could not escape Popesku's surveillance or get out of the house without being followed, and thus leading the Gestapo straight to his friends. He would stay here; he had always known as much. All he had to do was engage the attention of Popesku and the SS long enough for the plane to land and take off again. At ten he decided to draw the enemy's fire to himself and went up to Popesku, who was leaning calmly against one of the drawing room windows, and was even thinking of suggesting a game of chess to Romano. Romano took Popesku by the elbow, swung him round towards himself, and struck him hard in the face, calling him a traitor, a Nazi, a collaborator and a number of other names which felt like dry stones in his mouth. Then he led him to the telephone. Popesku, trembling, unsure what to do or say now, informed the Gestapo that Romano Woltzer, von Meck's locations assistant, was a member of the Resistance, but that just at the moment he, Popesku, had him under control, and von Meck and Wanda had just called and said they would be back in an hour or so. The bewildered Boubou, the confused Maud, and the equally disconcerted Ludwig and Lucien watched this scene unfold before their eyes as if it were part of a bad film, badly constructed, badly made, with a bad plot, bad actors and bad dialogue. It struck Romano in the same way.

The SS arrived ten minutes later, and the headlights blazing all around the house confirmed Romano's forebodings. He would only have to hold out for an hour or an hour and a half, put off talking as long as possible, and that was that. He would never see Constantin again; that was that, too.

At ten o'clock, Wanda realized that Romano would not be coming. At twenty past ten, when the English plane arrived and landed quietly in the grassy field, just as the landing beacons lit by the Resistance were dying down, Constantin realized it too. All the same, he went to the plane in spite of himself, helped Otting into it, and then Wanda, and stood there with his hand on the fuselage, hair blowing in the wind of the propellers, looking at them. His eyes were glowing, thought Wanda, glowing like a big cat's.

"Come on," she said.

"But . . . Romano . . ." And Constantin gestured, a gesture indicating the fields and woods from which no Romano would appear.

"M. von Meck," said Otting, leaning out, "M. von Meck, surely you're not going to stay here on account of that little terrorist who is a pansy too, if you ask me, with his dyed hair? Are you?"

Wanda quickly placed her hand on Otting's knee, but Constantin had already put his head inside the cabin, and was looking at the man.

"That little terrorist who is a pansy too," he said, "is going to get himself killed, all alone, so that you, *you* can kill millions of people at a single blow, do you understand? He will very shortly be dying for you, Herr Doktor Otting . . ."

There was moment's silence, a strident silence, one might almost have said, so fast were the propellers turning, so anxious was the pilot to take off, so much did everyone want the plane to leave, and so strongly did Constantin feel himself gradually digging his feet into the ground, digging in from heels to ankles, unable to leave without understanding why, without knowing why.

"Constantin," said Wanda, "please, please get in! Get in! I couldn't live without you, Constantin . . . come on!"

Constantin shook his head.

"I can't," he said. At this point Otting, who had flinched from Constantin's words as if they were a blow and had retreated, leaned forward again. He had the face of a dour puritan redhead, an unattractive face, but at that moment it wore a reasonably conciliating expression.

"I'm sorry, M. von Meck," he said. "I didn't know he was such a friend of yours . . ."

"Nor did I," said Constantin. And he stepped back, letting his arm fall to his side. As if the plane had been kept there solely by him and his hand, it moved forward, raced over the ground, rose suddenly above the forest and disappeared into the sky. For a moment, one last moment, Constantin thought he saw tears flowing over Wanda's face like rain, like a downpour, a downpour of tears, and throbbing regret for her body, her voice, her eyes, her love went through him. He set off for the forest, swaying on his feet, got back into the Talbot and started off again.

He had always been fond of that Talbot. Perhaps she sometimes tended not to hold the road when he pushed her hard, when he asked too much of her, but otherwise she was a faithful friend. And now her engine roared and purred and flung her around the bends like a ballerina, a rather awkward, pretentious ballerina but a good girl all the same. Gradually, God knew why, he found himself recalling a story Romano had told him: what the devil was it about? Oh yes, Romano in his caravan in a field near a village in Hungary, and his father playing the guitar, and that vast, immense and endless plain, with the sky very low and a line of trees along the banks of a rather sluggish river. And Romano stretched out beside a girl, looking at that low sky, listening to the guitar, and a fire in the distance, a fire in the grass, with that strange odour such fires have of the woods and sadness and solitude, whether they burn in Hungary or California or New Zealand. That acrid, soft and piercing smell, and Romano with the girl, and his father playing the guitar a little way off, and the low sky . . . what *was* this story whose point he couldn't remember? Was it about Romano bedding his first girl, or Romano's last caravan, before he lost his family? He could not even remember Romano's memories any more, he couldn't remember anything, anything at all except this road which was so long that it seemed it would never come to an end, and the fact that the car was gradually eating it up; he was going to get there, he was going to find he didn't know exactly what, but he was making straight for what he had to do. And for once Constantin von Meck knew what he had to do — even though what he had to do was the worst thing in the world.

He raced down the drive, slammed the door of his car, and invlountarily stood to attention all by himself as he saw soldiers and messengers milling around everywhere, weapons shining and passing each other in the dark. Poor Boubou Bragance, he instinctively thought, before going up the steps to the door with a clipped, precise, meticulous, correctly military tread, those steps up which he had cheerfully run like a young man with Romano so many times before. He pushed open the door and waved aside the soldiers' crossed bayonets with the lordly authority conferred upon him by his fair complexion, reddish fair hair and moustache and his blue eyes. He walked through the big drawing room, and had time to notice Boubou, lying where she had fallen in a chair, looking drawn, unkempt, dishevelled, her face already swollen, an indecent sight yet again in her torn dress, but despite herself on this occasion, Boubou who had the time and the incredible courage to wink at him and say hoarsely, in a voice like an ancient bird's, "Hullo, Constantin!" before his strides carried him on, taking him to the study, which he knew must be the place appointed. He made for its door, and the soldiers outside gave way of their own accord before his blond arrogance.

Constantin shouted "Heil Hitler!" with conviction, opened the door, closed it again, and latched it before leaning back against it. The room was all in shadow, its one powerful angled light being trained on a chair to which all that was left of Romano was tied. His head was lowered, and at first all Constantin saw was the dyed fair hair, its dark roots looking twice as long as they had been that morning. Around him stood two German soldiers in shirts already stained with blood, two impeccably dressed officers, smiling and smoking, their caps on the table, and on the other side of that table, a lamentable and ridiculous figure like a tourist who had lost his way, in shorts and sandals, was the trembling and pale Popesku. At the sound of the door opening, one of the officers put a hand swiftly to his hip. Constantin stepped forward into the light, and the sight of his own hand firmly holding the large pistol stopped the officer's. Constantin looked at Romano's back and bowed shoulders. Romano raised his head, and in that unspeakable face Constantin saw the eyes, clouded and dull with pain, focus on him, recognize him, and he thought he saw a gleam come back into them, an expression of love, a great and imperishable love, a look in which pleading and gratitude mingled, authority and tenderness, with the light of something Constantin had always dreamed of seeing some day in another person's eyes. He dropped his arm to Romano's throat, that young, sunburnt, smooth throat across which he had fallen asleep only the night before, amused and confident, not knowing that he should have watched over that throat for nights on end with eyes open, mouth open against it, hearing and feeling the pulse of love itself under that soft skin. Constantin fired into the centre of Romano's throat, into the carotid artery, and the blood gushed out at once, all over the disfigured face it hid as the head fell forward on the chest again, showing first the fair hair, then the dark roots, and then the nape of the neck. The soldiers and officers began shouting and swearing, but their shouts were drowned by Popesku's scream, a dreadful, shrill scream as Popesku held out the palms of his hands as if to stop Constantin's avenging bullets: as if Constantin had any notion of revenge left, as if he still knew what revenge was, as if he still knew what Popesku was.

The door rattled behind him. He was afraid of being suddenly captured, and violently thrust the pistol into his mouth, so fast that the sight of the gun grazed his upper lip in passing and hurt him, even annoyed him. "Shit," he thought, but already there was a vast explosion inside his skull, an explosion whose echo he did not hear.